# DAY ZERO
# FAMILY MATTERS

Library of Congress Control Number: 2019905329

ISBN 978-0-9914702-5-9
10  9  8  7  6  5  4  3  2  1

Covers by Terry Fogarty
Edited by Judith Swain

www.DayZeroBook.com

*For Judy.*

# DAY ZERO FAMILY MATTERS

Written by Charles Ingersoll

Edited by Judith Swain

# 1
## *Headspace*
Day Zero minus 2 – 6:27pm EST

Jude Sawyer couldn't believe what Doctor Rick had asked her to do. It was bad enough he had advised her to cut back on the drinking and flush the anti-depressants two months ago. Now, she was supposed to ask her girlfriends what they thought of her parents? What the hell was that supposed to accomplish?

"Come on!" Jude slammed her palm on the center of the Toyota Corolla's steering wheel. The horn blared at the old lady driving like it was Sunday. "The pedal on the right is the gas! Jesus!" The horn helped. The Buick LaCrosse with the handicapped placard hanging from the rearview mirror performed a minor miracle by speeding up a couple miles per hour.

With another catastrophe adverted and the old woman continuing to accelerate ever closer to the speed limit, Jude returned her hands to the "ten and two" positions. Her friend, Cecilia, told her the classic driving position was actually a modern misconception and could break a driver's wrists or arms if the airbag deployed. Fat chance of any bodily harm in this car. Not only did the Toyota not have airbags, it didn't even fucking have power steering.

Her cellphone rang. She may not have a new car fresh off the assembly line—or even a decent one—but Jude would be damned if she didn't keep up with the latest in cellular technology. The larger screen of the new iPhone sitting on a makeshift holder on the dusty dashboard showed the caller as Virginia—a goofy, half-drunken, slit-eyed grin and a margarita depicting her in her natural state. Jude

1

swept her long curly auburn hair off her face before tapping the green "answer" button. "What's up, Ginnie?"

"Hey, girlie," Virginia's voice slurred back. Apparently, she had started her boozing earlier than usual today. "I just wanted to see how the headshrinker went."

"It went," Jude answered.

"He finally give you the green light to drink with me again?"

"Not yet." After Jude had announced to her friends she was swearing off alcohol for the foreseeable future, she had been sad to discover some of them didn't associate with her as often as they used to. At least Ginnie was still making a concerted effort. Jude was thankful for that.

"He figure out all your issues?"

"Almost. He says you're a bad influence on me."

"Well," Virginia said, then paused a moment before finishing, "duh!" They both laughed, having known each other since the second grade at St. Rachael's Catholic Academy. The irony was Ginnie *was* a bad influence on her, but Jude had never shied away from any dark twisted road. They had plenty of history together.

"Hey," Jude said, already hesitating.

"Hey, what?"

"Umm... the shrink told me I'm supposed to ask you something."

"Okay?" Virginia voice was a bit tentative, drawing out the second syllable in mock exaggeration. "And?"

Jude let out a deep breath. "What do you think of my dad?"

"He's cool, I guess... for a dad."

"Umm..." Jude didn't know how to respond. When Doctor Rick told her to ask her friends about what they thought of her parents, he told her to not ask any leading questions to skew the answers back.

2

He had definitely shackled her in how she could navigate this conversation.

Virginia must have felt the need to fill the silence. "I mean, he is a little strange."

Jude jumped on the chance to open the crack further. "Yeah? Whatcha mean?"

"I don't know," Ginnie replied with measured hesitation, even with her current level of liquid courage. "He always kind of skeeved me out, I guess. Remember our sleepovers in high school?"

"I remember. Why did he skeeve you out?" Jude was starting to talk like Doctor Rick. He was always answering questions with an endless string of more questions of 'Why do you feel that way?', 'What happened next?', 'Could you have approached it a different way?', or 'Why do you think that is?'.

The sound of Virginia taking another sip from her early cocktail was crystal clear through the phone, even if it was a little distorted when mixed with the Corolla's rusting muffler. At least Ginnie wasn't drinking straight from the bottle. She was a classy broad. She finally answered with, "He looked at me weird sometimes. Made me want to cover up with that stupid lion of yours."

The annoyance of the old lady in the Buick had been forgotten. What replaced it was a flood of images of all the times her dad had come into her room during sleepovers with her school friends. He never had a qualm about telling them dirty jokes, a beer bottle between his knuckles and a half-burned down cigarette pressed into the corner of his smirking mouth. He had always seemed to forget there was an understood, albeit invisible, line where high school girls shouldn't hear dick jokes from someone's father. A memory of Ginnie hugging Jude's oversized stuffed lion when her dad came into the room hit her. Finally, Jude asked, "Is that why you stopped coming over?"

"Kinda," Ginnie said after another swig.

"I guess Doctor Rick is more insightful than I gave him credit for."

"I hope so. I heard he ain't cheap. And, by the way, the bill for my services will be in the mail tomorrow. Be sure to keep an eye out for the postman."

"Does anyone say *postman* anymore?"

"Only the cool bitches!"

"And, you think you are one of the cool bitches?"

"Yep!"

"You can be happy in the knowledge that you are half-right."

"Yeah, I am pretty cool! Talk to you later. You shouldn't talk on the phone while you're driving. Bye." The phone disconnected with three beeps.

Jude was suddenly alone with her noisy muffler, her tangled thoughts, and the flashing red glow of Buick Lacrosse brake lights. This old lady was going to be the death of her. Unless that old bitty and her Buick turned soon, Jude would have a very long three miles until she could start the already notoriously arduous hunt for a parking spot close to the apartment complex. With Ginnie's admissions about her father and this shitty commute home, she was starting to feel the nagging pull of the humble beginnings of a migraine.

## 2
# *This Just In*
Day Zero – 1:11pm EST

The volume on the television was cranked up so loud Jude could hear it clearly through the wall between the living room and her room. Thank God her migraine from after her last appointment with Doctor Rick had dissipated to a tolerable level after the first two days. Ginnie had not called her back since her car-bound question about her folks. That had been disappointing, but Jude had decided to give her space. A CNN report finally drew her out from her room.

Mom sat in a frayed high-back wing chair. That chair had occupied the corner of the living room for as long as Jude could remember. She wouldn't have been surprised if someone eventually told her the family had brought it over from Holland. In contrast, Mom watched her shows on a state-of-the-art flatscreen television Jude and her brothers had bought for her last Christmas. With her failing vision and hearing, the best in technology increased Mom's viewing enjoyment and decreased her complaints. An added benefit was the television took up a hell of a lot less room than the old massive transistor tube model.

"… the fire here at R&R has raged unabated for three days. The result of an underground gas main rupture, according to an R&R spokesman, the fire you see behind me has engulfed the warehouse and has countered any attempts by local firefighters to subdue it. As of today, R&R announced it would let the fire burn itself out, concerned the continued battle between the blaze and local engine companies could result in unnecessary injury.

"Carl Stack, ABC 7, reporting from Farson, Wyoming."

The on-scene reporter disappeared, replaced by a young in-studio female anchor. "Thank you, Carl," the anchorwoman responded. "In related news, as the winds push the smoke east from Farson toward Cheyenne, Casper and Medicine Bow, R&R has asked Wyoming's governor to bring out the state's National Guard to assist in possible evacuations. R&R still claims the warehouse holds no hazardous materials that would affect public health. The company, known for its decades-long work as a defense contractor with the United States government, asserts it is only looking out for the safety of the public…"

"Jesus Christ," Jude's brother Jimmy said from the couch next to Mom's chair.

"Watch your mouth," Dad warned from the table in the adjoining dining room. "Remember where you are."

Jimmy didn't bother to glare at his father, instead continuing to keep his eyes on the TV. Dad wouldn't have seen Jimmy's look of animosity anyway, since the wall behind the couch separated the living room from the kitchen and obscured the view to the dining room. Jude could see them both, but they couldn't see each other. Jimmy tightened his grip on the walking cane between his legs, the rubbing sound of the lacquered wood audible over the volume of the newscast. Jude's skin turned cold as Dad gave her an appraising head-to-toe look before returning to his newspaper. She wished Doctor Rick hadn't forced her to talk to her girlfriends about him. Hearing how they all felt about him made living here under his roof worse.

"…In other news, a rash of attacks has been reported on the outskirts of Rapid City, South Dakota. Local authorities have reported several young men and women, experimenting with an LSD-laced batch of the drug Ecstasy, have shown aggressive behavior as a result of drug-induced hallucinations. When local authorities arrived on scene, the officers were forced to resort to Tazers and non-lethal measures to subdue the group. Several officers were injured and sent to local hospitals with contusions and bites, resulting in the dispatch of the Rapid City SWAT team to bring the tense situation to a close. All suspects are now in the Rapid City jail awaiting arraignment."

Jude knew Jimmy wanted to say the Lord's name in vain again, but also knew he wouldn't. Even though he was twenty-years-old and almost as big as his father, he would keep quiet. There was a hate there between them. Dad hated that he had produced a defective boy whose left side was palsied, and Jimmy hated his father for hating him. Jude's brother probably would have stood up for himself had his body not betrayed him at the genetic level.

"...finally, on a more upbeat note, Biskist the German Shepherd returned home ..."

Jude didn't hear the rest of the broadcast. Her father came over and put his hands on her shoulders. "Are you holding up okay?" he asked her.

Jude peeled herself away from under his fingers and gave him a pained smile. "I'm okay." She wasn't okay. Ever since she spoke to Ginnie and her other girlfriends about her father, her mind had been reeling with how much her perception of the world had been skewed. She thought she had been living her life in the first person, but now realized she had been watching each day like Mom watched her news from her worn chair.

While Jude hadn't heard any of the story after the newscaster started talking about the dog, she did hear the absence of the newscast when Mom turned the television off altogether. "When is

Michael coming home?" she inquired. "He should have been here by now."

"He's on late shift," Dad said.

"Again?" Mom replied. "Well, at least I still have a son coming home."

Jude's familial anger flared up with her mother fanning the proverbial flames. She glanced at the subdued Jimmy and even caught her own reflection in one of the many mirrors hanging around the house. "You have five children, Mom."

"Only four now." Mom ignored her outburst. "And, you're moving out, anyway."

"I'm always going to be able to talk to you, Mom. That's what phones are for."

"Don't sass your mother," Dad intervened again.

He went to touch her again, but Jude walked over to the couch and sat down next to Jimmy in order to avoid contact. He switched his cane over to his weak side as she cozied up to him. The tension was thick in the living room. Jude glared at her father, but he turned away before catching her stare. She was sure he wasn't even aware of all of the irrevocable damage he had done to her. Probably why she had resorted to excessive drinking and gravitating to a wild child like Ginnie in the first place. And, her mother? She just sat quietly in that chair—unless she was poking Jude with her own passive aggressive barbs—as if it had the ability to protect her from the outside world. Everyone sat under a cone of silence. This family was great at keeping their mouths shut.

'Only four now,' her mother had said. That was the most Jude had ever heard her say on the subject of her oldest son. Neither parent was willing to discuss having lost Matty during his second tour in Iraq. They had ghosted through the funeral with nary a word or a tear. It was as if his death was just a temporary thing and he would come through the door again any day. In their eyes, having Andy still in the armed forces in Europe was almost as bad. Dear old Mom and Dad chastised him for staying abroad after Matty's death. They tried to guilt him into believing Mom was in poor health, assuming—or maybe wishing—he would forsake the Corps in favor of returning home to his parent's side.

Jude figured Mom and Dad wondered what they still had to be proud of. Look at what they had left. A crippled son who was a physical disappointment—who would never leave home for a career in the Armed Forces, but would be a constant reminder of the deformity they had made. Their second son had chosen to follow in his older brother's footsteps instead of caring for his parents. And, the cherry on top, a daughter who would rather abandon her parents than be dutiful and at their beck and call. Yep, the Sawyers were a perfect example of all-American family dysfunction.

The door opened and closed with a slam.

"What's up, family?" youngest and preferred son Michael called out from the foyer.

"Nothing," Jude replied, stilled pressed against Jimmy's good side. "SSDD."

## 3
## *Fiddler on the Roof*
Day Zero – 5:29pm EST

The sun dropped a little bit in the western skies, partially hidden behind a layer of low hanging, graying clouds. The roof always allowed the best views. The city sprawled out past the parapet, low apartments and multi-level residences slowly giving way to more retail-oriented establishments. It was only in the distance the taller buildings rose out the skyline in dull silhouetted relief.

Jude sat on a plastic milk crate, sliding the heels of her flip flops against the packed gravel. This was one of her favorite spots to find a little solitude, but she wasn't the only tenant who liked to come here. The aluminum frame of a lawn chair leaned against the raised edge, the nylon strips for the seat having been torn away long ago. In the far corner, where it didn't fall into shadow by a newly constructed high-rise apartment erected late last summer, a raised vegetable garden sprouted tomato and heirloom cucumber plants spiraling around a wire trellis.

"I knew I would find you up here," a voice came from behind her. "You'd be up here in a hurricane, hell or high water."

Jude knew her parents wouldn't look for her up here. That was one of the reasons why she chose the rooftop in the first place. They only made the climb at dusk on the Fourth of July for the firework shows blasting throughout the neighborhoods and over the downtown skies. The roof was primo for the annual spectacle.

The gravel stomped, crushed and slid around, then repeated several times. Jimmy made his way over to her. He looked around for something to sit on, spying a folded-up step stool leaning against the brick enclosure of the roof access door.

"Fuck," Jimmy said under his breath.

Jude turned around as he angled himself and his cane toward the door. "You want me to get it for you?"

"No," Jimmy said too suddenly and abruptly, before taking a breath and a pause. "I can get it. Thanks."

Several moments passed before he finally snagged the handle of the step stool in the crook of his good elbow and shuffled his way back to where Jude was sitting. He allowed her to take it off his hands, literally, and open it up so he could sit down. He wiped the sweat from his forehead with his sleeve and let out a long cleansing breath. "Well, that was work."

"You okay?"

"Yeah. Yeah. All good. Just needed to get out from under the clouds swirling around in the apartment."

"What?" Jude replied in mock disbelief. "You mean the archangel Michael didn't shine up his halo to raise all spirits up?"

Jimmy let out a hearty laugh before catching the rest with a hand over his mouth. Jude loved to hear him laugh. The genuine ones usually evolved—or devolved—into hilarious snorts. And, right now, he needed something to smile about.

"I think this shit on CNN has Mom spooked a bit," Jimmy managed to get out once the humor drained out of him enough to speak. "She's totally going old country superstitious down there."

"Ya think? I've had to deal with her longer than you, kiddo."

"Well, it ain't my fault that I happen to be younger and prettier." He tapped his cane against the aluminum tubing of the step ladder, his weak hand curled up in his lap.

Jimmy was younger than her but missed being the youngest son by one conception. Gross! That privilege went to Michael, the beautiful and perfect angel conceived to make up for the birth defects Jimmy was born with. Michael was the strong male child Mom and dad had prayed for. They must have prayed extra hard since they had been cursed with an inferior girl and a cripple after two strong and healthy sons.

"I'd still rather be you," Jude admitted.

Jimmy held up his cane in his strong fist and tried to raise his palsied arm to match. "You sure about that?"

11

Jude thought about the way his father touched her shoulder for a few seconds too firmly and for too long. She thought back to how Ginnie had blurted out that one alcohol loosened word when asked about him. A single word encapsulating how Jude felt about him now, too… skeeved.

Jimmy took in his sister's silence, knowing not to pry further with any comments or quips. Instead, he set his cane against the inside of his good leg and fished out a worn pack of Marlboro 100s from his shirt pocket. The foil crinkled in his fingers. The waft of somewhat stale tobacco drifted over to Jude's nostrils, making her lips pucker in a Pavlovian way. Jimmy held the mostly empty pack up to Jude. "You want?"

"You know I can't."

"Do I?"

She slapped him on the arm, crippled or not. "Remember when I went up to Niagara Falls with Eddie last year?"

"Yeah."

"Remember when I told you we had a fight on the drive up and his solution was for me to fucking calm down with a few puffs of a cigarette?"

"Uh huh."

"What I didn't tell you was that those couple puffs turned into a pack-a-day habit within a couple of weeks after I got back."

"No shit?"

"No shit. I can't just take one drag, Jimmy. I'll get obsessed with how to get the next one… and the next."

"So," Jimmy theorized, putting the pack back into his breast pocket, "cigarettes are like Lay's potato chips. You can't smoke just one."

That comment warranted another slap in the good arm. "Asshole."

A series of faint pops carried to Jude's ears from far off on the north end of the city. Dogs started barking as a result, startled by the sudden fireworks. The sun drifted further down toward the horizon, the determined celestial body never pausing from noises made by mere humankind. Jude turned her face upward and closed her eyes, warming her skin in the waning sunlight. It certainly wouldn't give her the first suntan of the season, but it would provide a measure of solace for however long she could manage to hold onto it.

"Love ya, sis," Jimmy said out of the blue.

Jude smiled, soaking in that declaration of brotherly love along with the remaining rays of the sun. After the third police siren of the evening grew louder as it passed the complex before receding again into the east end of town, she replied with her own three little words, "You're a dork."

4
## Re-opening Wounds
Day Zero – 11:04pm EST

"... *of the protesters have come over the barricade...*" a man said off-camera. Jude and her Mom watched as the earlier reported CNN news coverage was being dissected. "*...and seem to be ignoring the orders of the National Guardsmen.*"

The footage continued. One of the bloody protesters rushed over to the closest Guardsman and made a grab for his rifle, the Guardsman batting the protester's hand away and shouting for him to stand down. The protester stumbled, but caught his balance

13

quickly before biting the Guardsman on the thigh through his fatigues.

"Did that asshole just bite that guy?" Jimmy asked from the hallway.

"Shssh," both Jude and Mom said with engrossed annoyance. The bitten Guardsman screamed and slammed the butt of his rifle into the back of the protester's head. A fellow squad mate pulled the protester off, the biter coming away with a chunk of thigh meat.

"What the fuck?" Jimmy muttered.

Neither Jude nor Mom bothered to correct or scold him for his vulgarity—not this time, at any rate. Jude's mouth was agape and Mom had both hands over hers. "Oh my God," Jude whispered.

"*Oh my God,*" the reporter continued, "*the protesters have attacked the Guardsmen. Truly out of their minds…*"

The video was shaky, but the camera was still locked on the action in the middle of the street. The protesters surged over the concrete rail and converged on the soldiers closest to them. When rifle butts to the head didn't quell them, the soldiers opened fire on the crowd.

"*The soldiers have been overrun! They have opened fire on the civilians. I can't believe this…*" the reporter on the scene yelled. No one in the Sawyer household said a word. Jimmy sunk to the arm of the couch, not taking his eyes off the screen. Nobody blinked as the remaining Guardsmen retreated from the scene.

"*… the soldiers are down! The guardsmen are down! The crowd is… oh my God… they're eating the soldiers… what the hell?… Louie, let's get the fuck out of here!*"

Louie must have seen some extreme shit in his day to continue holding a steady shot of the carnage. Civilians ran toward the lens. The video shook for a moment longer before the image spun toward the ground, the camera recording a pair of sneakers on the asphalt. The reporter spat out curses as he and Louie ran down the block. A sudden screech of metal and a loud bang followed. The camera steadied again, auto-focusing on the interior floorboards of what Jude assumed was their news van.

The feed turned to static before cutting back to the NBC affiliate. Ron Williams, the anchor Mom had always watched for what she said was his 'John Forsythe looks', looked like he was about to lose his dinner in front of his viewing audience. Julia Wong, the token female on this newscast as far as Jude was concerned, stared at the desk with her loose-leaf notes wadded up in her fist.

"Ron?" Ms. Wong asked, her eyes still downward.

"Uh..." the veteran anchorman uttered. Not his most Pulitzer Prize worthy statement, but probably the most relevant and poignant word he could have said to capture the feelings of anyone watching. "I..." That was the last thing Ron Williams said because, at that moment, the power went out in the apartment.

"Are you shitting me?" Jude heard her youngest brother yell from his bedroom down the hallway. Even if Mom had registered Michael's curse, she wouldn't have reprimanded the young angel. The hierarchical favoritism was very apparent in the Sawyer household.

Michael soon loomed in the hallway. The light on his phone splashed across the hallway shelves and living room end tables filled with Hummel figurines and knickknacks. Mom had always said the figurines were placed was where they could be best appreciated. Everyone else in the household knew those the figurines were in the spots where they were most likely be knocked over and broken. Of course, when Jude had bumped into one of the shelves at thirteen-years-old and broke one of Mom's favorites, she was dragged over her father's knee and given a belt whipping in reparation for her transgression. At the time, it had seemed she had been given a few more lashes for her trouble—probably just for being born.

"Mom," Michael called out. "What the fuck's going on?"

Jude looked at her Mom and watched as she snapped out of her shocked stupor enough to shield her eyes against the glare of the light on Michael's phone. She cleared her throat and stood up, ignoring the hand Jude held out to assist her in the darkness.

"Where's your father?" was her answer.

## 5
# *Good Little Soldiers*
+1 Day – 12:02am EST

*Where's your father?* was Mom's answer to any problem she couldn't deal with, three words she had spoken several times since the power had gone out. Admittedly, Mr. Horace Sawyer was a man of many talents. He had been the repairman and the superintendent of the apartment building before this one. He had worked on boat and small aircraft motors. He dabbled in photography and painting. But, probably, the most honed skill Jude's father possessed was his ability to drink pretty much all comers under the proverbial table.

"Why isn't he home yet?" Mom asked, wringing her hands with the handkerchief she always had up her sleeve like a stage magician.

"Dad don't need power to open up another bottle of beer, Mom."

"Jimmy," she retorted, "just because your father isn't here doesn't mean you can say disparaging things about him. Show some respect."

In the soft yellow glow of the fat candles Mom had stored for such blackout emergencies, Jude saw Jimmy wringing the top of his cane with both hands. He clenched his jaw several times before visibly swallowing down Mom's comment to his gut. It would have plenty of company in the pit of his stomach with the rest of his angst.

"I'm sure he'll be home soon," Michael said from the recliner \ off-limits to all of the Sawyer kids—except him, apparently. Jude remembered at least a dozen occasions where she had received a smack on the back of the head from Dad after finding her too comfortable in his chair. With only the couch, Mom's high-back chair, and the recliner able to fit in the living room—plus, a narrow coffee table between the couch and the television—it was either sit in the forbidden recliner, fight for space on the couch or relegate her boney butt to the too-thin thread-bare rug.

"He needs to be here in case something happens," Mom said.

As soon as her words left her mouth, three police cars raced down the block with their sirens shrieking in the dead of night. The living room windows were the perfect vantage point to see the world beyond the walls of the apartment. While it would be great to have a bird's eye view from a higher apartment, living on street level did have its advantages. Any time she had been grounded to her room—which had been a lot—her friends still came over to visit with her at the bedroom window. Jude had found the loophole in her punishment. She was in her room. Her friends were in the flowerbeds. The defense rests.

A commotion stirred up outside. The Mexicans who lived in the apartment across the hall were now drinking Coronas at the corner under the dead lamppost, lining up their empty bottles around its base in an ever-widening ring. Jude imagined her father lining up his own empties on the bar top, each bottle a good little soldier who had sacrificed its life blood for the ongoing frontal assault on his liver.

A gunshot cracked outside. Someone screamed. Several men started yelling at each other. The noises were way too loud and close for Jude's comfort. She decided to find something suitable to defend herself with in case someone decided to take a run at the windows in her father's absence. Jude left her mom sitting in front of the coffee table flickering with a half-dozen candles in order to take a look in the kitchen. Trying to keep the noise down and avoid disturbing anything in the tidy kitchen, Jude lifted a ten-inch cast iron skillet from the stovetop. It was substantial enough to cause plenty of damage on the skull of an intruder, but she knew her arm would quickly tire. She slid it back on the burner and stepped over to the prep counter. The butcher block seemed to hold the perfect bladed weapons. She pulled out the Santuko knife from the block. It had a smooth shaped handle and a seven-inch blade. There wasn't a tang or hilt—whatever you called the piece of metal separating the blade from the handle—to keep Jude's hand from slicing straight into the blade if she exerted enough force against someone. She put the knife back with the others. A meat tenderizing mallet would be more serviceable and was already shaped like a weapon without the likelihood of inflicting damage to its owner. It didn't have the heft of a real hammer since it was made from cast aluminum, but Jude figured it was the safest as a threatening deterrent.

"You going on a rampage?" Jimmy asked from the doorway.

"No," Jude said defensively, her voice having an unintended whine to it.

"Easy, killer," he said, raising his good hand up in surrender.

Jude realized she was brandishing the tenderizer in an aggressive way, holding it with the head pointed at Jimmy. She dropped it to her side. "Sorry."

"No worries, warrior princess. It is getting cray out there. If this goes on for too long, people are going to run out of booze and start getting really mean."

"What if someone tries to get in?"

"Then," Jimmy said, pulling back an aluminum bat beside the doorway, "if they get past the welded window bars, we bash in some skulls."

"You gonna be able to lift that thing?" She regretted the words as soon as they left her lips.

He braced his back against the door frame and raised up the baseball bat like a barbarian's club. "Hell, yeah."

After a few seconds, Jimmy dropped the tip of the bat to the floor with a thump and a silence fell between them. It wasn't a quiet of the uncomfortable variety, just one between siblings that came from years of growing up under the same tyrannical rule.

The wall phone rang. Neither of them was shocked or surprised there was an incoming call after midnight, even with the power out. It was a normal occurrence anytime their father was out of the house. The miracles of modern technology had forgotten landline phones still carried low-voltage electricity through them direct from the phone line itself.

"Answer that phone," their mother called out. "Tell your father to get home!"

Michael walked up between Jimmy and Jude, slapping the receiver up off the cradle of the rotary phone. He grabbed it in mid-air and slung it to his ear. "Hello. Sawyer residence."

We all watched Michael listen to whoever was on the other end of the phone. It was usually the desk sergeant at the police precinct telling one of us Dad had forgotten how to get home or he had been on the losing end of a bar fight. "Thanks, Hank. We'll be right there." When Hank called, it usually meant Dad had overstayed his welcome at the bar.

"Where's your father?" Mom asked.

"Dad had an accident."

"Oh my God! What happened?"

"Hank said that someone banged him up pretty good in the alley before some guys broke it up."

"Glad someone came to help," Mom replied. "That's good. Right?"

"I hope so," Jude replied.

"I'll go get him, Mom."

"Thank you, Michael."

"Yes, 'Thank you, Michael'," Jimmy mocked him.

"Hey, don't hate me because I'm a beautiful human being, big brother. Give me Andy's bat."

Jimmy handed it over and received a soft slap to the cheek as a reward. Michael winked at Jimmy and Jude before heading down the short front hall with the bat in one hand and his keys and iPhone in the other. It only took a few seconds before Michael had locked the door behind him, leaving all of them in a different version of familiar silence. This one, unfortunately, was filled with dread and tension.

6
## *The Weak Side*
+1 Day – 12:37am EST

The yelling and police sirens had grown louder and more consistent, now joined by sporadic gunfire from the other side of town—probably the retail area and the downtown. Those always seemed to be the first locations to be looted and ransacked.

"Can't believe he took my bat!" Jimmy complained from the couch. He sat with his hands folded and his lower lip extended in a pout. Very unattractive for a man.

"It's Andy's bat," Jude reminded him. "Don't be so melodramatic." Mom had abandoned her chair in favor of alternating peeking through the blinds and pacing the hallway between the living room and the master bedroom. She carried a small candle with her, the glare from the flame obscuring her view out to the street every time she looked out. "You know you would see better if you didn't stick the candle so close to glass, don't you?"

"I can see fine, Jude."

"Okay, Mom." Jude held her tongue against saying anything else. These verbal battles were rarely won, and this battle wasn't worth taking the field for.

"What's taking them so long?" Mom's pacing continued.

When Mom finally drifted off toward the bedroom again, Jude shifted on the middle couch cushion and swept her legs under her to look at Jimmy head-on.

"Yes?" Jimmy drew out his words for maximum effect. "Can I help you?"

"What the hell is wrong with this family?" Jude whispered, still worried about attracting any commentary from Mom.

"You just starting to speculate on that issue, Jude? I've been asking myself that question since me and my awesomeness sprang out of the womb. Of course, I've been bitching about a lot of things since way before I knew bitching about stuff was a thing." He shifted as best he could to face Jude, pulling his leg along with his good hand. "Bullshit body, though."

Jude reached out to his weak arm but he pulled it back before she made contact. Jude was an idiot, knowing he had an aversion to being touched anywhere where he was atrophied.

BAM! The front door banged open.

"Some help here!" Michael yelled from the front hall. "He ain't getting any lighter!"


7
## *The Prodigal Son Returns*
+1 Day – 12:37am EST


Jude sprang up from the couch, pulling Jimmy up with her. Mom hurried through the hall, her sleeve brushing against several of her Hummel figurines on the elbow height shelf. One even rocked back and forth a couple times. Jude watched as it finally settled back on its base. Thank God. She didn't need to be blamed for anything else tonight.

Michael lumbered from the foyer to the dining room, dragging Dad with him. A vein stood out on her brother's forehead as he struggled with Dad's slumping weight. It wasn't dead weight, but it was damn close.

Mom stopped short. She stifled a gasp from behind one cupped hand. The flickering candle in the center of the dining room table left Michael in shadow. Jude's father, on the other hand, was in full amber illumination. Blood caked his left cheek from his temple to the collar of his work shirt. His eyes were open, but glazed over. The candlelight danced across them.

Jimmy limped to the kitchen. Water started to run from the tap at the sink. As muscular as Michael was, he was forced to lean Dad against one of the straight-back chairs.

"Come on, Jimmy" Michael demanded.

Jimmy came from the kitchen with a hot wet dishcloth in his hand and a dry dish towel over his shoulder. He held out the dishcloth to his brother.

"Don't you dare use that cloth, James," his Mom warned from the edge of the living room. She had ventured no closer, but she had straightened up a little taller as she regained some of her authority over her apartment and the things happening within it. "Go get the rags your father uses to sop up after the washing machine leaks."

Jimmy alternated a look between his drunken, swaying father and his younger brother straining under his weight, the dripping washcloth hanging in his weak hand.

Michael hiked up Dad. "Just hurry up."

Jimmy tossed the washcloth back into the kitchen sink and made his way past Jude. He had to sidestep around his glaring mom. Apparently, her disappointment in her son was enough to distract her from the proud bleeding, staggering mess propped up in the dining room.

"Jude?" Michael asked with a huff. "You wanna help me out here?"

Jude was paralyzed, standing between her parents. She tried to make her mouth work. Tried to say something explaining why she couldn't move... neither toward her Mom nor her Dad. She knew she should be helping in some way, but couldn't connect that thought to any motor functions.

"Jude…" her father gurgled.

That single word, filled with weak disdain and a sustained anger developed over years to perfection, got her body moving. She rushed over to the opposite side of Michael, pulled out one of the dining room chairs, and placed it sideways in front of them. Michael maneuvered their father around in order to ease him into the chair. It creaked back a few inches on the linoleum.

"Watch the floors," Mom warned.

Jimmy returned with several rags draped over his arm. He tossed one of the wetted towels—from under the bathroom sink faucet, she guessed—to Michael who adeptly caught it. Once Jimmy made it to the dining room, he dumped the dry rags on the table.

"Don't get my tablecloth dirty." Mom continued to be rooted to the spot where the hallway and living room met. Jimmy clenched his jaw against barking back at Mom for admonishing him for his apparent misguided attempts to help. Jude didn't have such filters, unfortunately.

"Jesus Christ, Mom," Jude cursed. "Leave Jimmy alone! He's helping. More than the bitching you're doing." The snap cowed Mom back into stunned silence, but instantly flared up a gasoline fueled fire pit full of fanned shame and guilt in Jude's belly. Catholic guilt had always been the default underpinning in the Sawyer household, courtesy of the Pope, the Roman Catholic Church and St. Angus of the Mount. Mom and Dad also had their own ways of driving spikes of disappointment into their children. Maybe that was why Matthew and Andy had joined the armed services as soon as they had come of age.

Michael wiped the blood from their father's face and neck with the wet towel. Once it was soaked red, he handed it to Jude. She took it to the kitchen sink to rinse out while Jimmy handed his brother a clean towel. Jude turned on the hot water, letting it become near scalding before running the towel under the stream from the faucet. After her hands turned pink, Jude finally wrung out the towel. Red splashed around the basin and swirled down the drain. Jude was sure her mother would have some choice words about any blood residue come tomorrow. She wrung out the towel twice more before handing it off to Michael.

"Thanks. Take this one." Michael continued to wipe off their father with the new towel while she stood there with the second bloody one. If any blood dropped to the floor, Jude was unaware of it. Dad was starting to look more human again, even if his body was slouching more against Jimmy and threatening to topple completely off the chair. Michael took a step back and appraised his work. After wiping Dad's neck a couple more times, he handed the towel to Jude. "A couple scratches. Nothing too deep. They're already clotting. Just need him out of that shirt and he should be good enough to sleep it off."

"Take it off and bring him to the bedroom," Mom said with authority. In spite of her reactions tonight, she'd dealt with Dad's escapades many times over the years. They all had experience dealing with the drunken aftermath. Guiding him to bed so he didn't wander around the apartment was a common occurrence. The bloody mess was the only new development.

Michael peeled off Dad's button-down shirt and handed it to Jude. She had been relegated to hamper duty. A woman's work was never done, apparently. Michael lifted Dad off the chair—with

Jimmy's awkward help—and dragged him across the apartment toward the bedrooms.

"Don't hit any of the Hummels," Mom ordered.

The boys sighed and turned sideways enough to shuffle their father against the wall opposite the precariously placed breakable knick-knacks. They managed to get past the ceramic German-born boys and girls without incident, the porcelain children's eyes wary and watchful. Yep, even the Hummels looked worried about what could possibly happen next. They had already witnessed a lot. Maybe, too much.

Jude had picked a hell of a year to stop drinking and taking her pills.


# 8
## *Cool to the Touch*
+1 Day – 4:36am EST


Jude was nudged awake by whispers and a random tap on the bottom of the only foot not under the covers. She pulled her leg back under the blanket in an attempt to ward off further requests to get out of bed.

"Wake up… get up."

Jude pulled away the covers from her face and stared at the dark room. Without the illuminated blocky numbers of the digital alarm clock or the glare of the street lamp outside the window, it was near impossible to figure out how early in the morning it was. It seemed liked their father had been cleaned up and put to bed just a couple minutes ago.

"Uhh…" Jude moaned. "What?"

Jimmy smoothed out the covers at the edge of the bed before plopping his ass down next to Jude. "It's too quiet."

"You woke me up for that?" Although groggy and irritated at Jimmy, Jude perked up her ears and cocked her head. There was no whoosh of cars passing by or the blaring of angry horns. The yelling, barking and sirens from earlier had gone eerily silent. The warbling of mourning doves nested in the tree on the corner had ceased. The coos of the pigeons who usually clicked along several of the poop-stained window ledges... gone. It was as if the loss of electricity had sapped the energy from the entire world.

"Yeah" Jude finally answered, "it's quiet."

"It's weird," Jimmy muttered.

"You're weird. It's not like the lights have never gone out before." Jude propped herself up against the headboard, punching her pillow in an effort to fluff it up. She tried to flick a foot at Jimmy's ass in an act of playful defiance, but never got close since his ass pinned down her legs under the covers.

"It's different this time."

"Dad coming home all ghoulish didn't help any."

"Probably." Jimmy chuckled. It sounded resigned and defeated rather than being filled with any mirth. Jimmy had always held his head high and gave off positive vibes through everything he had been saddled with, both physically and psychologically. But, even the strongest tree can only bend so much before breaking, right?

"Everything will be okay," Jude offered, scooping up Floopy in her arms and hugging it to her chest. The oversized stuffed lion had always been a wonderful fuzzy and squishy source of comfort for her. Her dad had bought it for her a long time ago during one of his bouts of alcohol abstinence.

"Sure." Jimmy shrugged. "When the lights come back on everything will be just perfect again." His voice lacked any belief of his words. As much of a positive influence Jimmy had been to her, she had forgotten he sometimes got lost in the melancholy of his own existence. Having both a body and parents betraying him at every turn was exhausting.

"You want Floopy?" she asked.

"Nah." He shook his head, but did crack the slightest of smiles. "Thanks, though."

The floors in the hallway creaked. She hugged Floopy tight enough to force his head to lop to one side. Was it already time for her father to get ready for work? She hoped not. His daily routine was to check in on her, tucking the covers up to her chest and grazing his fingers along her shoulders while she pretended to be fast asleep. She always felt him staring at her while she concentrated on keeping her breathing light and even. Jude was sure one day her father would call bullshit on her pantomime, scaring the fuck out of her. But, he hadn't so far. She was glad Jimmy was here as a deterrent.

The bedroom door opened. Jude realized she had dug her fingers into Jimmy's thigh a moment after she realized it wasn't her father at the door. She looked up at her brother with apologetic eyes. He gave her an understanding nod, even if he winced a little when she let go of his good leg.

Mom took a step into Jude's room and cast her candle around. While not an active participant in the arcane rituals of her former high school life and boasting a fairly stark bedroom, Jude still had a collection of posters she was proud of—Avenged Sevenfold, Disturbed, Five Finger Death Punch and Evanescence. The only other furniture besides the bed was a three-drawer dresser forcing her to keep her wardrobe fairly sparse. Anything not fitting there—

even though she used the KonMari method—ended up under her bed or in one of the storage containers stacked up in whatever corner she had available. Her Mom stared at the blindfolded skeleton surrounded in fluorescent green smoke and chains, the words 'Welcome to the Family' written across the bottom of the Avenged Sevenfold poster. The look of disgust and worry for Jude's mortal soul on her Mom's face was comical... and almost endearing.

"The power's still out, huh?" her Mom stated as a rhetorical question.

"Yep," Jimmy answered, hiding a smile from everyone but Jude. "Thought you were Dad."

"Let your father sleep," Mom advised. "He had a difficult night."

"Sure." Jude said, relieved the loss of power offered at least one day of interrupted routine. She rolled her eyes, fully aware the gesture was hidden from her Mom by Jimmy's body. Yeah, her father's night had been difficult, alright. Of course, all of his difficult nights were a string of unfortunate or undeserved events sewn together by a mix of self-righteous indignation and alcohol.

"I'm going to shower and dress" Mom told them. "It's my day for yoga at the Y."

"I don't think the Y will be open today," Jimmy advised.

"But today is my day for yoga," Mom repeated.

Jimmy opened his mouth to assert some measure of rational thinking, but quickly thought better than to start an early morning argument he had no chance of winning. Jude patted him on the thigh, both to soothe the fingernail marks she had left behind and to commend him on his use of restraint.

Mom left the room in pursuit of preparing a fresh pot of percolated coffee before her announced shower. No instant coffee in this house. Heavens, no. It would be absurd to think a Keurig would make life any better. Jude had tried to get one for the family—her included, of course—but her mom made her take it back to the store before anyone had a chance to try it out. That had been a sad Christmas on many levels.

"Still weird," Jimmy stated.

"Yes, she is."

"No." Jimmy shook his head. "The fact Dad isn't up."

Jude looked at her brother with a blank stare. "He was a bloody mess."

"And, every fucking day he is up at the same time. No matter what."

Jude mulled that over for a moment. Jimmy was right. No matter how late he stayed out or how drunk he was when he got home, you could set your watch by his uncanny ability to be up for work scant hours later.

"Should we check on him?" She hated the words as soon as she spoke them. It was amazing how indoctrinated she was toward family and how strong the shackled servitude was to the patriarchy. She sighed and pushed her feet into Jimmy through the blanket. He grunted, but didn't move. "Come on, Jimmy. Move if you are feeling so strongly about this."

"Yeah. Yeah." Jimmy scooted to the edge, leaned himself up on his cane, and headed to the door. Once he was clear, Jude flipped over the covers and swung her legs until the soles of her bare feet touched the cold floor. She shivered and pouted, touching the abandoned warm covers longingly. With a more deliberate sigh—and, maybe, more of a cleansing breath—Jude got to her feet and padded to the door. Jimmy led the way down the hallway, past the always-poised-to-tilt death-trap shelf of Hummel figurines, past the one bathroom the entire family shared, and the opposite doors to the boys' bedrooms. Even with Matty gone and Andy still deployed overseas, Jimmy and Michael were forced to bunk in the same ten-by-twelve bedroom across the hall from Matty's empty bedroom—and shrine. At the end of the hallway was the closed door to their parents' room.

In the kitchen, Mom was opening cabinets and banging them closed. Dishes from the previous night were clicking against each other as they were being put away. Mom was always meticulous about the condition of her culinary sanctuary. Here, on the other end of the apartment, Jude pressed her hand and cheek against her parents' bedroom door. It was cool to the touch, too. Jude didn't bother to knock, sacrificing politeness for discretion.

The interior of the master bedroom—only called that because it was the largest of the bedrooms by four more feet on one side—was dark and stuffy. Piles of papers, shoe boxes, and a massive dresser filled one wall. The queen-sized bed barely fit in the room with a night stand on either side. The door to the closet had been removed years ago and replaced with a curtain because it had banged against the nightstand. There was the distinct musk of the familiar smell of camphor from the mothballs Mom used to guard against the fabric-devouring insects. There was also a metallic copper taste in the air from Dad's shirt from last night. As was so out of character, Dad was still asleep. His hulking form was still under the comforter. Maybe the scrape at the bar did worse to him than anyone thought. Jimmy stood at the door and gestured for Jude to go ahead.

"Cowardly son of a bitch," Jude whispered in a hiss.

"Yep." Jimmy wore the badge with honor, giving his sister a salute with his cane.

Jude moved to the side of the bed. She reached out to the covers, but pulled her hand back before touching them. She whispered, "Dad." He didn't stir. In fact, he was much quieter without his usual warbling snore. Jude reached out again, this time rocking his arm back and forth.

"What are you doing?"

Jude jumped back, letting out a yip.

Her Mom stood in the doorway, her hands on her hips. "You let your father sleep!"

Mom's raised voice also did nothing to rouse her husband. He didn't grunt, fart, or roll over. Jude put caution and possible retribution aside, whipped back the covers, and put her hand on her dad's bare bicep. She didn't bother shaking him, quickly pulling her hand back to her own chest and backing away. "He's cold, Mom. He's cold."

# 9
# *Where the Hallway Ends*
+1 Day – 5:21am EST

"I can't believe Mom was sleeping next to him," Jimmy said in disbelief, sitting in the same chair their father had the night before.

"Or, that she didn't realize he was dead," Michael added from where he leaned against the doorway to the kitchen. He had a cup of Mom's percolated coffee in his hands. "Creepy."

"Umm hmm," Jude commented noncommittally from the floor in front of the apartment's worn steel front door. She couldn't believe he was dead. Her own father was gone and she had no fucking idea how to feel about it. She was disgusted at herself for the sense of relief she felt knowing he wasn't going to get out of bed again. Their mother was holding vigil in the bedroom. Let her. Jude couldn't think of any reason to go down to the end of the hallway to see him again.

"Gotta get him out of here sooner than later," Jimmy advised. "We can't keep him in the bedroom. It's weird."

"Easy enough, bro." Michael pulled out his iPhone and started typing on the screen. Within several seconds, he pressed the screen with authority and held the phone up for everyone to hear.

The phone rang twice before it clicked over to a recorded message, "We're sorry. The directors at Sampson & Sons Funeral Homes are currently assisting others. We understand you are grieving and may be in need of counseling. Please leave your name and number and we will return your call as quickly as we can. Thank you."

Jude expected the message to segue to a beep, but after two clicks the line suddenly disconnected to silence. At least a land line gave a steady dial tone to coax the caller into taking further action.

Michael stared at the phone for several seconds before using his thumbs to select the next funeral home to call. This time, he held the phone to his ear. He gave Jimmy and Jude the thumbs up and a smile before his triumphant was stricken into a frown. He shook his head. "Another recording."

"Shouldn't you leave a message?"

"I would've, Jimmy, but it said the inbox was full and disconnected me. What the fuck?"

Jude half-listened to her brothers' tele-communication plight, suddenly distracted by the bedroom door at the end of the hallway. It was a very long hallway. Had it always been so far away? How had Jimmy and Michael dragged their father's dead weight that far?

33

But he hadn't been dead last night. As unresponsive as he had been, he had still stumbled a leg or two forward while they had lugged him through the apartment.

The door was closed. No sounds came from the other side. If their mom was crying, she was doing it more softly than what could carry to the rest of the apartment. The door was closed, true, but it had always been closed as a matter of fact. It was their parent's private space—off limits to any of the kids. For the Sawyer kids, it was like the apartment ended when the hallway did. The master bedroom was simply a place discussed as whispered stories of urban legend.

The door burst open, revealing a swallowing darkness beyond swirling with hissing smoke and roiling with enormous shiny shelled insects.

Fuck! Jude's legs pistoned up. She slid up the door, the palms of her hands and her back pressed against it. She tried to draw in a breath, but her lungs had collapsed with the weight of her terror at the sight of the snapping leviathans at the end of the hallway. Her startled brothers glanced over at her for a second before Michael returned his attention to his phone. Jimmy limped over to Michael to supervise his online progress.

The smoke and insects parted the darkness. Dad emerged from the bedroom. He stepped out into the hallway, still wearing his undershirt and work pants. His feet were bare and he wiggled his toes when they touched the cool floor. The blood had returned, oozing freely from the cuts at his temple. He paid it no mind as he shrugged back into the blood-stained dress shirt he had worn for his night out. He straightened it by lining up the second button and buttonhole. The blood had dried into the fabric, too saturated to soak up the fresh fluid streaming down his neck.

"You don't think a little bar fight was going to slow me down forever, did you, pumpkin?" Jude's father asked. Each syllable gurgled from his throat as he spoke. He might have punctured a lung from a broken rib. It wouldn't have been the first time he had suffered such severe internal injuries. The last time he was rushed to the emergency room, his appendix had burst on the operating table. That had been a close call.

"Don't worry about me, pumpkin," Dad said. "Nothing a little on-the-job scotch can't cure."

Her father left pale red footprints on the floor behind him as he walked toward Jude. He stopped at her bedroom and stood in the doorway. He smiled at her before disappearing into her empty room. The door at the end of the hall was still filled with the oily shimmering blackness. She was startled as he quickly stepped out to the hallway again, a smile plastered on his face. He brought his left hand up to his nose and breathed in deeply the scent of something on his fingers. "Your mom wanted another son, but I was happy to have a daughter. Did you know that?"

Her father passed the point of no return—the precarious Hummel shelves. Jimmy and Michael paid him no mind as they continued to look at the iPhone. Their faces were lit up in a ghastly white as their eyes darted across the information on the screen. The man Jude had despised since she had turned twelve-years-old walked across the living room, licking his cracked lips and leering at her with bloodshot eyes filled with flecks of red and gold. "My sweet, sweet girl."

Jude screamed.

Michael and Jimmy jumped in surprise, their heads snapping toward her. Jude slapped her hands over her mouth, her breathing ragged through her runny nose. Tears fell across her clasped fingers, running down her arms to her sleeves.

Jimmy rushed to her side, half-falling to his knees because of his bum leg. He hugged her. "What's wrong?"

Jimmy's hug left Jude's cheek on his shoulder and the sightline to the bedroom clear. Michael looked on, the phone research forgotten. Her father had vanished. The bloody footprints had disappeared and their parents' bedroom door was closed tight.

She stared at the door.

It burst open, making Jude yip in fright. Jimmy held her tighter with his strong arm. Jude wrapped her arms around him and buried her face in his chest. She didn't want to see her father again. She had seen enough.

"Did you call 911?" Jude's mom asked as she rushed toward Michael. The bedroom door was open, pale weak sunlight starting to burn across the room. "They'll come, right?"

Apparently, the decision to stop the drinking and anti-depressants wasn't enough. She needed to stop taking the sleeping pills, too.


**10**
## *Poor Connections*
+1 Day – 5:57am EST


The Sawyers sat around the dining room table, Jimmy having no compunction about sitting in the chair of his dead father. His cane was propped against the wall, Mom having already yelled at him for leaning it on the table. God knows the cane might scratch an edge. Of course, the scratch would have to have been made from the cane's rounded handle rubbing through the linen table cloth through the felt table pad to the lacquered oak. Jimmy had promptly used and dropped this logic as his defense after it fell on Mom's deaf ears—per usual.

Michael put the phone on the table center runner and pressed the call button, making sure it was close enough to Mom to hear. He placed a mostly empty flavored water bottle in front of him. The phone came to life with its warbling ring tone. Jude leaned in and stared at the screen as if it would reveal to her the secrets of the universe. What they heard next was nothing so earth shattering, but was like the beam of a lighthouse when out in a rowboat in stormy seas.

"9-1-1, what is your emergency?"

Everyone exhaled but did not reply.

"9-1-1, what is your emergency, please?" The voice was pleasant, but far from enthusiastic. The strain of several hours of work surely had bled into her voice.

"Uh," Jimmy finally spoke up, leaning even further onto the edge of the table. "Yes. Hi."

"What is your emergency, sir?" Jude could hear the din of what sounded like dozens of other emergency operators dealing with their own dire situations. She thought she heard a scream in the background, but played it off as her current overactive imagination spiked by an ill-advised sleeping aid. The operator's voice suddenly lost all pleasantry as she spoke to someone else on that side of the phone. "Another fuckin' five-year-old playin' on the goddamn phone."

"Wait!" Jude yelled.

"Yes?" The operator waited.

"Yes," Jude found her voice again. "Our father died."

The operator's voice softened a little. "Sorry, ma'am."

"What do we do with him?" Jimmy asked from the other side of the table.

"Yes, sir. I understand. Our emergency first responding teams are currently overwhelmed, sir."

Mom looked around the table at each of her kids. She leaned in and spoke at the phone. "My husband is laying in the bedroom, right? When will you be here to take him?"

"Ma'am," the operator advised in a tired voice, as if she had given this advice several times today, "if you provide your contact information and address, we will schedule a pick up."

A pick up? Sounded like something Goodwill would do for the old clothes people wanted to donate. Should they wrap her father up in a few commercial garbage bags from the super's basement storage room, wrap Dad up and leave him at the curb? He was a piece of garbage, sure, but he was still a human being.

"How long do we have to wait?" Michael asked after giving the operator our information.

"Unknown at this time, sir. Someone will contact you as soon as they get you on the schedule."

Jimmy asked the practical, if morbid, question. "What do we do with him in the meantime?"

"Sir, keep him in as cool and dry a place as possible."

*Like a potato*, Jude thought. Her father was now akin to a starchy tuber plant. She thought back to the first time her mom had told her to clean a basket of potatoes in the pantry after she came home from school. After she had changed into her play clothes, Jude had pulled out the basket to find the potatoes were alive, having sprouted creepy new fleshy roots all over their gritty skins. They had stared at her with their dark swirling eyes, angry at her for tearing away their appendages and their attempts to flourish. Angry at her for torturing them as she ripped away their newly-formed limbs.

"...thanks...bye..." someone said.

The sound of the call disconnecting brought Jude back into the present. The 9-1-1 operator had told them to keep her dad in a cool dry place. The curtains in the master bedroom would have to be drawn. It would be the best they could do. Since they had no power, they had no means of actually keeping Dad cool. Protection from the sun would have to suffice. And, keeping that damn door closed.

# 11
## *All's Quiet on the Western Front*
+1 Day – 10:34am EST

Jude expected the apartment would take on an ever-strengthening rotting smell, with an oppressive and sour taste sticking to the tongue that couldn't be washed away with any amount of Gatorade or ginger ale. In reality, having a dead body in the apartment wasn't as bad as she had been conditioned to believe from all the movies she'd watched or the pulpy literature she'd read. Regardless, she refused to step foot in the master bedroom in spite of any coaxing or cajoling, content enough to sit in her own room.

While her worry the harbinger of death and the body in the master bedroom would eventually come for her seemed to stay unsubstantiated, there were more tangible and sinister forces at work. Mainly... time and boredom. After the call to the 9-1-1 operator, Michael and Jimmy had argued over how to handle the body. Mom had chimed in about making sure they respected their father by not disturbing any of his things—as if all of the Sawyer children had their greedy fingers ready to snatch up all of Dad's worldly possessions. It really did speak volumes about what Mom must think of her offspring.

After a while, Jude tired of sitting in her room. She did not own a battery-powered transistor radio and worried about how long her phone battery would hold out before it lost the battle against a powerless charging wire. She looked at the phone and tapped the dark screen to verify—for the tenth time—it was set to airplane mode to save the battery life. Jude toyed with shutting down the phone altogether until an emergency but couldn't actually bring herself to do so. Slipping the phone into the back pocket of her jeans, she followed suit by stepping out of the apartment unnoticed. The door clicked softly into place behind her, leaving her brothers, mother and the shell of the father she once feared inside.

The hallway on the first floor of the five-story building complex was empty, as lifeless as the apartment she had just escaped from. There were only four apartments on the first and second floors versus the six occupying each of the other four floors. The designers or architects had left room for the two-story glass atrium serving the tiled lobby and main entrance. Anytime the power grid went out and the temperature started rising inside, people would typically congregate for a bit of breeze and gossip. So… maybe everyone was outside.

Jude peeked out the double doors. No one was on the sidewalk. It was a weekday and most people would probably be at their offices in search of corporate generators or commutes to where power still flowed. She thought she heard something in the far-off distance, but by the time she stepped out to the stoop the sound had faded away… if it had ever happened at all.

The traffic lights strung across the intersection swayed in the faintest of breezes, proof the world was still spinning in spite of the blackout. A ripped open cardboard case of Bud Lite beer overflowed with empty crushed aluminum cans. A few other brands of beer had snuck in there, as well. Between the case and the lamp post was the completed and surprisingly intricate circle of Corona bottles, spiraling out in a counter-clockwise swirling design. Drunk people could be very artistic or morally questionable. The latter was the case with her father.

The sound of fabric brushing past the prickles of a thorny Crepe Myrtle bush came from over Jude's right shoulder. It was followed by gruff advice. "You shouldn't be out here by yourself."

Jude turned around at the sound of the voice. Still in a black tightly-cinched bathrobe and matching slippers, Mr. Emery looked out of place on the sidewalk, especially with no other pedestrians to distract her from his attire. His brown hair was combed over with a low part, plastered to his scalp in an effort to make his appearance a bit more youthful. He wasn't old by any stretch, but Jude had always gotten the feeling he was a bit vain about his looks or, maybe, he just lamented the passage of time and detested the ravages it had exacted on his body.

"Hi, Mr. Emery."

"Hey, kiddo."

"A bit empty out here, huh?"

"Yep." He looked up the rest of the block before gazing past Jude's shoulder toward the intersection. "Maybe... too quiet." He chuckled at his own stretched out words, probably quoting a line from one of the movies he loved so much. She never got his humor but he had always been kind to her when her parents were being... themselves.

41

A blare of sirens came from several blocks away. She exhaled a ragged sigh of relief. "There you go. At least there's still some life out here."

"Good thing, kiddo. We should go back inside, though. The radio says to stay inside."

"You have power?" Jude asked hopefully.

"Nah. Just my transistor radio. Always got fresh batteries. Don't want the radio to die and end up missing the Sox. How about you?"

"No such luck." Mr. Emery had offered her a good segue with his 'don't want the radio to die' comment but, for some reason, she didn't want to mention the fact her father had died during the night. She imagined the dialogue.

*"Don't want the radio to die, you know," Mr. Emery said.*

*"Speaking of dying," Jude retorted. "Did you know my dad died? Hey-yo!"*

She shook her head, just wanting a few more minutes of normalcy. Was that too much to ask? Mr. Emery and his wife had always opened their home to her, giving her a safe haven from whatever troubled waters she was wading through. But, once she crossed this line, she was sure the support she had been afforded by Mr. Emery up to now would be replaced with pity.

Mr. Emery gave her an appraising look. He probably knew there was something going on inside her head. "Like I said, the radio said to stay indoors until everything calms down."

Jude scanned the streets. At the far end of the next block, she spotted three people bumping into each other on the sidewalk. Really? Wasn't it a little late in the morning to still be sloppy drunk and staggering into each other? With no electricity, it seemed some people felt it necessary to let go of their restraint and wisdom. Any excuse to keep the alcohol flowing down one's gullet, she supposed.

Her smile soured as their drunken strides reminded her of her father. Her dead father. "Should probably do what they're saying, then. Don't want to be out here anymore, anyway."

Mr. Emery's smile faded for a moment, but then perked up again. "Well, come on. I'm sure I can find some music on the radio for you. And, I do have those double-stuffed Oreos you always loved."

"I'm a little old for cookies, Mr. Emery."

He looked at her like she had just traded State secrets to the Russians. Then he smiled. "You are never, ever too old for cookies! Now, let's go get some."

The drunkards on the next block had closed the distance to them by half, pretty quick for a bunch of boozed-up degenerates. Jude was suddenly filled with a renewed and burning hatred for anything alcohol-related. She was torn as to whether to take the empty cans and bottles inside or kick them over into the street.

"You coming, Jude?"

In the end, Jude didn't retaliate to the alcoholic evidence. She didn't clean up the mess. She didn't make a huge anger-filled spectacle at other people's bad decisions. Instead, she followed Mr. Emery back inside with the promise of music and cookies. And, maybe—just maybe—a continued distraction from the reality of her life.

## 12
## *Milk Does a Body Good*
+1 Day – 10:57am EST

Mr. Emery's apartment was sparser than the Hummel and bric-a-brac lined walls of the Sawyer home, even though the apartment floorplan was laid out in much the same way. The only difference was Mr. Emery's apartment was a two-bedroom version. The hallway was non-existent, only needing enough length to provide for the closed bathroom and two bedroom doors. That was a relief. The living room, with its one couch against one wall, a dark flat screen television elevated on a vintage trunk on the opposite wall, and the new addition of a distressed painted wood coffee table between them, made the space more spacious than the last time Jude had been here.

"What happened to the Vespa?" Jude asked, Mr. Emery rummaging in the kitchen panty for the baked goods he promised.

"Street legal, baby!"

Jude let out a much-needed laugh, unable to resist Mr. Emery's enthusiasm for the moped—correction, an Italian brand of scooter manufactured by Piaggio, as Mr. Emery had always been quick to point out—he had slowly reassembled in the middle of a tarp in his living room. "At least you have your living room back again."

"Feels a little empty in here now," he said as he brought out a tray with a plate of Oreos and two small plastic tumblers of milk. He saw Jude appraise the selection and spoke up after he set the food and drink on the coffee table. "If the power doesn't come back soon, the milk is going to spoil anyway, right? Might as well enjoy it while it's still cold."

"Can't argue with your logic." Jude grabbed the closest tumbler of milk and plucked one cookie with her other hand. She dunked the cookie—as any good connoisseur would—and stuffed it in her mouth.

"Bravo!" Mr. Emery plopped onto the couch and grunted as he reached forward for his own milk and a stack of four creamy-filled cookies. He settled back and balanced the stack of cookies on his bare knee. He dunked the top cookie into his glass of milk with one quick motion before popping the whole thing into his mouth. He practically bit his finger in the process. Once the milk-softened cookie dissolved enough, Mr. Emery swallowed it down and cleared his throat. "How's the family holding up without the conveniences of modern technology?"

Jude stopped her second cookie in mid-dunk. The distraction of the visit and the Oreos were supposed to keep her from thinking about her dead father. She tried to navigate the question with an elusive answer. "Michael and Jimmy are obsessing with who can keep their phone battery the most charged while still using them constantly."

"And your folks? I know your mom is all about her tablet these days."

Fuck. "She's okay. Probably more worried about the meat spoiling in the fridge if the power stays out too long. Just like the milk." Jude's stomach turned at the thought of a certain slab of meat rotting in the bedroom.

"Oh, yeah! She's certainly all about her kitchen!"

"Yeah," Jude agreed, hoping she dodged a bullet just as she tried to stifle a yawn. "All about her kitchen." The cookie suddenly disintegrated and disappeared into the milk, leaving her finger and thumb with only a wet mush between them. "Shit."

"Whoopsie."

Jude looked at the wavering Oreo as it bumped up against the sides of the glass, appearing and disappearing into the murky white. Figures. Jude reached for another cookie. She hovered her hand over the plate for what seemed like an endless moment of indecision before she clenched it into a fist, returned the glass to the tray and retracted her arms to hug herself.

"You should drink it all down. The cookie mush at the bottom will slide right out of the glass."

"No, thanks." Her heart was racing, but she could barely keep her eyes open. The stress of the last twenty-four hours had wreaked havoc on her.

"You alright?"

"Peachy."

"Listen," Mr. Emery said. He put the remaining stack of cookies in his robe pocket, his leg still exposed. He scooted over to the center couch cushion. Putting his hand on Jude's knee, he continued. "Whatever is going on, you know you can talk to me. You know I've always been here to listen to you, even when your parents weren't…" He mulled over his choice of words, considering what wouldn't show disrespect to the Sawyers in front of her. "…weren't receptive, let's say."

"I know." Jude continued to hug herself. "You've always been kind to me. Ever since I was a little kid."

"The Emery and the Sawyer families go back a long time. Way before I lost Lindsey. You and your folks have been a godsend to me these last couple years."

"Glad we could be there for you, Mr. Emery."

"So, how can I repay my debt to you, Jude? What's troubling you?"

Jude looked at the bedroom door. It was so much closer to the living room in this apartment. She heard something bumping around on the carpet behind the door. "Did you hear that?"

"No. I don't hear anything." Mr. Emery squeezed her thigh above her knee cap.

"Must be my imagination"

"You've always had a very active imagination."

"That's what my mom always says." The scraping and thumps against the door continued, but Jude tried to block them out. As a distraction, words flew out of her mouth before she could stop them. "My dad is dead."

"What? Oh my God! Are you okay?" Mr. Emery said in disbelief, sliding closer to Jude and wrapping his arm around her shoulders. Mr. Emery had always been a good friend—always there to listen to her constant gripes about school, siblings, parents, and life. He always had cookies or some other pastries ready for her when she visited him. She felt safe in his arms, comforted by someone outside the family who didn't look at her as a pest or a genetic mistake. She leaned into the material of his fuzzy robe and took the hand he had on her mid-thigh into hers.

"He just passed away during the night, you know? He came in late after a bar fight, mom and the boys put him to bed, and he was just..."

"Gone?"

"Yeah," Jude replied meekly. "This morning."

"I'm so sorry, sweetie." Mr. Emery squeezed her tighter and pulled her in closer against him.

"Mom was sleeping next to a dead body." She cozied up to him, her eyes very heavy.

"Oh my God." He kissed her three times on the forehead. "My poor little girl."

Jude cried for a moment, not realizing she had done so until the warm salty tear drop cascaded down her cheek. She sniffled and Mr. Emery rocked her back and forth. She grabbed a fistful of the soft fuzzy terry cloth of his robe. Another thump came from behind the bedroom door—this time loud and hard enough to shake the door in the frame.

"What the hell?" Jude stared at the door.

Mr. Emery's now-free hand slowly, but deliberately, traveled north of her mid-thigh toward the place friends and neighbors should know better than to visit. He kissed her again on the forehead, breathing in the scent of her hair before he let out the faintest of sighs.

"What the hell?" Jude repeated, this time at Mr. Emery's actions. Her heart rate tripled. The adrenaline roared through her veins as she pushed him away, twisting away from his hugging arm and groping fingers.

"Fuck!" Mr. Emery held his hand to his now-bloody mouth. She had inadvertently split open his lower lip with a head butt in her effort to get away. Good. Creep. "I've always been a good friend to you."

"So, you thought groping me was a good re-payment?"

Mr. Emery, showing surprising speed and agility, bounded from the couch. The belt of his robe loosened. One of the flaps peeled back to reveal everything from the waist down. He wasn't wearing underwear. He had been wearing nothing at all.

"Sick fuck!"

"You watch your language in my house, bitch! Lindsey didn't allow that talk and neither, will I!"

But, he just said, 'fuck', didn't he?

Another thump at the bedroom door.

Distracted, Jude didn't realize Mr. Emery had cut off her route to the front door. Shit! "Get out of my way!"

"You don't say a word to your mother. I'd say the same about dear ole daddy, but he ain't gonna listen to you anyway, is he?"

"Never did." Jude's shock and disgust gave way to anger. "Now, get out of my way!"

Mr. Emery must have heard the weight of her words, each one a sentence unto itself. Or, maybe he saw a different look in her eyes. He didn't move aside, but his smile faded into a thin grimace. Blood trickled down his chin. He licked his bloody lip as he balled up his fists.

Jude bent her knees and lowered her center of gravity as Mr. Emery rushed her. Both flaps of the robe billowed back like a superhero's cape, revealing his rigid manhood and putting it on full display. She snapped up a leg and connected the top of her foot square into his testicles. He howled as he crashed into her. They both went down, Mr. Emery on top. Jude cracked her head against the hardwood floor. As she tried to clear her head of stars and her lingering sleepiness, Mr. Emery's hands went to her breasts. She slapped them away, but his weight pinned her down at the waist.

"Get off me!" Jude pushed against him. He grabbed at her chest again. A drop of blood fell from his chin to her exposed neck. Something else of his was pressing into her groin.

The doorknob to the bedroom rattled. Jude strained her neck to see what was going to burst through. Mr. Emery looked up at what Jude was looking at. She shot her right hand down between her legs and squeezed the first things her fingers found. Emery howled again. Jude dug her fingernails deeper into the fleshy ball sack. This time,

Emery rolled away in pain. Jude rolled the opposite way and got her feet under her.

She shot toward the door. Something tripped her up, slamming her against a dining room chair. She grabbed it to steady her feet under her. Something darted at her. Jude swung the chair behind her, catching Emery square in the shoulder. It wasn't enough to knock him out, but he slammed into where the walls of the living room and dining room met. His head snapped back as his teeth bit into the plaster. Blood spurted from his mouth as he slumped to the floor.

Jude stood above him. She wrung her hands on the rails of the chair back as she tried to decide what to do next. He had tried to defile her as she opened herself up to him. He had used her vulnerability as an opportunity to take advantage of her. Had he planned on raping her? Had he been naked under his robe ever since he met her outside?

"God knows what shitty things Mrs. Emery had to put up with married to you. You probably put her in an early grave. She must be much happier now." He groaned. She lifted the chair and swung it down on Mr. Emery's back. She pulled it off him, lugged it above her head again and drove it down onto his back again. She screamed with each hit. There was a satisfying crack, either from the splitting of wood or the breaking of a rib or two—maybe both. She didn't care which was true.

Suddenly exhausted, Jude backed away with the chair in tow, dragging it across the dining room floor with her. A trail of blood followed from one of the legs each time it touched the floor. The leg had plenty of blood and a few tufts of hair still attached. When she passed the kitchen, she noticed the half-empty bag of Oreo Double-Stuffed cookies, the half-gallon container of 2% milk, a metal spoon, and an open container of over-the-counter medication. That motherfucker had laced her milk with crushed up Sleepinal pills. His underwear was bunched up in the middle of the tiles on the kitchen floor. She stared at the Hanes boxer briefs. Then her gaze fell back on the plastic bottle of sleeping aides. A small pool of blood had formed at the bottom of the chair leg.

She changed directions, crisscrossing the trail of blood back onto itself like a loose braid. Emery was still breathing—heavy wet rasping exhales and gurgling inhales. He twitched the fingers of his outstretched left hand. She stepped on his wrist, forcing his fingers to curl up. Breathing deep, Jude swung the chair off the floor in a huge arc. Emery's blood cast off the chair leg and sprayed onto the wall and ceiling. She drove the chair down on Emery's shoulders with all the weight of her body and force in her limbs and back.

The back legs of the chair broke off. Jude left it broken in a heap on his back. She didn't look in the kitchen this time as she staggered past the doorway, the adrenaline draining off of her as quickly as Emery's blood had dripped off the chair onto the floor. She didn't pay attention to where she walked, smearing the blood on the floor as she focused all of her remaining energy on getting to the door. When she pulled at the doorknob, the door didn't open. She fumbled with the deadbolt latch and the doorknob lock for several seconds before she was able to open the door and free herself from the apartment.

The lobby was filled with fresh air and freedom. It was still empty. Thank God for small favors. Jude wouldn't have been up for answering questions about why she'd been in Emery's apartment. Even though there was a stale haze to the lobby as the late morning sunlight streamed in from the lobby windows, the air had never tasted so good on her tongue or smelled so sweet as she breathed it in through her nostrils.

She was lucky to be alive—more importantly—happy to be alive.


## 13
## *Hyperbaric Chamber*
+1 Day – 11:21am EST

The lobby was bright. Too bright, in Jude's opinion. When had all that sunlight decided to come in? What stupid architect decided making their lobby a fucking two-story hot box was the way to go? Stars exploded behind her eyes as the sun's rays reflected off the chrome mullions. What asinine engineer signed off on that brilliant idea? The last thing she needed was another migraine to come on.

She shook her head in an effort to clear both the cobwebs and the shards of light from her brain. Her body was threatening to shut down on her, forcing her to brace herself against the painted walls as she walked. When she made it to the bank of mailboxes, she still managed to scoff at the trite design on the floor—dark brown circles of mosaic tiles intersected by a crimson and tan four-pointed star on top of them. A compass point to nowhere. She shook her head, shielded her eyes from the painful glare, and walked the ten feet from Mr. Emery's apartment back to her own.

The apartment door was locked. She didn't have a key. A soft mew came from her throat, a sound she didn't recognize as her own. The Sleepinal laced in the milk battled hard against her fading adrenaline. She was foggy, but still hyper focused. The metal numbers of the apartment leapt off the door at her, their edges sharp enough to cut her if they chose to. She patted the too-often painted door softly, leaning her wet cheek against it. Male voices reverberated inside, the low rumbling sound of her brothers. Hearing them filled her heart with a glowing gladness to be home—even if she was on the hallway side of the locked steel door.

Home. All her friends grew up in houses, thinking it would be cool to live in an apartment. Why would anyone want to live in a place without its own yard? Never being able to call a place your own. Something to defend, something to call 'yours'.

The voices stopped inside the apartment, replaced by a series of taps and slaps. Chains rattled and bolts retracted from metal. The door opened. Jimmy looked at Jude. "You look like shit, sis."

Jude couldn't keep her ironic laugh inside. She stepped across the threshold and flopped her arms across his shoulders. He reeled back a step—cane and all. She finished it off with a sloppy kiss on his cheek next to his nose, comically close to his lips. "Thanks."

"Eww," Jimmy stepped back another few steps from his suddenly too-clingy and too-affectionate sister. He wiped his face of her slobber. "You alright? Looks like you're leaking."

Jude wiped her own cheeks. It wasn't slobber to be found there, but hot stinging tears of innocence truly lost. Mr. Emery had been a good family friend—had acted like a good friend. He had always been someone she could complain to about the angst in her day. All the while, he had been an attentive and congenial host. All the while, he must have thought his kindness would make her an easy target for... what? An intimate relationship? Sex? Rape? Was his lecherous intent planned from the moment they had first met? Or, maybe, the loneliness from losing his wife had left him damaged. *Sure.* There must be a good excuse for Mr. Emery to be the way he was.

*Get a grip, Jude!* she shouted to her inner monologue.

She pictured just how attentive Mr. Emery had been to her all those years, even before his wife died. A stray brush of his fingers across her back as he passed by, a squeeze on the knee lingering too long. Her memories of him suddenly were sharper and much less innocent. All of it seemed like an elaborate long con just needing an opportunity for when the world was quiet and he had her to himself. *Fucker.*

She finally realized she hadn't answered her brother yet. "It's the damn glare from the lobby. You know how sensitive my eyes are."

"Your eyes aren't that sensitive," Mom called out from the living room. There it was. Mom's perfect timing for souring any mood—the moment of warmth from her sibling affection with Jimmy crushed by the cold, hard edge of her mother's practicality and intolerance for whiny and weak nonsense. A woman's role, in her mother's opinion, was to follow her husband's instructions, care for him and the family without complaint, and live a stoic existence. She never showed any sympathy for Jude's real ailments or illnesses. When her menstrual cramps had been almost debilitating, her mother had told her the same as she was saying now…, 'Your cramps aren't that bad. Stop being a baby. It's all in your head.'.

"Okay, Mom," Jude said through gritted teeth. Jimmy gave her a look. He understood the ignorance and indoctrination existing between generations in the Sawyer household. Even with his cane and half-paralyzed body, he had always been expected to just—what most coaches in baseball parlance would have described as—'walk it off'. He shrugged, not having any better answers for their mother's singular drive to take on all burdens and remain quiet about it. Although, that never seemed to stop her from complaining about everyone else's inability to do the same.

"You got some red paint flecks on your face or something, by the way," Jimmy commented. "You hanging around rusty dumpsters again?"

Cast off from Mr. Emery or the bloody chair? "Probably crap falling from the trees in front."

"How is it out there?" Michael asked from their father's recliner.

"Quiet." That asshole Emery had made the tacky joke about it being 'too quiet' outside, but it had been an accurate comment. The lack of pedestrians and vehicles—and noise of any kind, more specifically—had been unsettling. No birds had chirped or first responder sirens had blared, not even the faint sound of dog barks. All of the noises from the previous day were just gone. It had been eerily quiet. Other than those drunks she had gotten a bad feeling about, the outside world had paled.

Now, the apartment had taken on the same aura. Jimmy's eyes drifted to more of Mr. Emery's flecks on her neck. Michael, losing interest in his siblings altogether, returned to scrolling through Instagram on his phone. Mom stared at the blank television, her hands in her lap.

Wonderful, Jude thought. Apathy was contagious.

Or, maybe, it was despair.


**14**
## *Corridor*
+1 Day – 1:59pm EST


Four-hundred and eighty-two.

That was the official number.

Four-hundred and eighty-two minutes. Twenty-eight thousand nine hundred and twenty seconds. Eight hours and two minutes. That's how long it took to lose hope. After the 9-1-1 call and the promise someone would come to take her father's body away, all Jude could now do was sit at the dining room table and stare at the closed bedroom door at the end of the hallway.

The sunlight streaming through the three plate glass windows in the living room bathed Mom and Michael in a wash of dusty brightness. They seemed unaffected by the events of the last several hours. Michael was engrossed in his social media apps. His battery was going to die soon if he didn't curb his usage before the power came back on. He was a blessed individual, but even he couldn't make the life of a crappy smartphone battery extend out indefinitely. Jimmy was gone, having retreated to the temporary solitude of his shared bedroom.

Jude stared at her parent's bedroom door. The sunlight from the living room didn't penetrate that far into the hallway. The sunlight—like an angel touching at the feet of the righteous—allowed a swatch of light to creep across the floor to the bottom of her other brothers' bedroom door. That door was closed, too, serving as the threshold to her parent's shrine to the overseas-deployed Andy and her dead brother Matthew. The rest of the hallway graduated back into dim darkness, the sunlight not bothering to illuminate the corridor leading to a slowly decomposing body.

The body of her father.

Even with her eyes adjusted to the stale gray of the hallway, the fucking door stared right back at her. Wisps of black smoke seeped from the edges between the door and the frame, filling the end of the hallway with darkness. The smoke didn't rise to the ceiling, but clung close to the floor to trickle along the baseboards.

SLAM.

The door shook in its frame.

Jude gasped, unable to move. Her feet were firmly entrenched into the sucking floor bubbling under her chair. Her mass had multiplied to such a degree her shoulders slumped from the weight. Her lungs could barely take in a breath, the atmosphere in the apartment like the crushing depths of the ocean. The dark ground fog raced out across the floor, advancing and receding like the soft waves of a lake slipping across the sands of a beach.

"You're a stupid girl." The words reverberated through the fog, emanating from behind the door. Jude still didn't move. The world tilted forward several degrees as the edges of her vision went dark. The apartment tried to slide her toward the bedroom. She braced against the edge of the table to keep from hurling toward the gaping darkness. She would probably careen into the shelf of Hummels on the way. Mom would be furious if she did.

Her breath was caught in her throat. She tried to cough it out or swallow it down. Her body had forgotten how to process oxygen. How long did it take until the brain completely blacked out from lack of oxygen? Jude had ignored her high school science teacher when he had explained biological mechanics. She was, indeed, a stupid girl.

"No love for your dear ole dad?" the smoke asked.

*He was a sperm donor*, Jude thought back at the swirling darkness. It was the only response she could manage as her throat could only produce a series of strange mewing sounds.

"But... no love?"

Jude's father had worked several jobs to provide for his family. That would be admirable except for the fact he pissed a large sum of it away on frivolous toys like a fishing boat and a beat-up Cessna he claimed he won in a poker game. Jude had clothes, food, and a roof over her head. She couldn't claim otherwise. But, love? She wasn't ready to admit to that.

Another slam resounded against the door. A puff of dust broke loose from above the door frame, mixing with the swirling air and smoke. She would have to call Mom out on her poor dusting abilities, knowing she focused much of her cleaning energies on her menagerie of figurines. Apparently, the top moldings of the door frames didn't rank high on her list of dusting destinations.

"Love?" the smoke reminded her with a whisper.

"No," Jude whispered back. There had been no love. Not the love her other friends enjoyed from their folks on a daily basis. Not the support needed to propel a child forward in their young development. There had been only criticism and disappointment from her Mom and Dad. They hadn't understood their "old world" ways of childrearing would produce offspring filled with as much resentment and bile as them.

"No love?" The smoke rose up in a singular pillar, poised with expectation. The only love Jude's mind could conjure up was of her father's early morning ritual of letting his fingers inappropriately linger along her skin—far too inappropriate for a father/daughter relationship as she was finally realizing.

"No!" Jude seethed with a rising anger.

The column of smoke recoiled at her answer. It fell to the floor as if its backbone had just evaporated. It retreated to the master bedroom, sucking itself back through the crack under the door.

"No!" Jude repeated the word, happy to be able to draw in another breath.

"'No,' what?" Mom asked from her high back chair.

The hallway was back to normal, dim and filled with the judgmental eyes of figurines with no business being in a high-traffic area. Fucking Mr. Emery's Sleepinal must still be in her system.

"Nothing, Mom."

"Quit being so melodramatic, then."

Jude stared at the door at the end of the hallway, a foreign idea starting to take shape. She feared the new thought, but her curiosity for what it could become was greater. "Sorry, Mom."

## 15
## *Coins in a Wishing Well*
+1 Day – 2:31pm EST

Jude rummaged through the top drawer of her hand-me-down dresser. It had been painted and distressed over the years, come upon at the curb by her father during one of his more adventurous drinking jaunts. He had always been proud to regale people of been able to lug it twelve blocks without breaking a sweat—and that only one of the drawers had fallen out during the trip. Jude touched its chipped lower corner. She traced her fingers over the etched lines of 'Matthew wuz here' on the top surface. Jimmy had scrawled it into the wood with the handle of a spoon some years ago. When she had asked her brother why he had put his brother's name on the carving instead of his own, he shrugged and told her he was trying to throw any possible accusers off his trail. Jude remembered thinking Jimmy's rationale was both brilliantly maniacal and tragically flawed.

She closed the top drawer, irritated she hadn't found what she was looking for. It should have been in with the rest of her jewelry collection—as sparse as it was—but her quarry eluded her so far. The next stop was the narrow drawer in her nightstand. It was filled with currently useless charging wires, two tubes of unsealed ChapStick, a few cough drops and numerous discarded wrappers. Several wrapped condoms were at the bottom of the drawer currently going to waste. What Jude was looking for was not to be found there in that mess, either.

"Damn it. Where are you?"

She closed the drawer. There was no closet in her room. She was lucky the bedroom was able to accommodate the twin-sized bed, dresser and nightstand. She considered herself lucky she had her own room at all. Having to share the room with one of her brothers in a bunk bed situation at her age would have been a bit fucked up— in her opinion.

She patted the back pocket of her jean shorts. No wallet. She moved to the hooks screwed into the door. Several scarfs adorned them in a swaying hanging menagerie. Her black purse hung by its strap in the middle of the sea of knit color. She unzipped the top of it without taking it off the hook. There wasn't much inside, but Jude still had to burrow her fingers around to locate her wallet. Why was it the smaller the purse, the more difficult it was to find anything inside it? *One of the cosmic jokes of the universe*, she guessed.

Aha!

Jude pulled out her wallet, unsnapped it, and opened up the bi-fold. Ignoring the credit cards with too much debt on them, a driver's license she was finally putting to good use, and seven dollars in singles, she poked her finger into the extra slot behind the credit card holder.

She pulled out the oversized flat metal coin. It had been her father's. It was something he had been proud of… at the time before the coin came into Jude's possession. A triangular field on the round coin was emblazoned with the number 6. A band along the outside edge read, 'To Thine Own Self Be True'. It had been Dad's 6-month AA sobriety coin.

He had tried to get himself clean. He had tried to stay sober. He had been trying to be a better person... a better parent. But Mom didn't understand what it was like to be an alcoholic or what it was like to have an alcoholic mind. When he had proudly shown off the coin to the family, Mom had declared her husband cured. A few nights later, Mom had insisted a little nip of wine at dinner would be okay—since he was cured of his disease. It didn't take too long before that single sip turned into more... and then into a lot more. Months of work destroyed by the act of a single swallow. Mom understood what being an alcoholic was about as much as she understood what Jude and Jimmy endured living in a house where parental nurturing didn't exist.

She closed her hand over the coin and made a tight fist around it, wishing the simple act of applying the right amount of pressure would make things the way they were. She closed her purse and opened the door. A dark form loomed in the doorway, startling her. "Jesus!"

"No." Jimmy shook his head and pointed at his chest. "Jimmy. My name is Jimmy."

"Your name is Pain in The Ass."

"That's always been a favorite of mine, too. Without a doubt."

"Weirdo."

"Also, a good one. Whatcha doin'?"

Jude shrugged, afraid to give voice to what she was planning. Was she being stupid or sentimental? Was this going to be a futile gesture Jimmy would think was ridiculous?

"Tell me."

"I was going to say my goodbyes." She held up the coin between her index and middle fingers. "Maybe get some closure... or something... I don't know." She began to backpedal as soon as she heard the words coming out of her mouth.

Jimmy looked at her, his cane tapping on the floor.

"What?" Jude asked defensively.

"Nothing," Jimmy replied. "You want company?"

## 16
# *In Repose*
+1 Day – 2:46pm EST

They stood at the closed bedroom door. Jimmy tapped the bottom of his cane against the door frame. It was a steady rhythmic rap quickly grating on Jude's nerves. "Stop."

"Sorry," Jimmy apologized. "You know how I get when I'm nervous."

Jude gave her brother a sideways glare and shot back with some patent-pending sarcasm. "Nervous? Ya think?" She gripped the sobriety coin in one fist and reached for the doorknob with the other. Her hand recoiled when a faint thud sounded from the other side of the door.

"What?" Jimmy asked about her hesitation.

Had Jimmy not heard the noise? Of course not. It was all in her head. Smoke hadn't poured into the hallway through the cracks in the door earlier today. There was no evidence of dark soot under the door or gray ash on the floor or any of Mom's most cherished children—the Hummels. It was all going on in her head, most likely the after-effects of being drugged by a neighbor.

She reached out to the doorknob again, this time closing her fingers around its faceted surface and squeezing it as tight as she was gripping the coin in her other hand. She turned the knob and opened the door. She was prepared for the loud creak as the door swung open, the hinges having done so for as long as she could remember.

What she wasn't prepared for was the smell. It wasn't rot or a gagging deterioration from her father's body. The horror flicks were quick to fill a room with inferences of vile and vomit-inducing odors. Her mouth was assaulted instead by the oppressive taste of burnt-down cigarettes, heavier with the heat billowing out of the room into her face. The lack of air conditioning made everything in the air more pungent—mothballs in the closet, the cedar from the hope chest at the foot of the bed, the faint yeasty aroma of too much beer on too many clothes and, Jude was sure, coming out of every expired pore of her father.

Jude exhaled sharply and stepped into the room. Jimmy moved in behind her, but lingered at the door's alcove while she walked over to the bed. The lamp from Dad's nightstand was on the carpet. Maybe that had been the thump she had heard? She picked it up and placed it on the yellowing lace doily Mom thought would make the apartment appear classier. It was several more seconds before she worked up the nerve to sit on the edge of the bed next to her father.

Jude didn't know what to say. She looked back at Jimmy, now little more than a silhouette at the door. She couldn't will her eyes to drift over to her father's face—at least, not yet. Finally, she cleared her throat and grounded herself by gripping the coin tighter. "Hi, Dad."

Was that it? Was that all she could muster? She knew she needed to 'nut up' as her brother Matthew used to say. She tried again, this time holding up the coin. "I remember when you got this coin, Dad. I was young, but I knew what it meant for you to get this. Six months is a blink of the eye, I know, but I knew you worked your ass off to get that far…" Jude let her words trail off, not knowing what she really wanted to say or what words would magically close the fissures that had grown into chasms between them since that sip of wine at the dinner table. "…it could have been different, you know. If you would have stuck with it, you would've been a better person. I know you would have. I saw the progress you were making. I could see it, plain as day. We were different together, you and me. You were trying. Things were better. Why couldn't you have just kept…"

Jude stopped again. She knew Jimmy was observant and the smartest of the siblings. The question was whether he was smart and observant enough to realize what their father had really done to her. The morning routine was a butterfly kiss compared to the other, more treacherous, thing her drunken father had done to a trusting daughter. She cleared her throat again, wishing she had brought in a glass of water along with the coin.

She placed the coin inside her father's fingers. They were starting to stiffen, but they were still flexible enough for Jude to close them around the coin that had been a talisman of sorts to her. She leaned in close to his face to keep her words between them.

"I know there was something wrong with you at a fundamental level. I know a father would never touch a daughter that way. Not if there wasn't something wrong with his brain to start with." She squeezed her fingers over his. "I don't know if I will ever be able to forgive you. I may never get there. But, for those six months, when you were trying your absolute best to heal yourself, I was proud of you." Jude let go of his hand, wiping a tear away from her cheek. The fingers loosened around the coin. That was okay. She hadn't expected his body would hold onto it.

Jimmy limped over to the foot of the bed. "You good?"

Jude shrugged as she stepped away from her father's body to where Jimmy held his ground at the end of the bed. She didn't know if anything would help, but was finally able to look at her father's body. "Time will tell, Jimbo."

"Good an answer as any." Jimmy put his good arm around her waist and gave her a hug. "And, stop calling me Jim–"

"Shit!" Michael bellowed a curse about something again. Maybe the battery on his phone finally went dead. The youngest Sawyer considered himself less of a person without his phone. "You gotta see this!"

Jude took one last look at the body on the bedspread. The fingers had closed around the coin. She had heard the human body started the rigor process around eight hours after death. It was possible her father could have been dead for that long.

"What's he going on about?" Jimmy asked rhetorically. She realized he hadn't seen Dad's fingers close around the coin. Maybe, that gesture from beyond the grave had been just for her. Jude felt some of the weight lift off her shoulders. She would continue to carry guilt and shame with her, but she felt a touch lighter—at least for the moment. They turned toward the door. "Come on. Let's see what Michael wants."

Thump.

Jude and Jimmy stopped and looked over their shoulders at the same time. The lamp was on the floor again. Something glinted from the carpet next to it. It was the six-month sobriety coin. Jude moved to retrieve the coin in order to put it back in her Dad's hand, but stopped in her tracks when he rolled over.

"Christ!" Jimmy exclaimed.

"Dad?" Jude was unsure of what she was seeing.

Her father slowly dragged himself to his feet, his fingers twitching and his left leg a little slower to get his weight under it. It was too dim to see him clearly, but his eyes and mouth were open.

"Jude! Jimmy!" Michael was still hyped up with something in the living room. Sorry, bro. There was already something fucked up happening right here in the master bedroom. Their father heard Michael and growled, ignoring the two offspring right in front of him. Typical. Dad sniffed the air, the growl becoming a moan as he took an unsteady step forward.

"What the fuck?" Jude instinctively pulled Jimmy behind her as they took a step back toward the door, keeping the distance between them and their dead father—a dead man now somehow upright and staggering toward them. He sniffed the air, a mewing sound choking through his throat. His eyes fell on them—only for a moment— before surveying the rest of the dim room like he had never seen it before.

Feet slapped on the hallway floor, coming toward the bedroom. Michael slid to a stop at the doorway, his silhouette making the room darker. "People are coming back from the dead!" His eyes darted between the people standing in the room, one more than he had expected. All he managed to utter was, "Who's this?"

The next few seconds unraveled as if she was watching a movie in slow-motion. Dad immediately dismissed Jimmy and Jude. Could have been the sudden change in light or the quick movement at the door. Michael was yelling about the dead coming back from death, anxious to fill in his siblings about what he had discovered while scrolling through his social feeds.

Dad showed surprising speed and agility. He lunged past Jude and Jimmy, knocking them to the floor. He howled as he leapt at a startled Michael. His knees landed on Michael's stomach, who finally snapped into action and tried pushing him off.

"Stop all that noise!" yelled Mom from the living room.

Dad's fingers ripped through Michael's shirt and dug into his skin. Somehow, his blunt fingers squirmed through Michael's muscles to wrap around his collar bone. Jude gasped as Michael screamed. Her feet wouldn't move. Paralysis had been added to the fight or flight responses. She stared in abject terror as Dad snapped his neck forward and bit into Michael's beautiful face. Michael stumbled backwards and disappeared back into the hallway, Dad still perched on his chest.

Jimmy crawled over to the door and swung it closed with the rubber capped bottom of his cane. Smart. The door squeaked loudly, latching into place a moment before something thumped against it. Jimmy sat with his back against it as the final deterrent against Dad's re-entry. There were several loud thumps before Dad lost interest and went back to Michael.

"Help me." Michael's whimpers and whispered pleas could be heard clearly through the door. Jimmy put his cheek and hand against the door, his eyes squeezed tight.

"Stop this tomfoolery right now!" Mom shouted from her living room chair. Feral growls quickly drowned out Mom's orders until her own screams trumped both Dad's groans and Michael's cries of pain. Jude stifled her own cries, fearing Dad would somehow remember he found her more appealing than her brother and mother.

17
## *Wedge*
+1 Day – 3:43pm EST

Jude and Jimmy sat alone in their parent's bedroom. Jude covered her ears with her arms, her fingers intertwined behind her head. It had done little to drown out Mom's high-pitched, blood-curdling screams. Now, with the apartment quiet again, Jude found the air in the bedroom difficult to inhale. It was laden with the stench of mothballs, cigarette smoke, and alcohol—now with a scent of copper and the faintest whiff of both dead and torn open flesh.

The decomposition had not been obvious when she had entered the bedroom, having been distracted with her intention of fostering closure with her dad. But, the smell hadn't been that bad. She remembered distinctly making a mental comparison to how people reacted in horror movies when she entered the bedroom... a lifetime ago. The stench must have been kicked up when Dad started using those rotting atrophying muscles, the smell seeping out through the pores of his skin in death just like the alcohol had bled through with his sweat in life.

Her dad was dead... but somehow alive. She could hear him banging around the apartment as if he had just come home from a bad day of work and a shittier evening at the bar. He thudded against the door a few times, Jimmy still using his slight frame to ensure dear ole Dad didn't burst through the door.

"Jimmy," Jude whispered, her voice barely audible. He didn't react to her voice, making her think he hadn't heard her. Jimmy stared at the space between the bed and the closet. The lamp was still on the carpet. So was the sobriety coin. She didn't need to see them to know they were still there. At least, those inanimate objects hadn't decided to come to life. She leaned forward and cleared her throat as quietly as she could. Still nothing from her brother. She was forced to raise her voice. "Jimmy!"

"What?" he muttered, shifting his eyes to her.

Jude pointed at the doorknob and pantomimed him turning the latch for the deadbolt. Yes, their parent's bedroom had a deadbolt. Jimmy looked up at it from his seated position. He reached up with his weak hand, slapping at the thumb turn with his fingers. They slipped off, his knuckles tapping against the door. "Fuck."

Something slammed against the door. Jimmy rolled away, his flight response in full swing. He scrambled on his hands and knees toward Jude, leaving the door unguarded. He had even left the cane on the carpet in front of the door. Dad slammed against the door again, his moans growing more insistent. The door shuddered in its frame. The doorknob wiggled back and forth. It wasn't enough to unlatch the door—at least, not yet.

The knob turned more. Jimmy pushed himself against the outside wall with his good leg, bumping against the dresser and causing Mom's must-have knick-knacks to clink against each other on the top. Just more worthless glass and ceramic junk she had found so valuable. He wrapped his arms around his knees.

Jude halved the distance to the door before it burst open. Dad roared as he slammed his shoulder against it. Jude jumped backward in panic. She landed on her ass, her head cracking against the front of one of the dresser drawers. This time, the figurines on top did not just sway against each other. Several bumped to the front edge and fell on the carpet. They didn't break. Except the one falling directly on top of her head.

"Shit!" Jude covered her head against additional falling ceramic angels. For a moment, she felt a pang of worry Mom would be cross at her for destroying some of her favorite things.

Dad's massive blue-collar body, with years of manual and menial labor to show for it, was caught between the frame and the half-opened door. Jimmy's cane had wedged perfectly between the door and the wall opposite it. One of Dad's arms and his right shoulder was past the frame, but his other shoulder was wedged solidly behind the door. Being stuck did nothing to dampen his efforts to get into the room. The cane moved a few inches left or right each time Dad reared back to slam against the door again. Eventually, the cane would fail and she and Jimmy would be trapped. "We gotta get that door closed!"

Jimmy didn't move. He didn't even acknowledge what she had just said. Unless, of course, one counted hugging oneself even tighter as a result of the spoken word. Fucking useless.

Slam! Dad made a run at the door again. This time he twisted his shoulders around in an effort to get both arms through the doorway. If he managed that, the rest of his body would slip through more easily.

Jude didn't think.

She reacted. Grabbing the fallen lamp, she ripped off the shade and wrapped the electrical cord around her hand before marching at the gurgling and snapping marionette wearing her father's skin. His eyes showed too much white... plus, a lot of gold and red. She drove the base of the lamp into his upturned face. The front bottom teeth and one of his canines disappeared into his gaping mouth. Dad howled at her. It wasn't the sound of pain or even outrage, but of a primal feral desperation to get from one side of the door to the other.

"Sorry."

She raised the lamp up and swung it down with all her flailing strength. Dad's face became more unrecognizable with each blow. His growls tapered off into a failing whimper, each strike punctuated with an apology Jude barely heard from her own lips. Once Dad's face was an oozing bloody pulp—and no more sounds escaped his throat—Jude threw the lamp back toward the bed. It landed next to the sobriety coin, a splatter of gore coating its surface and staining the number 6.

She needed to get the door closed, currently wedged between her dad and the cane. She didn't have the strength to move the cane, so she took a different tactic. With her ass on the carpet and her back braced against the wall, Jude placed her feet against each of Dad's shoulders. She scooted into a more powerful angle and pushed her legs out with a grunt. Dad wasn't moving. He was not a rolling stone after all. She pushed again. Her foot slipped off Dad's shoulder and squished into his crushed and draining head. Her sock turned an instant and wet dark red.

Goddammit!

Finally, Dad slid a few inches toward the hallway. He was probably lubricated by the pool of still-slick blood seeping under him. His arms thumped against the floor. His fingers twitched across the surface like the pins of a player piano against the scrolling music sheet.

He could grab her ankle any second! In a panic, Jude pistoned her legs as hard as she could, practically kicking her father back into the hallway. She scrambled onto her hands and knees to move his arms to his chest to clear the doorway. Michael's body was laying in its own pool of blood close to the living room. His lifeless blue eyes stared at her, demanding an explanation as why Dad had attacked his favorite son.

A thump from the living room.

"Mom," Jude called out. She opened the door wider for a better view. The bottom of one white socked foot stuck out from behind the edge of the hallway wall, turning sideways before slipping out of view. Mom grunted. "You okay, Mom?"

Jimmy continued to make himself as small as possible, pressing his knees against his chest and his back against the wall. Another grunt from the living room made Jude refocus on what was happening in there.

Mom was getting rickety in her old age, even with the weekly yoga. She finally shuffled into view. Nobody could deny she was one tough old bird. Her silhouette cast a shadow toward Jude, the afternoon sun at her back from the bank of living room windows. Mom staggered right, her shoulder knocking squarely into the shelf of Hummel figurines. The entire shelf tilted from the wall before pulling away altogether. The figurines fell to the floor, shattering. For once, Mom paid them no mind.

"Mom?" Jude asked. *Your Hummels are broken.*

A low gurgle was her only reply.

"Mom?" Jude's plead choked her words. *Please be mad about your Hummels.* Mom's gurgle rose up into a warbling growl. Her stagger became a disjointed twitchy trot.

"Shit." Jude slammed the door closed. It wouldn't latch. Dad's crushed head was still blocking the threshold. She pushed him farther into the hallway. Mom was already past the door to Matthew's room—without even a glance in that direction. "Shit... shit... shit."

Mom lunged at her. Jude slammed the door in her face, the latch barely able to seat against the strike plate before Mom's ruined cheek and gaping mouth thumped against the other side. Jude twisted the thumb turn and heard the deadbolt click into place. It was probably the most wonderful sound she had ever heard in her life.

Mom rammed against the door. She scratched against it. She sniffed the bottom of it, sensing Jude on the other side. The growls turned into snarls, then inhuman roars. The roars turned into more ramming against the door. The scratches turned into bloody fingers skittering under the door.

Jude wept. Relentless, but unfelt, tears fell down Jude's cheeks. Strained and high-pitched cries ripped through her raw throat. Neither the tears nor the wails did anything to relieve her mind against this unthinkable new reality she found herself in. She feared her mind just might end up snapping in half as a precautionary measure.

# 18
## *Entombed*
+1 Day – 5:58pm EST

The scratching and sniffing at the door had tapered off a bit, diminishing to the point where, at times, Jude thought Mom might have lost interest in getting behind door number one. Monty Hall surely would have been happier to give away a new car instead of the two blood-splattered and shocked adult children trapped in their undead parent's dead-bolted bedroom.

"Michael," Jimmy whispered to himself. His arms hugged his knees to his chest, his eyes staring off to a dim, far corner of the room.

Michael was lying dead on the hallway floor with his insides now on his outsides. Dad had eviscerated him, clawing through his chest and stomach before she had crushed his skull. The image of the carnage and Michael's accusing blue eyes made bile creep up into Jude's throat. She controlled her breathing through her nose and swallowed her gourd back down the best she could. Thank God for the therapist. Had she not had a year-and-a-half's worth of sessions under her belt already, odds were good she would have lost her shit already.

Jimmy, on the other hand, didn't look consolable, and Jude wasn't sure if she knew how to help him. Jimmy was all the family she had left in this fucked up world. She grabbed his cane from between the door and the alcove wall and slid over to where he was still pressed against the chest of drawers. She squeezed herself next to him, wedged his cane between his arms, and put her arm around his shoulder. "How you doing, kiddo?"

Jimmy replied with a choked groan, shifting his weight to lean into Jude's body. Small miracles.

"We'll get out of this, Jimbo," Jude assured him, probably said more to assure herself. They were trapped in this room. A reanimated killing machine waited on the other side of the bolted door. The windows were barred and useless as a means to escape. The door was the only way out… and Mom's only way in.

The cane trick wouldn't work against Mom like it had worked to wedge Dad. She was much smaller and would slip quickly through to disembowel the two of them. Jimmy wouldn't be able to hold the door while Jude bashed her Mom's brains in, not with his obvious disadvantage. The opposite was also true. While Jude would be able to pin Mom between the door and frame, Jimmy might not have the strength to kill her with only one good side to work with. Jude didn't want to chance it.

"Andy," Jimmy whispered.

The only other Sawyer brother possibly still alive, deployed somewhere in Eastern Europe the last she knew. Had this nightmare reached across the oceans, or was this a special punishment just for the American people? God knew the people deserved whatever the universe deemed appropriate as reparations. It required repayment for the atrocities and ignorance the government and its citizens felt was their birthright. But ghastly, hungry life after death? That seemed simply too cruel by any standards.

"We'll get out of here," Jude said. "I promise." The promise had to be made, even if she didn't fully know how in the hell she was going to make it a reality. The windows were out. They would have to face the door and Mom—eventually.

Mom.

Could she even be called that anymore? What was sniffing outside the bedroom was a warped, palsied version of their mother. It was feral, more apt to lunge at her on all fours instead of upright like a dignified human being would. Apparently, all of a sudden, death was not the end. It certainly wasn't as glamorous as reincarnation where the body goes on to do better works in the next life. What happened to people who had more red marked in their Ledger of Life than black? Jude had imagined they would become dung beetles or something in the next life. She had never imagined they would return immediately in this life as grotesque hungry caricatures.

Mom returned to sniff at the door, scratching at the bottom edge. It only lasted for a few seconds, but it was still unnerving. Jude and Jimmy were in a dire circumstance. The up-side was the bedroom was a bunker. The negative was the apartment only had one bathroom. The idea of an en suite—bathrooms connected directly to master bedrooms or, what HDTV calls owners' suites —was only a luxury reserved for the rich and their lavish lifestyles. Eventually, Jude would have to face her mother to get her and Jimmy out of the apartment. Plus, she had to pee.

"Matthew." Jimmy was still whispering the names of their siblings, living and dead.

Jude gave him a tighter comforting hug. She was not the typical emotive older sister. Jimmy must have been confused by her gesture because he twisted slightly away from her hug to better cycle through his brothers' names. It figured.

Matthew had always the strong and reliable one. He was the one all of the younger kids looked up to. His death in the Middle East was a blow none of them had truly recovered from. If a better angel like him could be felled and shitty abusive parents could prosper, where was the true justice in the world? Matthew's body and belongings had been transported Stateside. A coffin in a hanger under a draped flag had trumpeted his return. Mom and Dad hadn't let any of them see his body. They had kept closure for themselves—which had been fucking bullshit. And, immediately after, they had brought all of his gear and personal effects back to the house and turned his room into a shrine to his successes and eventual death.

"Matthew."

"I know, Jimmy." It had been all about Matthew in life. He had been the prodigal son. The slayer of oppressors. The golden boy. He who could do no wrong in his parent's eyes. All of the other kids were pale imitations—always compared to the design of the perfect first-born son. A fucking shrine of his trophies, medals, the flag the Marine Corps presented to Mom at his funeral, his...

Jude stopped for a second and furrowed her brow. She thought it through carefully. Yeah. All of Matthew's effects had been delivered to the family. That included the Beretta he had bought with his own money after basic training. How could she have forgotten about Matty's sidearm? He had taught her to fire it, for Christ's sake! She and Jimmy were a dozen feet away from being able to defend themselves against the monster outside the door. The problem with that was they had to first get past the monster in the hall in order to get to the gun to get past the monster in the hall.

Fuck her life.

# 19
## *Family Squabbles*
+1 Day – 7:21pm EST

"Come on, Jimmy," Jude coaxed. "It's time to go."

Jimmy muttered something indecipherable, which was better than reciting his brothers' names like a mantra. Jude held her breath as it seemed likely Matthew's name would slip past his lips again, but she gracefully exhaled when Jimmy shifted his weight and grunted a semi-intelligible, "Bullshit."

"It can work. We just have to get to Matty and Andy's room."

"Why?" Jimmy's monosyllabic response was filled with doubt and fear. It was also direct and to the point.

"Matty's Beretta," Jude replied. She beamed when Jimmy straightened up a bit, his hands falling away from the knees he had been determined to press into his ribcage. "I totally forgot about it."

"Mmmhmm." It wasn't much of a response, but Jimmy was definitely more interested in hearing the details of the plan Jude was cooking up.

"You open the door for me. I push Mom back so we can get to Matty's room. We get inside, get the gun, and finish this."

"How?"

"How what?"

"How do you fend off Mom?"

Good question. Jude had mulled that over while the sunlight had dimmed from behind the edges of the heavy window curtains. She had run through all sorts of scenarios. Back Mom up like a tiger in a three-ring circus—no chair. Push her back with the mattress—too bulky. Use a weapon to bash her brains in and negate the need for the gun at all—she wasn't ready for another round of that. "I'm still working on it."

"Work faster."

"Any ideas would be appreciated." Jude shrugged. At least Jimmy was now engaged in conversation. The need for self-preservation finally rose out of his subconscious to beat away the shock and paralyzing grief. The fear couldn't be overcome, but it could be harnessed to fuel the adrenaline needed to pull off this half-cocked asinine plan.

The sun sank. The room dimmed more, the curtains no longer needed to keep the afternoon sun at bay. Dad loved—had loved—to sleep in almost complete darkness. With his erratic work schedule and late-night into-the-wee-hours bar-hopping, it had been important nothing disturb him while he caught up on his often-fitful slumber. Like waking a sleeping bear with a pointy stick. It had not been wise to ever rouse him with childhood shenanigans.

"The curtain!" Jude exclaimed.

"What?"

"The curtain," she repeated. "Mom won't be able to see us if we throw the curtain over her. You open the door, I net her and push her out of the way, and we make a break for Matty's room."

"Brilliant idea."

That was Jimmy's way of saying it was a dumb idea. Unfortunately, it was the best plan she could come up with. They couldn't stay in their parents' bedroom forever. Jude needed to pee.

She got up and went to the window. Without any care or worry for the rod, Jude ripped the curtain off the rings. Several snapped off and pinged against the wall. Another one bounced off her head. The rod itself clattered against the window and the nightstand.

Mom's snarls renewed from the hallway.

A pigeon crashed into the glass from outside. Jude jumped back a step, cringing. Except, it wasn't a rat with wings. A man with sunken eyes and pale skin slapped his hand against the window. He looked homeless, but he was wearing a fresh Polo shirt and what looked like an expensive wrist watch. Jude opened her mouth to ask for help, but closed it again when the man opened his own—and spit dark bile and blood on the window. The hand slaps smeared the gunk around the glass, thankfully obscuring his face from hers. She turned her back on the dead man, hugging the curtain against her chest and returning to Jimmy.

He was just now getting to his feet again, stumbling a few steps before stopping and banging his fists against his thighs. "Guess I shouldn't have let them fall asleep. Now, both legs are tingly."

"You're a dork, Jimbo." Jude waited. After a minute, he had walked around enough to give her a nod and make his way to the hinge side of the door. She stretched out the curtain, facing the door and taking in a deep breath.

"Ready?" Jude asked too loud. Fingers scratched against the other side—maybe as a response.

Jimmy nodded. He turned the deadbolt thumb turn. It snapped back with a deafening loud click. Mom slapped against the door. Luckily, the latch held. Jimmy reached for the knob. Jude lifted the curtain in front of her, low enough to see over the top of it. She shifted from foot to foot and nodded back at Jimmy.

He mouthed the countdown... three... two...

Jimmy never got to one.

The latch broke and the door burst open. Mom rushed in and tackled Jude at the knees. Mom snapped her teeth against the coarse heavy material of the curtain, Jude feeling the power of her jaws through it. She dropped the curtain over the thing that used to be Mom. "Run, Jimmy!"

Jimmy didn't actually run, but he did manage to limp quickly. He performed no heroic hurdling as he swung the door wide and hugged along the frame's edge until he was in the hallway. The combination of fear, adrenaline, and hours of sitting on the floor made it awkward enough for him to stumble through the hall without tripping over the curtain or their parents. Mom-thing sensed Jimmy scooting past her. She writhed toward Jimmy, but only managed to tangle herself up tighter under the make-shift net. Her guttural noises grew louder as she was unable to find the most-direct route to warm flesh in either direction.

Jude pushed the struggling bundle aside, hearing a soft bump as Mom-thing's head hit the door frame. She didn't opt for skirting around the twisting thing under the curtain. Instead, she went for the heroics and leapt over it. Heroics? What the fuck was she thinking? She landed on the other side of the squirming fabric. Score! She tripped over Dad's thigh and landed hard on the palms of her hands, feeling a jolt up her arm as she came nose-to-nose with the sightless, ruined face of Michael. Shit!

"Come on!" Jimmy's tone was frantic and out of breath. He wasn't in the hallway, so he must have made it to Matty's room.

Jude scrambled up to her feet. Or tried to. The floor was still slick with blood from Dad's hallway attack on Michael. Mom-thing roared behind her. Jude's legs got her going again, her eyes not wanting to see if Mom-thing had escaped the curtain. Or if she was about to grab her ankle. Jude slipped once more in the blood, but managed to use the wall to stay upright.

Her brain screamed that monsters beneath the bed and under the stairs were real, not just the conjuring of dark fairy tales and stories of boogeymen going bump in the night. That cautionary tale bullshit was just parents trying to keep naïve children in line and foster their obedience. Part of a mother and father's job description was to protect their children and keep them from harm. The Sawyer parents had failed miserably on that front.

Jude was tripped up again and sent sprawling. Mom-thing had grabbed at her ankle with fingers raw from scratching at the bedroom door. The curtain draped around her waist, being dragged along with her as she crawled over Dad. Now, he was just an obstacle for her new obsession. Fuck! Fuck! Fuck! As Mom worked her way up Jude's ankle, the curtain slipped off and made a make-shift shroud for Dad. Rest in peace.

"Move it!" Jimmy's voice got her brain out of neutral and slammed it into first gear. She turned over and kicked at Mom-thing's forehead, aiming away from her mouth and all those drooling, dripping white teeth in their blackened gums. Mom-thing lost her hold on her ankle, clumsily trying to grab at the other leg. Jude crawled backwards over Michael's body, trying to put another barrier between them.

Jude bumped into something. Arms hooked under her armpits. She let out a yipping scream. Mom-thing slowed to sniff at Michael's body in spite of Jude's outburst.

"Quiet," Jimmy hissed in a whisper in her ear. "She's distracted."

Jude covered her mouth with her slick hands. She pedaled her legs until she was upright again. Jimmy stepped backwards and guided her into the bedroom. He swung her around and slammed the door behind them. There was no lock on the door so he inched over the nightstand enough to catch the corner of it. The children's bedrooms hadn't been reinforced to doomsday bunker standards like their parent's room had been.

Jude dropped onto the pristine and tightly made bed—probably the first person to do so since the bedroom had been closed off. Only a slit in the heavy curtains displayed the sun's oblivious descent to the western horizon. Mom must have gotten the drapes in bulk, because Jude didn't remember any of the bedrooms having them before her brothers' deployments.

Jimmy pulled out an old white T-shirt from Matthew's dresser drawer and tossed it to Jude. "Wipe your face."

Jude looked up at the mirror over the dresser and caught her reflection in the gloom. Her face was pale and she had dark circles under her eyes. Shit. Jude didn't ever remember having dark circles before. The return of the dead to life seemed to be bad for her complexion. But, what Jimmy had referred to had nothing to do with her tired eyes. She had a red blotchy handprint across her mouth. It would have been almost comical if not for the fact it had been painted on using Michael's spilt blood. She wiped away at it with the dry shirt—saliva seemed to be in short supply at the moment.

"Did I get it?" Jude asked.

"It'll do." Jimmy appraised her face.

"What?" Jude asked several seconds later when she couldn't stand his stares any longer. "What did I do now?"

"Why didn't you lock her in her room?"

Shit. Good question. Why hadn't she done that? She had the opportunity when she vaulted over Mom to get into the hallway. One well-placed kick and Jude could've closed the door and locked her inside. Then there would have been no need to rush to Matty's bedroom for his gun or fend off a snarling and snapping deteriorated version of their mom stalking around the hallway.

"Sorry," Jude finally said, her shoulders slumping a bit.

"Hey, I didn't have the balls to stay and help."

"I told you to go."

"Doesn't mean I had to listen to you."

"Yeah. For once in your life you actually did what I told you." Jude chuckled for a moment before a sniffing sound came from the crack under the door. She couldn't help but smirk at the absurdity of being locked in another bedroom with a reanimated corpse outside the door. Staring at the barricaded door brought with it a realization.

Her parents were dead. Every decision she made from now on would bring with it its own consequences wholly resting on her shoulders. Plus, she was the oldest Sawyer left. She had to take care of Jimmy. She both loved and hated her brother. He was the only one who knew what being a damaged Sawyer was like. His existence had also made her the butt of plenty of jokes by her friends. Regardless, she understood Jimmy was all she had left. And, she would be damned if she let anything happen to him.

"Let's get down to business, Jimbo," Jude said with more resolve than she was used to having at her beck and call.

**20**
## *Shot in the Dark, and You're to Blame*
+1 Day – 7:50pm EST

Matty's service sidearm had been easy to find. It had been laid to rest on a doily in front of a steel-framed picture of him taken after his graduation from the Marine Corps War College. Yep, Matthew Sawyer had been the oldest and the best of the Sawyer brood. Andy had emulated him and set off on the same career trajectory. Jimmy and Jude, unfortunately, had lived in their brothers' heroic and selfless shadows for as long as they could remember. Then came Michael—the fortunate son—where all parental hopes and love had been bestowed.

Jude hefted the M9 Beretta's heavy, but comfortable, weight. Yeah. This weapon would see them through. While she reacquainted herself with the weapon, Jimmy looked for the Beretta's spare clips...

...*"Magazines, not clips."* Matty reminded her again.

*"Fine,"* Jude said with mock annoyance. *"Magazines. Whatever."*

*"I don't want you to embarrass yourself if you ever come across an actual gun enthusiast."*

*"Yeah,"* Jude agreed. *"We wouldn't want that, would we?"*

*"Nope."* Matty sat on the bed, grinning at her.

*"What?"* Jude was embarrassed by his jovial nature and piercing eyes. It was as if he could bore right into her blemished soul.

*"Nothing. Really."* Matty shrugged. *"You doing okay?"*

*"As good as one can be living in this family."*

84

*Matty nodded. He understood what being a Sawyer was like. He had just been lucky enough to have the skill and brains to rise above it and follow his own path. Serving his country with honor just happened to be something Mom and Dad could brag to the neighbors about.*

*"You did good at the range," Matty said, expertly turning the conversation into something more positive. He was a master at keeping her from being mired in wallowing self-pity. Well done, sir. Well done.*

*"Thanks," Jude replied. "I had an okay teacher."*

*"Yeah, he's pretty handsome, too."*

*"He's okay looking." They both laughed at that, knowing it was more true than false. He had never fallen into the trap of resorting to using his looks and charm to get what he wanted. He was smart, an amazingly empathetic person, and humble to a fault.*

*"Agreed." Matty turned the empty Beretta over in his hand. "Hey. Do you want to learn how to disarm someone?"*

*"Uh," Jude said, "duh!"*

She smiled thinly with the memory of the magazines versus clips debate—and the two hours of brutal disarming training. That had been one of the best times she remembered spending with her oldest brother, firing at the range and disarming each other. Maybe, it had been because they had found commonality. Matty had grown up and had charted his own course. He had been an adult—a man. Someone who had seen the world and knew what was out there for himself—and for her. He had always drilled into her that she had the same potential. He had reiterated the same sentiment the last time they were together—the last time she had seen him alive.

Jude fiddled with the magazine, having it turned around backwards. She was finally able to slam it home into the grip, making that satisfying click when it locked in. Movie action heroes didn't ever make that mistake when they loaded their weapons. Sigh. She had never considered herself an Alice or Ripley before. There must have been a first time for them, too.

Mom-thing sniffed and scratched at the door. Jude pulled back the nightstand while Jimmy reached for the doorknob, his foot bracing the door in case Mom-thing tried to burst through again. Jude squared up her stance and aimed the Beretta at a low point in the door. She nodded at Jimmy. His eyes went wide, but he nodded he was ready, too. He counted down with his weak hand, his fingers quivering.

Three...

Jude hoped this plan was their best option.

Two...

She was an idiot to believe she was actually ready for this.

One...

*Don't open that door!* She wanted to say, but couldn't even breath the words. If she couldn't speak, would her fingers betray her in another second when she needed to pull the trigger?

The door swung open. Mom-thing sat up alertly on all fours. She sniffed the air. She smelled warm-blooded meat, looking directly at Jude. This was Jude's opportunity. She tried to pull the heavy trigger. Nothing happened. It was too hard to pull. She tilted the Beretta. The safety was off. The weapon was loaded. Mom-thing crawled one step across the threshold.

"Shoot," Jimmy mouthed, although it was louder than he anticipated. Mom-thing became agitated and pressed into the door, pinning Jimmy against the wall. She swiped a hand around the edge. He hissed.

Jude couldn't figure out the Beretta.

Safety off... magazine loaded...

Shit! She hadn't chambered a round. She tilted the weapon and pulled back the slide. The click was loud, instantly catching Mom-thing's attention. She snarled at the sound and glared at Jude's silhouette in the shadowy room.

"Shoot her!" Jimmy had abandoned any semblance of stealth.

The hammer was cocked.

The round was chambered.

Jude pulled the trigger as Mom-thing leapt at her. The room lit up in a strobe of yellow. Mom-thing was cast in a terrifying flash of light. Her mouth was agape. Her fingertips had been whittled down to bloodied meat, her eyes wide and coated with a cloudy white film flecked with red and gold. A hole appeared at her hairline.

The room went dark again. Jude's eyes couldn't adjust in time to see Mom-thing crash into the front of her legs, bowling her over onto her stomach with Mom-thing under her. Jude twisted away, fearful another bite or scratch was coming her way. She retreated to the doorway to cover the still shielded Jimmy, the Beretta coming up level.

No sniffing. No scratching. No snarling. Just a feeling it was okay to breathe again. Jude usually didn't trust her own judgement. But, this time, as the room filled with a cloying smell of copper and earthy rot, Jude found herself believing everything was going to be alright. Jimmy was safe. She had escaped any harm, except a bruised ego from her gun snafu and being knocked onto the floor. They had a gun, lots of bullets, and a secure apartment.

Uh oh!

Jude rushed to the bathroom, barely registering the bodies of her father and brother. Slamming the door behind her and wrestling her jeans down to her knees, she fell hard on the toilet seat. Even though she had been in discomfort for God knows how long with the need to urinate, her body had locked down her thruways. She concentrated on her breathing and the small cracked hexagon-shaped tiles at her feet. Several agonizing seconds later, a burning sensation spreading between her legs added pain to her impatience—her body having decided peeing was on the approved list. Dribbles became a torrent as Jude was finally able to relieve herself. If nothing else, this moment of relief was proof there was still good in the world.

## 21
# *Scrubs*
+1 Day – 8:47pm EST

Jimmy sat on the couch in the near dark. Jude sat next to him holding his hand in hers. The Beretta was on the seat cushion of the high back chair—where Mom would have been sitting about this time to watch America's Got Talent. Well, these two American kids definitely had talent… that's for sure. Although, Jude might have got an X from Howie Mandell for lack of comedic content.

Michael's body lay on the floor in the hallway with blood and shards of Hummel figurines strewn around him. Only part of the curtain shroud could be seen as it draped over Dad. In another few minutes, she wouldn't be able to make out the outlines of the bodies at all. That didn't matter. There was no amount of blackness that could make her or Jimmy go down the hallway again.

"We both could sleep in my room," Jude offered, stifling her own yawn. The adrenaline had worn off ages ago. She felt drawn out. Her body was buzzing with a soreness seeming to block out everything else. It made it much more difficult for her brain to stay sharp. She needed to shut down... just for a little while. That wasn't too much to ask, was it?

"Nah," Jimmy said with a weak shrug, "I'm good here. You go."

"Okay." Jude squeezed his hand tight. "Love you, Jimbo."

"Love you, too, big sis."

"Okay." Jude got off the couch—a feat unto itself—and fought to keep a wash of dizziness from overwhelming her. Once the wave of lightheadedness had passed, she reached down to grab the Beretta. "I'm taking this, if that's okay with you."

Jimmy shrugged again. "Whatever gets you to sleep at night."

Jude laughed a little. Jimmy smiled thinly. Both were too exhausted to emote much more. That was alright. Jude's brain wasn't up for an emotional exchange anyway. "Okay, Jimbo. Let's get some sleep."

"That won't be a problem," Jimmy agreed. "And, sis?"

"Yeah?"

"Quit calling me 'Jimbo'."

"We'll see what tomorrow brings. Good night."

She turned to go to her room. As a last-ditch idea, she grabbed the afghan blanket from the back of Dad's reserved recliner. The throne was now vacant. Jimmy was the last living Sawyer son and could lay claim to the family mantle. Although, Jude did have the gun and could easily wrestle control from him.

What a silly thought.

Jude pulled off the blanket and shook the crazy thoughts from her head. Dragging it across the floor, she draped the blanket over

Michael's body. She couldn't take seeing his lifeless blue eyes anymore. Dad had been shrouded by Mom's curtain. She was enshrined in a tomb of her own making. It was only right Michael was given proper respect and attention after death. She thought to mutter a few parting words for Michael—something worthy of the floating pyre at a Viking funeral or the passing of a beloved Pope of the Vatican—but her addled brain could only come up with one word. "Sorry."

Jimmy had already pulled up his legs up on the couch. He turned away with his knees bent and his arms hugging one of the two decorative throw pillows. The bottoms of his socks were black from the dirty floors of the apartment. She would have to remember to get him a fresh pair.

Tomorrow. It could wait until tomorrow.

Tonight. Sleep.

Jude went to her room. The bed called to her. *Not yet.* She put the pistol on the nightstand and stripped off her sweaty and bloody clothes. She even stripped off her bra and undies. She grabbed a hand towel and a half-full bottle of water from God-knows how long ago. She poured the water onto the towel in a generous amount, spilling more than she should on the floor. Staring at the mirror in the last slivers of daylight, she wiped away the grime, sweat and blood still clinging to her skin. She started at her face and worked her way down her arms and torso. She splashed more water on the towel and scrubbed everything else she could reach again, this time more vigorously. The red from the blood she rubbed off was replaced by the raw skin she left behind.

A flicker of light through the window caught her attention—coming from the alleyway between two neighboring buildings—before it winked out completely. She stared into the alley, but the light did not return. That left her naked, shaking and crying in the darkness. She dropped the towel to the floor, grabbed a fresh pair of undies from her drawer. Followed by her favorite well-worn night shirt. It once had a graphic of a kitten on the front, but the kitty had disappeared a long time ago.

She was exhausted, but her mind was still racing. The other half of the sleeping pill she had taken before was still on her nightstand. She needed sleep. There were dead bodies strewn all over the apartment. It was only half a pill. It was only half a dose. She really needed sleep. She grabbed the pill between her finger and thumb and dry-swallowed it. Everything would be much better in the morning. It had to be, right?

Jude plopped her fatigued body on the covers of the bed. The box spring squeaked its opinion about her added weight, those springs almost as old and tired as she was. She curled up in a fetal position, burying her head into Floopy's coarse fur, rocking herself back and forth until consciousness finally drifted away from her.


**22**
## Garbage Day
+2 Days – 12:00am EST

Thump.

Jude was cold. Sleep had always been elusive. That was why she had swallowed a sleeping pill to ease her into unconsciousness. But, even with the pill, the weariness from the emotional stress, and the bleed-off of adrenaline, she was wide awake.

Thump.

Unable to sleep, she had decided to investigate the noises she kept hearing. She stood at the mouth of the alleyway across from her apartment—the same alleyway where the last moments of shining dusk had been captured. The brick walls of both apartment buildings were grimy with decades of dirt, soot, and particles of air pollution finally drifting back to earth. Somehow, street artists hadn't discovered the alley, the walls still virgin of spray paint. Maybe, they only liked clean canvases. Both sides were adorned with the twentieth century's own answer to industrial art—wrought iron fire escapes. One of the upper platforms had pulled away from some of its mounts, listing into the space between the buildings like a twisting skeleton. Obvious attempts had been made to brace the failing metal exterior stairs with struts and ropes, but the section was too far gone to be saved by such ambitious, but still amateur workmanship.

The alley was surprisingly clear of debris or stray garbage bags. Dumpsters lined both walls in an alternating pattern, with twenty to thirty feet between them. The setup allowed for smaller vehicles to weave through the rudimentary maze without having to worry about losing a side mirror.

The brickwork, while grimy, still held a polished sheen on the surface of its red clay roots. The mortar between the bricks still showed flecks of bright white nuggets of cement. A thin rivulet of water trekked its way to a small square storm drain, its drips echoing as they fell through the metal grates. All of the windows facing the alley were open, dark square blemishes on an already soiled surface.

The interiors of the apartments would be very hot without operating AC. It had been an unseasonably warm spring, and tonight had not gone against script. The edge of a single lace curtain drifted out from one of the open windows, clinging to the coarse brick for a few moments before it tore itself away and curled back inside.

Thump.

Something bounced off the plastic lid of one of the dumpsters at the far end of the alleyway, tumbling in a flopping heap into the center of the cracked and pock-marked asphalt. Was someone throwing their garbage out their window? Maybe it was an elderly woman who wasn't able to use the stairs with the elevators being out. Another bag of garbage dropped from above. Thump. It hit the edge of the same dumpster and careened off toward the wall out of sight.

Thump. Thump.

More garbage landed on the dumpster lids behind her. Jude couldn't see any of the culprits who were shoving bags out their windows, but more bags of varying sizes dropped out from a cloud of hazy darkness above her.

Thump!

Garbage slammed into the top of the dumpster next to her. She yelped and jumped back. The bag bounced off the now dented lid and rolled to her feet. She gave it a kick in retaliation for scaring her. The black plastic bag started to stretch.

"What the hell?"

The plastic turned white, tearing once it reached its transparent breaking point. A gray arm poked through, just as white as the plastic. Another arm came out. The tear widened.

"Shit! Shit!"

A head and shoulders slid through. The man wasn't alive... but was. His face was sheared off at the forehead, nose and chin.

Thump. Thump. Thump.

More bags fell onto the alley floor. More of them were tearing open. All were filled with the living dead—hungry things focused on her. They crawled out all around her, their near-paralyzed vocal cords emitting a chorus of a mewing need. She was trapped in the center of it all, a hundred feet from either end. Men, women, and children dragged the remnants of their Hefty-style body bags along with them. Extricating themselves from their plastic prisons was secondary to their pursuit of living flesh.

A child of no more than six swiped at her leg. Jude instinctually stomped on the little girl's forearm. The bones snapped and the limp arm was dragged back to the child-thing's body to hang limp against her leg. Another man-thing dove forward with a growl in his throat and splayed fingers ending in bloody stumps at the second knuckles. Jude screamed, wishing for the Beretta still on her nightstand. She retreated a few steps.

Something pushed her from behind. She yelled out again, having backed into the rusting extended ladder for one of the fire escapes. She grabbed the highest rung she could and pulled herself up. Her legs didn't want to help her climb, paralyzed with the fear of a dead flesh thing grabbing her by the ankle to pull her back down. *Fucking help out a little, you goddamn legs!* She scrambled up the ladder to the first platform, then scurried up to the second landing to be sure the things couldn't get to her. Then to the third, just to be absolutely sure.

She was safe.

Thump.

Rotting animated bodies slid their way down the stairs from the platforms above. Jude went to the railing and looked up. The entire fire escape was filled with the undead, reaching down at her. The weight on the iron contraption made it list even farther into the alley.

Fraying ropes snapped. Metal bolts screeched away from their brackets. The fire escape was failing. It was failing her. It swayed and slammed into the opposite wall. Jude lost her footing and pitched over the side. She flailed her arms as she fell through the open air.

The things below her reached up.

The things above reached down.

Jude reached out toward a railing miles away. She missed, plummeting toward the hands and teeth of mindless, but single-minded, seething hunger. Tearing fingers sunk into her. Their teeth ripped flesh from her bones.

Jude screamed for her worthless life.


23
## *Drug-Induced Dreams*
+2 Days – 3:12am EST


Jude felt the scream clawing up from her throat. She bolted upright in her bed, her body exhausted from the effort. She clutched Floopy so tight, her stuffed companion's head was in danger of popping off. Her skin was slick with sweat, both from the heat in the room and the nightmare terrors the sleeping pill had concocted from her already addled mind. "Goddamn it, Floopy," she whispered into her lion's ear. "Can't I ever get a fucking break?"

The lion had no answers for her. He never did. But, at least, he had always been there when she needed him most. Her muscles ached terribly from the tension of the fall in her dream. It took too much effort to pull away from her stalwart plush companion, her arms reluctant to pry away from the comforting fake fur of the king of Jude's room.

It wasn't night anymore, but it wasn't morning, either. When she had gone to bed, she knew it had been a few minutes after midnight. The perfect time for the supernatural... when yesterday still clung to every second of the clock, even as today wrestled to pull itself out of the misted muck of tomorrow. There were moments where both overlapped the same space and time, enveloping and entwining with each other.

The dream was already fading back into Jude's subconscious, becoming difficult to remember. Jude looked around her dark bedroom. She had no idea what time it was. The midnight of the dreamscape had become whatever witching hour it actually was. The time when demons, devils and all other supernatural beings were said to be at their most powerful. Jude wondered what other spectral entities would decide to haunt her for their entertainment.

"Just want sleep." She shook Floopy to redistribute some of the batting back into a less-lumpy shape. Once looking like a cartoonish lion again, she plopped him on her belly and leaned him against her bent knees. "Is that so much to ask?" Floopy cocked his head to the left inquisitively, but said nothing. "Yeah. You're probably right. Too much to ask."

Limping footsteps padded around the living room. Jimmy was up at this ungodly hour, too. She hoped his sleep had been more restful than hers. After propping Floopy up next to the pillow, she swung her legs out of the bed. Her muscles ached. Her joints were stiff. Sleep still had a hold of her blurry vision and tearing eyes. She definitely needed more rest.

She wiped the excess sweat off her body with her discarded shirt. Damp nightshirt and undies were exchanged for another set of clean undies and bra. Laundry would have to be done soon, somehow. Clean socks, denim jeans and a tank top finished off her ensemble. Hair back in a ponytail holder. Viola! Done... and done.

Something of glass origins fell to the floor and shattered. Was there anything left of their mother's collection that could be broken? There were the Boyd's Bears figures on the living room table with the lamp. They had escaped the first wave in the Great Figurine Purge. Apparently, they were destined to be wiped out in a secondary attack. Jude guessed she should step in to save the bears from extinction.

Opening the bedroom door, Jude stepped out into the hallway. She kicked the head of one of the decimated bears hard enough to send it bouncing off the other wall. Oh, well. Jimmy wasn't in the living room, his cane still propped against the couch cushion. The dining room and foyer were empty, too. She guessed the bear had fallen to its death all on its own. Jude's powers of deduction were pretty sharp in spite of the fitful sleep, so she padded toward the kitchen.

"Jimmy," Jude called out softly. The last thing she needed was to scare the crap out of her brother in the middle of the night. She rounded the corner where several of her mother's tchotchkes adorned the walls between the kitchen and dining room. A framed painting, brought home from a trip to Poland many years ago, rattled as she brushed past it. Jude made sure it wasn't going to fall off the wall before dismissing it to look into the kitchen.

Jimmy was at the other end of the galley looking out the window. He was cast in black silhouette as he leaned against the frame, the outside world surprisingly bright and sharp compared to the dim outdated kitchen interiors. The moon was earning its pay tonight. A rack hung from the ceiling with all manner of pots, pans and skillets. They hung too low for Jude's comfort. She always had to skirt around them or duck under them to get to the stove. Another detriment of being a tall woman. She hated being a tall woman.

"Anything good out there?" Jude asked.

Jimmy didn't answer, but shrugged his shoulders.

"You want me to get your cane?" Jude asked, hating the way the words tasted as they left her lips. This simple utterance of kindness sounded condescending and flagrant, serving perfectly to point out his palsy.

Jimmy turned, his face still obscured by those fucking hanging pots and pans. He wasn't as tall as she was, but the pots would still clank against his forehead if he didn't duck down under them. The problem was his limited mobility didn't allow for him to easily crouch down at the knees or at the waist to do so. So, he did what he always did, sidestepping toward the refrigerator to go around the cookware. Mother had never bothered to relocate anything, even after it became apparent Jimmy would have trouble with them. Her opinion—shared by Dad, too—was Jimmy would figure out how to navigate through the apartment on his own. They had said if he couldn't figure that out, he would never be able to get around out in the world. Jimmy, with years of practice, made it around the pots and pans with only two of them clinking against the side of his face.

"Ouch, bro," Jude said, sucking in air through her teeth. She knew it was Jimmy's weak side and that he didn't feel much there, but it still looked like it hurt. "You okay?"

Jimmy tripped over his stumbling feet, sprawling out at her. *Shit!* Jude reached out to catch him. His lips contorted down on his palsied side. His eyelid drooped almost closed. His skin was pale with dark circles under his eyes. He looked up at her, his good eye zeroing in on hers. He reached out to her, but fell face first onto the linoleum floor.

*Damn it!*

Instead of getting up, he crab-crawled toward her. Jude backed up out of the kitchen. He was moving strangely—that is, more so than usual. He looked up at her, his face a reflection of the moonlight glinting off the sheen of the hanging aluminum pots and pans. His lips peeled back to reveal dark gums. His eye was bloodshot and flecked in gold. *Like Dad!*

Jude bumped into the dining room table, the edge slamming into the small of her back. Jimmy didn't mind as he pursued her on his hands and knees. She overturned a chair as she retreated across the living room. He quickly scurried around it. *Fuck! He's fast!* His hands slapped on the floor in front of her. The gun was too far away. Her legs didn't work right, causing her to trip and fall down to his level. He climbed over her ankles. She brought her legs up to her chest. A warbled gurgling sound came from his lips. She kicked out with both feet. His neck pushed into his shoulder blades. Something tore. Or, maybe, it snapped. His face thumped against the floor between her legs.

Jude scooted back. Her shoulder hit the end table. Another figurine tipped off the edge and broke as it hit the floor. It had been a bear in a canoe, but both were now in two pieces. Jimmy stayed where he was, his forehead still against the floor. The crown of his head stared back at her, revealing the earliest stages of balding.

She rolled up on her knees, not taking her eyes off her brother's body. Once on her feet, she backed up into her bedroom and rushed to get the Beretta from the nightstand. She hopped up on her bed with her legs curled up under her. There was no way she was letting any monsters grab at her from under the bed. She pointed the gun at the door and willed Jimmy to stay dead. She willed him to come back to the land of the living. How had he died and come back as one of *them*? Michael was still dead—he somehow had managed to stay dead. Jimmy hadn't been attacked when they had faced Mom-thing. How could she have possibly have killed him with a double kick to the face? His muscles were degenerative and atrophied, true, but was it possible his neck and shoulder muscles couldn't withstand the snap of her kick?

She pulled Floopy in tight with the crook of her free elbow, again leaning on him for the protection only a childhood talisman could offer. Even the Beretta paled in comparison.

## 24
## *Lady in Waiting*
+2 Days – 6:14am EST

Matthew had set the precedent by being killed overseas in a bullshit political war masked as democratic freedom. Now, the Sawyer apartment was littered with the dead bodies of the rest of the family. Dad lay draped with a curtain shroud deep in the hallway. Michael was closer, covered with a knit afghan Mom had worked on years ago. The tips of three of his fingers poked out from under it. Mom was on the floor in Matty's room, a bullet through the face by Jude's own hand.

Jimmy.

Jude sat on her bed. Waiting.

"Couldn't have killed him with one blow," she muttered in Floopy's ear. "I ain't got that much leg strength."

A few hours had passed since she had kicked Jimmy in the face. In that time, Jimmy had not staggered into the room to finish her or Floopy off. The only thing to finally invade her room was a cool morning light denoting the world still spun on its axis... even if her own personal world was spinning off of its own.

The Beretta sat on the comforter in front of her, the weight of it finally becoming too much for her to keep leveled at the door. People didn't realize how quickly the weight of a loaded handgun could feel like a stack of Bibles in the palm of your hand. At least it's barrel was still pointing in the general direction of the door. That was a win—of sorts—right?

Jude set her feet onto the floor and flexed her toes in her fuzzy socks. Her fingers found the grip of the Beretta. It was still heavy, but light enough to slip into the waistband in the back of her jeans. Hoisting herself off the bed with a bit of stiff muscular effort, Jude tiptoed to the open doorway. The action seemed hokey. She felt like a character in a Scooby-Doo cartoon, lurking toward a spooky hallway already filled with dead bodies. Thank God they were covered. There was something oddly comforting about not having to see their faces—or what was left of their faces. Something as simple as a sheet or blanket—or curtain—made venturing into the hallway just a bit less intimidating.

Dad and Michael were right where she had left them. She peeked around the door frame toward the living room. Jimmy was also right where she had abandoned him, his forehead against the hardwood as if he was kissing the floor. Dust swirled in the heavy air, the coolness of the night not having done much to alleviate the stale heat hanging throughout the apartment. The hallway was the worst, probably because of the claustrophobic confines and the smell starting to come from the Sawyer men. Mom had been decent enough to have had her final death in a room where the door could be closed. Thanks, Mom.

Jude side-stepped the congealing blood and figurine fragments to get to the living room and Jimmy. He didn't look like a monster. He just looked like a young man with limited prospects and a bad roll of the genetic dice. She crouched next to the body, careful not to get too close. There were no scratches in his bare skin or, worse, chunks of muscle torn from his body. There were several claw marks on his left pant leg, probably from Mom trying to get at him when he had been hiding behind the door. None of them had ripped through the demin. Jude pulled up the cuff, surprised at his smooth, unbroken skin. Still no reason for him to have died to come back as one of those things.

His socks were filthy. She remembered noticing that last night. But, in the morning light, she realized it hadn't been dirt staining the cotton. There was dirt on the dingy socks, sure, but it was blood that had coated them. On closer inspection, Jude found several porcelain Hummel shards plastered to the congealed blood and cotton. On a hunch, she pulled off both socks. On his weak leg—the one with no feeling—the bloody shards had embedded themselves deep into the calloused flesh.

"Shit."

That must have been how he had been infected. He had walked straight onto the shards. Shot the goddamn contaminated blood directly into his body through his soaked socks. He hadn't felt it at all. He had died in his sleep—the way she hoped to die—and had returned as an animated corpse.

It was just Sawyer family luck… to wink out of existence during their sleep. Jude was the last. Her entire family was laying at her feet, some dead by her own doing. There was nobody left.

She was free. Was it possible? Why did she feel good to have such a thought? Her family was dead around her, but all she felt was a sense of lightness and liberation. Her stomach flopped at how morbid this revelation sounded in her head, but her heart disagreed.

There was nothing left to keep her from living her life the way she wanted to—except for the pesky end of the world part, of course. She had one last opportunity to be something more—someone different than what her parents had expected. Fuck them. Fuck their expectations. She stood over Jimmy, pain in her heart and a Beretta tucked into the back of her jeans. The pain was a constant. The handgun was something altogether new.

## 25
## *Come to my Window*
+2 Days – 7:11am EST

The lobby was bright with the morning sun streaming through the windows with purpose. Jude stopped in the center of the compass—standing over a tile-inlaid circle with arrows pointing to the four corners of the map. It was not a true depiction of a compass since the lobby doors faced southwest. In spite of the inaccuracy, she stood in the center of it anyway, feeling the heat on her upturned face and bare arms. If she closed her eyes tightly and focused on the sun's heat long enough, she could almost forget everyone was dead. Almost. She took all her judgements back. The lobby was not a result of some chewed up architecture vomit. The inlayed mosaic compass was not stupid and hokey. The sun warming her skin through the two stories of windows was not a sweat box of ill-conceived design.

Jude stood on a precipice—of sorts. She tapped the Beretta against her thigh, fully aware the safety was flipped to the "off" position. Her finger had naturally gravitated to the trigger guard. 'Red meant dead,' Matty had drilled that saying into her. He had trained her well, being as much her drill instructor as he must have had endured in his own basic training. She would never be a sharpshooter, but she knew she could get the job done if push came to shove.

What she didn't know was how to feel about the consequences of pulling the trigger. There was no basic training for that sort of thing. Jude was sure Dr. Rick would have some good advice for how to feel and how to handle this much death and personal loss, but all she felt was an encompassing grayness. She sensed a mix of despair and relief swirling around in her head and heart. Her nerve-endings had been raked raw with a buzzing numb. While she was thankful she could feel the heat on her skin through the windows, Jude worried she didn't feel bad enough about what she had done to her parents. She had bashed in her Dad's head and put a bullet through her Mom's, for Christ's sake.

She felt more for the loss of her brothers. At least that was proof she still felt something. What had happened to Jimmy had been an unnecessary and undeserved tragedy. Michael, while arrogant and entitled, should have had his whole life ahead of him to correct his immaturity and to become a better man. There was no future for him now.

It was Jude's parents who had squandered a lifetime to possibly become better people—and had chosen to not bother with such frivolities. Either through ignorance or laziness, Mom and Dad had decided their own needs were more important than the needs of their children. That had been especially true for Jimmy and Jude, the two disappointing Sawyer kids who had lived in the shadows between the rock of a heroic first-born and a patriotic second son and the hard place of a privileged youngest son. Jude realized she did indeed feel something, just not what she expected to feel. Anger was a feeling, after all.

She would try to process her feelings later if she ever managed to sort them out. Now was the time to survive. She stepped to the lobby doors and pressed the exit bar. Learning her lesson from years of accidentally locking herself out of the house, Jude wedged the Beretta in the back of her waistband and propped open the door with a tall ashtray. It had always been conveniently placed next to a bush that had become yellow from the years of proximity to the smoke. It didn't matter she had her keys on her this time. Better safe than stupid.

The street was still quiet and surreal, the hustle and bustle of a mid-week, mid-morning day painfully absent. It couldn't all be because of the warnings of the emergency broadcast system, could it? People in this area typically thumbed their noses at anything the local government had to say about such things. A hurricane warning to evacuate homes a few years ago was largely ignored. When the storm blew east out over the ocean, those people who didn't leave their homes were validated into believing they knew better than those in control. And, when the evacuated residents returned to their homes and saw the government was wrong about the damage they had been sure to incur, they also became hardened into thinking they should have known better than to listen to empty warnings. People hated being told what to do, but they still needed law and order to keep from descending into anarchy. It was a strange juxtaposition of the human condition.

Jude walked to where Mr. Emery had approached her earlier, the beer cans and bottles still lined up under the street lamp. She couldn't bring herself to look down the block to the alley—the scene of her subconscious demise. Her fitful dream, while hazy, was still powerful enough to keep her from overcoming the irrational terror of it. Instead, she looked up at the brick façade of her own building. There was nothing remarkable about it, other than a bit of ornate cornice work between the second and third floors and less elaborate trim below the roof along the parapet. There were granite keystones over each window. Her father had taught her that. Her father knew— had known, she corrected herself—a little about everything... except how to be a loving parent. She guessed knowledge was more important than love, sometimes. Anger flared up again.

Most of the windows were closed and would eventually need to be opened to let in some fresh air. The sun would bake the building soon enough. The fourth-floor apartment on the right corner, unlike the others, had all its windows open. The curtains billowed out. The light material dragged across the sill and flopped outside to cling to the bumpy brick. Then a breeze picked the curtain up like a sail before sucking it back inside. The movement of the curtain lit up a bubble of fear in her belly

Jude didn't know who lived in that apartment. She thought it might have been a family of four, but it was a vague recollection at best. Someone walked by the window facing the sidewalk.

"Hey!" Jude craned her neck and shielded her eyes to get a better look at who was up there. The same colors and shape walked past the window in the other direction. Whoever it was managed to stay obscured behind the gauze of the swaying curtain. Jude yelled louder, "Hey!" The person reversed course a third time, but stopped short of poking their head out the window. "Come on. Hey!"

Finally, the person came to the window. He slapped his head against the upper pane and reeled back. Jude guessed she shouldn't have been so loud and insistent. The guy leaned down and stuck his hands and head out the window.

Jude's next attempt at communication was strangled in her throat. The man, with his body out the window to his waist, was missing one side of his cheek. Blood had dried and darkened on his T-shirt and the skin of his deeply scratched arms. He spat out something from his mouth. Blood... and something else. As the chunk unfurled and fell the four stories to the sidewalk, she realized it was the missing part of his face. She wasn't able to rationalize the chunk of flesh slapping against the sidewalk. Jude could only look up at the man-thing reaching out the window. He teetered too far out the sill.

Jude backed up a step. Was she having another nightmare? Or was it coming to life? Jude shook her head in disbelief. The man-thing flailed and growled. She backed up another step. The man-thing slipped out the window. Jude's heart seized as she watched him fall. An endless second later, he landed on his outstretched arms. They snapped at the forearms. His head exploded in a spray of blood, gray matter and skull fragments. His neck disappeared into his shoulders. It all happened in slow motion. The rest of his body balanced vertically for a moment before his legs finally swung down and toppled what remained of his body to the stained concrete.

Jude backed up toward the lobby. Toward safety? She didn't know how the Beretta got into her hand. She couldn't look away from the apartment as there was more movement at the adjoining window. Smaller silhouettes paced behind the curtain. She was sure they would want to see where their daddy-thing had gone. They would follow. They would come for her.

Aluminum cans scattered across the sidewalk. Glass clinked together. Some of it cracked or broke. Something grabbed her on the shoulders. She tore away, spinning around. She scurried away from the lamppost, scattering more empty and discarded beer containers across the sidewalk and into the street. A yellow-skinned man loomed over her, the lamp post in the way of his flailing arms. It would have been terrifying enough without the fact his intestines were hanging over his brown belt. The bulbous tubes of flesh draped past his crotch, still oozing pungent human waste from tiny tears in the lining.

The first gunshot was a complete surprise to Jude. She looked at the gun. Had she pulled the trigger? Had there been a report? Did the gun kick up in her hand? The gunshot had surprised the tall sidewalk-thing, for sure. The bullet sparked off the side of the lamp post and tumbled straight through the bridge of his nose. The round must have ricocheted inside his skull before it blasted out a huge chunk in the back of his head. He slumped backward. One of his hands slapped against the lamppost with a hollow thud before he landed amid the debris of the previously-held sidewalk drinking marathon.

A thump from behind her. One of the kid-things from the apartment had indeed splatted on the sidewalk. Her fingers twitched several times before finally going still. Thankfully, her long flaxen hair covered the damage to her head from the impact. The rest of the undead family moaned from the window, both trying to get out at the same time.

Other windows started to show movement. It could have been a trick of the light against the glass, but there was too much activity to dismiss it out of hand. Two splattered bodies from undead suicide in front of her. One man shot and killed by her own hand behind her. Swarming and agitated things in other apartments.

Death was all around her. How was she the only person still alive? She didn't need more reason to get out of here.

## 26
## *Gun Metal Gray*
+2 Days – 7:44am EST

She had left the undead on the sidewalk to rot, rushing back through the propped open door of the lobby and locking it closed behind her. Between the two locations, she had chosen to return to where her family lay dead on the floor in order to figure out her next move.

There was no life left in the world, either inside or outside the apartment. At least, that's what she could see. Was she still alive? Living... what an irony. Had she lived? Could someone say they lived when they had to carry the oppressive weight of a disapproving and domineering mother? Could the same be said about a father who was a bit too attentive to his only daughter, especially when they were alone together? Jude shook off the thoughts, not wanting to fall prey to the sucking quality of that particular rabbit hole. Could she simply move on now they were dead?

She sat at her normal spot at the dining room table. The 9-1-1 operator had told them to let the body rest at home until someone could dedicate strained resources to fetch him. A morbid thought until one thought back to when shot-down outlaws of the Wild West were stood up in pine coffins for all to see or when a body was set up for viewing in the parlor of the family home. It wasn't until after the American Civil War that the embalming of bodies became accepted and the funeral home industry became popular. Hell, people used to be buried on their own land. Something else her dad had taught her. There were four bodies now. She sure as hell wasn't going to be able to bury any of them under the concrete and brick pavers of the apartment's small courtyard.

The Beretta lay on the dingy table cloth in front of her. Mom had always complained about the cloth's yellow hue and its smattering of faded stains, defending its condition against her self-proclaimed excellent laundry skills. Two filled magazines lay next to the sidearm on the linens. Two full boxes of 9mm rounds sat next to the magazines. One hundred and forty-five rounds. Correction. One hundred and forty-three rounds. She had forgotten the bullet ripping through Mom-thing's face and the one ricocheting off the lamppost into the skull of the man-thing on the sidewalk. She only needed one of those rounds to make everything better.

Morbid thinking, certainly. A permanent solution to a temporary problem, her friends would have said. Of course, that was back when people didn't live in a world where the dead came back to life. Doctor Rick would agree with the anecdote's substance, certainly. She had tried to reach him on the wall phone, but there had been no dial tone. The phone had gone dead, in spite of the low voltage supposedly running through the lines. Death seemed to be the order of the day. Why not join in? Who was she leaving behind to mourn her tragic passing? Everyone had opted out before her, leaving her alone.

As least the Beretta was still with her.

She picked it up and felt its comfortable weight in her hand. It was a substantial weapon at two and a half pounds, but she didn't fear it. Matty had made sure she had handled it enough to get over her jitters. There was such a mystique around weapons. They were so small and insignificant looking, but could inflict such swift and decisive death. Her hands didn't break into a sweat when handling the Beretta anymore, but she had gained a reverent respect for its power. *Guns don't kill people. People kill people.* That was the saying, right? Bullshit slogans meant to minimize what guns could do. Firearms were instruments of death and destruction, made for a singular purpose. People made guns so they could kill things. Or, to defend their property and loved ones. Or, to kill as many not-dead things as possible in order to live another few minutes. She might only need one bullet to solve all of her immediate problems, but Jude still had one hundred and forty-two opportunities to live. She could always save the last bullet for herself.

It was time to start making a go at it. She had already prepared everything she needed to move out of this apartment a couple months ago, in spite of her mother's previous adamant angst and venom on the subject. All she had to do is get there. If the police ever came around to investigate, maybe she would come back to set the record straight. Or, maybe, she would just let them rot.

Sorry, Jimmy.

## 27
# *Give Me Shelter*
+2 Days – 8:01am EST

She had fit all of the light non-perishable snacks she could find in the kitchen and pantry into one of Michael's backpacks. It was heavy across her shoulders, several old bottled waters from the pantry lined along the bottom of the bag. Jude's studio apartment was across town. She hadn't worried about dragging any more clothes with her as she had already quietly moved most of what she owned into the trunk of her car a few weeks ago.

Once she was on the street again, Jude hurried the couple blocks to where she had parked. Thankfully it was in the opposite direction from the bodies on the sidewalk. Her brain was still trying to wrap itself around the two undead suicides, knowing full well they had been trying to get at her. Didn't they have any sense of self-preservation?

Jude tightly gripped the Beretta as she walked, not wanting to be unprepared if she ran into any more of them. The streets were a fairly straight grid system, allowing her to see a few blocks in both directions. She saw a couple people in the distance walking in the middle of the street. Instinctively, she started to raise her free hand to wave, but thought better of it.

She shrugged off her apprehension and approached a line of cars. She couldn't see her little beater of a Toyota, but knew it was parked past the phone company utility van. That was, until she was standing at the van's front bumper. Oil spots dotted the faded asphalt. Shattered glass shards twinkled across the road in the morning light, glittering like diamonds spilled from a velvet sack. Several feet separated the truck from the late-model Buick Regal parked in front of it.

"Fuck!" Jude screamed to no one in particular. She stood in the middle of the empty spot that had, up to last night, included her car and all of her belongings. She balled up her hands and waved the Beretta around, feeling violated and impotent. She gritted her teeth against more feelings she couldn't express in what Doctor Rick would have called, 'a healthy way'.

She grabbed her phone and clicked the button on the front screen. The screen remained black. The next thing she knew, the phone screen and body cracked on the edge of the curb. She had drained her battery hours ago, but had hoped to recharge it from the Toyota's car charger. Now, her blind rage had caused her to hurl the goddamn device into the gutter. She didn't bother to retrieve the phone, disgusted with herself. She could go back and get Michael's phone—it normally had a wicked good charge—but it was probably in his jean's pocket. She wasn't going back.

Think forward. What to do next?

No one had a car. Jimmy had never learned to drive. Mom had never driven a day in her life. Dad had been happy to walk to wherever he needed to get to—or take public transportation. Michael had gotten his license at fifteen but never worried about buying a car since he could take the bus any time he waited.

Public transportation. Duh.

The closest bus shelter was up the block from the apartment in the opposite direction, past the bodies on the sidewalk. She would have to cross the street to bypass them. Thinking so rationally about it hurt her brain.

At least it was a plan.

She walked up to the next cross street and jay-walked diagonally through the intersection under the slightly swaying—but not functioning—stop light to the opposite corner. The bus shelter was framed in with metal supports and tempered glass on two sides. An out-of-date poster for a Marvel movie from February had started to curl on the edges inside the metal case of the third sidewall helped to hold up the slanted roof. She was almost positive the movie was already out on Blu-ray. Jimmy had been raving about it like it was the Second Coming of Christ or something.

Jude waited for the bus alone. She sat down on the bench with the Beretta hanging loosely in her hands between her knees. The barrel tapped absently against her left leg. The backpack's weight pressed into her back as she leaned forward with her elbows on her knees. She was the only one out and about as far as she could tell. No cars zipped by. Actually, there were no cars at all. The morning air lacked the familiar smell and sound of diesel engines and car exhaust typically captured inside the shelter shell.

The weight of the world pushed down on her as the tears welled up from deep inside her. She covered her eyes, the body of the gun pressed into her cheek. She had bludgeoned her father to death. She had shot her mother in the face. She had kicked her brother hard enough to nearly decapitate him. Only Michael had escaped her wrath. All four of them were laying in their own filth and body fluids on the hardwood floors of the apartment she had grown up in. The home she had loved, but also had hated. She had killed her family because they had threatened her life and the life of her brother Jimmy. For all the good it had done. Jimmy had still ended up just as dead.

She unshouldered the backpack, unzipped one of the side pockets, and rooted around inside. Pulling out her hand, she held an amber pill bottle with a white cap. It was her prescription of Ativan. Based on the recommendation from Doctor Rick, she had stopped taking them altogether over a month ago. Jude popped off the cap and extracted one of the pills. She rolled it through her fingers before popping it into her mouth and swallowing it. If there was ever a day to jump off the wagon, it was today.

She wiped the sweat off her gun hand on her pant leg before wiping her eyes and cheeks with her sleeve. She held up the Beretta and looked at it in profile. Other than the foodstuffs in her backpack, this was really the only thing she had to remember her family with. Funny… the Sawyer family legacy and heirloom was a Beretta 9mm 92FS. Fitting, as the family history was wrought with disapproval, disappointment, anger, violence, and unwanted attention. Jude turned the gun over in her hands. She slid her fingers along its edges. A simple piece of machinery. Only a couple moving parts. A simple pull of the trigger. That's all it took to extinguish a life.

A father who liked to sneak into her room at night. A mother who wanted a son—a healthy son—and ended up with a bitch of a daughter, instead. Jimmy, a crippled brother whom she had loved—and despised, in some ways—who had to be put down. Feeling unloved compared to the angel named Michael. Matty, who had died in the hot sands a half-world away, had showed her how to use the Beretta clutched in her hands. Children all over the country had found their daddy's guns and figured out how to pull the triggers.

It would be so easy.

She had unrealistically hoped she would have felt a mental twinge from the pill, some quick nudge out of the downward spiral she had found herself in. Jude turned the gun barrel so it faced her. She looked at the single front sight, knowing a single white dot was painted on the other side. The end of the barrel was a gaping dark mouth. Like that of her Mom-thing before she had sent a flaming bullet into her brain.

So easy. A little bit of pressure on the trigger. Click. Blam. Forever darkness. No more worries about the weight of the world. No more worries about lost family. No more worries of pain, judgements or injustices. Jude put pressure against the trigger. The hammer cocked back slightly. A long loud hiss dragged her out from the depths of her own mind.

"You getting on?" a voice asked. Jude looked up from the bench. A mass of aluminum stared back at her. The idling bus's door was open, it's driver tapping the steering wheel and staring at her with a mixed look of impatience and indifference. "Come on if you're coming. I have a schedule to keep."

## 28
## *Unscheduled Stop*
+2 Days – 8:32am EST

The bus was empty.

Well... there was the driver, of course, but every passenger seat was vacant. That didn't keep the faint scent of bleach, stale sweat and urine from assaulting her nostrils. Hadn't she been assaulted enough for one lifetime? She walked to the middle of the bus as the driver pulled away from the shelter. After holding onto a strap for a block, Jude decided leaving so many empty seats between her and another living person wasn't what she wanted in that moment. She walked to the front and plopped down in the seat opposite the driver. She was forced forward at the waist, having completely forgotten a pack was strapped to her back, pressed between her and the seat.

"You may want to put that away," the bus driver said.

"What?"

"The sidearm."

Jude looked down at the Beretta in her right hand. She had forgotten about the weapon as quickly as she had forgotten about her pack. She stared at it for a moment, then started patting her body for a place to stash it.

"Try the backpack, young lady."

116

Jude slipped the pack from her shoulders and set it in the seat beside her. The placards on the tops of the seats stating, "Reserved for the handicapped and the elderly" didn't stop Jude from being rebellious enough to keep sitting there. She had zoned out big time about the Beretta. Maybe the pill was finally kicking in. Unzipping the pack, Jude put the gun in the front pocket where she thought she would have the easiest time getting at it if she needed it. Once done, she placed the pack on her lap and hugged it. Clearing her throat— as if she was worried she had lost her voice altogether—she spoke up. "What's going on out here?"

"Out here?" the driver answered with a scoff. "Who the fuck knows? You're the first person I've seen since pulling out of the depot. Lots of drivers calling out sick. Some not calling in at all. Shit. This isn't even my route."

"You see anything strange?"

"Strange?" The driver looked at her in the convex security mirror. "Besides a mass cancellation of drivers, I guess I would have to ask you what your definition of strange is."

Jude thought back to the swan dive bodies littering the sidewalk around the apartment building. She thought about her dead father and how he simply opened his eyes with the singular drive to attack his family. Of course, had she not wanted to exact some closure with him, Dad wouldn't have escaped the bedroom to tear out Michael's throat or Mom's face. She shrugged. "Just, out of the ordinary, I guess."

"Nah," the driver replied, his eyes still on her in the mirror. "All's well." He licked his lips, overcompensating the steering wheel left and right to keep the bus going in a straight line.

Something thumped on the roof. Jude snapped her neck toward the middle of the bus where she had been standing a few minutes ago. Another resounding bang resulted in the metal bending downward from the impact. Another metallic thud. Another dent in the roof. Suddenly, there was a rain of heavy objects crashing onto the top of the bus. Something slapped against the side window behind her. A burnt hand rubbed thick red and yellow fluid across the glass. More hands appeared at other windows.

"See?" the driver told her, still pulling the wheel comically around while the bus continued in a straight line down the street. The windows burst in all around her, hands and arms now joined by the gaping mouths and hollow eyes of the dead hanging from the roof. They moaned and growled, reaching out to her with their bloody and boney stumps of what used to be fingers. They twisted their shoulders to get their upper bodies through the windows. Shards of glass from the frame ripped into their grey flesh, but they paid the filleting no mind. Jude fumbled for the zipper pull. It was stuck in the fabric. She couldn't get to the Beretta in time. The first undead ghoul plopped onto the bench in the middle of the cabin. It scrambled up to its feet. It lumbered toward her, bumping against the seats and support poles. The zipper was still stuck. Jude backed up to the dashboard.

"Told ya." The driver was now a rotting version of her father—complete with huge grin, empty eye sockets, and a flap of skin pulled down from under his jawline to the right nipple of his bare chest. "Nothing strange at all!"

It was then the flood of undead finally grabbed at her shirt, her father's bellowing laughter filled her ears, and dread poured onto her already raw heart.

**29**
## *Rude Awakenings*
+2 Days – 8:32am EST

Jude still had pressure on the trigger. The hammer cocked back slightly. She gasped as the flood of her terrible waking dream tried to rush a scream into existence through her raw throat. All she could manage was a constricted squeak. She relaxed her shaking finger off the trigger. The hammer settled back into place. She dropped the gun into her lap and let the hot salty tears fall.

A torrent of shame, fear, self-loathing and an endless stream of other psychological violations poured from inside her, every painful hitch in her breathing a reminder she was still feeling something. The fact she couldn't find any glimmer of hope under the swell of other heavy emotions didn't bother her. Now was the time to feel everything else.

She didn't know how long she sat alone in the bus shelter. Whether waiting for the next bus to come or the tears to dry up, it really didn't matter. There was nobody to look at her with pity or to sit awkwardly next to her. A couple snot bubbles burst. A few ugly sobs erupted from deep in her throat. If she had been wearing any mascara, she would have looked like a human-sized raccoon. But, eventually—and without warning—the dam of emotion plugged itself enough to shut off the waterworks from a torrent to a trickle. Jude wiped the wetness from her cheeks, and the snot from her nose and upper lips.

The bus wasn't coming. It was absurd to believe things would be as they were before. In some small way, Jude took solace in that thought. Things couldn't go back to the way they were... but they could become something else—something different. Maybe, eventually…if she dared to hope, something better.

She got up—the backpack straps having never left her shoulders—and headed back toward the apartment. The place where her existence had been defined. She wasn't going back for the nostalgia. She needed a new ride and knew just where to get it.

## 30
# *Terrycloth*
+2 Days – 8:49am EST

Mr. Emery's apartment door, with its tarnished unit numbers screwed to the metal and the paint of several seasons encroaching on the edges of them, stood closed before her. It seemed to Jude she was constantly facing closed doors these days. She was beginning to truly dislike them.

She pressed her ear against this particular door and listened. No bumps, thumps, or groans came from behind it. At least, none she could make out. She knocked lightly on the door, searching for any life inside. After several seconds, she moved her hand to the door knob and turned it as quietly as she could. The act was futile. The latch's release was like a sword being pulled from a stone, a long grinding sound making her grit her teeth. Three deep breaths later, the door swung open with its own squeaky announcement to any resident still moving around inside.

While a bit obscured by the dining room chairs, Jude could still see the splayed left arm and leg of Mr. Emery where she had left him. When she was sure Mr. Emery wasn't playing possum, Jude slipped into the kitchen. The asshole's home-made ingredients were still sitting on the Formica counter.

The thought of grabbing another chair from the dining room set and destroying it over his back suddenly flitted across her mind. No. Back to the task at hand. She was looking for something small and very specific. The hooks on the wall directly right of the doorway were empty. She opened each drawer. Nothing but everyday silverware and cooking utensils. The ever-present catch-all drawer was filled with loose matches, Chinese food takeout menus, dish rags, random instructions booklets, washers, and an assortment of twist-ties. Every house had one of these drawers. Jude was pretty sure it was a requisite to create one the moment someone moved in. Regardless of the clutter in the junk drawer, she still did not find what she was looking for.

Damn it!

She exited the kitchen. Mr. Emery still lay with his head cocked at a strange angle against the corner of the wall. Unlike at her apartment, Mr. Emery didn't have a pool of blood spreading out under him. All of the damage from the chair on his back and shoulders had been absorbed by the terrycloth. She kicked him in the side, waiting for a response. Nothing. She kicked him again, this time a fair bit harder. Still nothing. That kick was more for her, anyway.

Jude knelt down. She didn't want to touch him but had no choice. She felt around the robe pocket on her side of him. It was heavy with something. She reached inside, but she ended up pulling out the three Oreo's cookies he had stuffed in the pocket earlier. Damnit!

The other pocket was under Mr. Emery. She grabbed at his robe sleeve and pulled. She couldn't slide the terry material out. It was caught on something. She grabbed his sleeve and grunted as she attempted to roll him over. She arched her back and strained. Once he was at the apex of the turn, he flopped over at her. She lost her balance and ended up on her ass.

"Ouch!" She hissed out in embarrassed pain.

Mr. Emery stared at her with a twisted grin on his face. He might have had the last laugh as her bony behind suffered another injustice on his floors. He could keep that last laugh. With his robe wide open, the stature of his manhood was embarrassing small. His revealed robe pocket was laden with something. She reached in and fished around to the bottom until her fingers grabbed something that jingled. She pulled out the ring of keys. This was her ticket out of here.

She held them up to Mr. Emery's blank stare. "You don't mind if I borrow these keys, do ya? It may be a little while until I can bring them back to you."

Mr. Emery's stare didn't change.

Jude smiled.

Mr. Emery's smile widened.

What the fuck? She crab-crawled away from him, keys still in hand. His mouth started to work and he shifted his eyes to follow her movements, a whispering sigh passing his lips. Was he alive? His body didn't move at all. There were no twitches in his fingers. No spasms in his limbs. But his face and eyes were pinned on her. His smile twisted, the corners of his mouth pulling back to his cheeks.

She stared at his chest for a full minute. His chest was not rising and falling. He was dead. He was another one of those things. His mouth opened and he tapped his teeth together. Then again. And again. It became a steady clicking sound, like an Old West Western

Union telegraph office. A low mewing came from the Emery-thing's throat, but his body still didn't move a single muscle toward her. Jude realized she had paralyzed him. She had broken his back to the point where he was a quadriplegic reanimated corpse.

She burst out in laughter, covering her mouth as a reflex for the sudden loud bray coming from her mouth. It didn't matter the edges of the keys poked into her cheek and lips. It didn't matter she had taken another life. The thought of Mr. Emery having to wait an eternity for someone with bare ankles to come so close to his mouth he could actually bite them made her laugh even harder. It was poetic justice. He had lain in wait for years for the perfect opportunity to molest her—or worse. Now, he could lie there forever with his exposed tiny flaccid member waiting for a meal that will never come.

Eventually, the laughter tapered off and the tears dried on her cheeks. The keys she needed were in her closed hand, digging into her palm. She had originally planned to move quickly through this apartment, but she decided to linger for a bit longer. It could have been considered morbid, but looking upon a neutered predator gave her sense of soul-cleansing satisfaction.


## 31
# *Princess Vespa*
+2 Days – 9:27am EST


The renovated lobby had been the talk of all of the tenants when it had been completed. Ironically, what most people hadn't talked about was the updated basement—complete with new laundry facilities, an exercise room, and storage… plenty of storage. Of course, in this day and age, it was still probably not enough square footage for all the crap people tended to accumulate. According to something Michael had googled once, there were more self-storage facilities in the United States than there were Starbucks coffee shops and McDonald's restaurants, combined. Whoever buys the most stuff wins!

Here she was, standing at the entrance to the storage area with the laundry room in the corridor behind her to her right and the exit door to her left. Ten individual storage cages were lined up on each side of five aisles. A cross walkway cut through midway, allowing for easier tenant access to quickly move between them. Luckily, there were narrow casement windows around the outside walls providing a bit of natural light into the space. Otherwise, this part of the adventure would have been as terrifying as dealing with her undead family.

She passed her apartment's storage unit. There was nothing handy in there... unless she wanted to take up film photography again. It had been another one of her father's passions. There were also several cardboard boxes, an old wooden sled with removable sideboards, and a wide array of hand and power tools. Instead, she stopped in front of a cage two units down from hers. The Emery's storage unit. It was not as cluttered as her own. It was filled up, too— one of several dozen tombs to things hoarded and forgotten—but was much more organized and tidy. In the middle of the unit was what she had come for.

The Vespa.

Mr. Emery had spent several months in his living room putting it back into working order. The scooter sat up on its kickstand, its chrome trim and glittery paint job beckoning her to give it a ride. The bike was exactly what she needed. Her impatience showed as she had to work through five keys before she found the one that opened the gate. But, once it was open, she rushed in and hopped on the bike. Its suspension system was tight and new, the paint reflecting the light coming through the high narrow windows. She rolled the Vespa forward out of the unit and into the aisle. The scooter's key was easy to pick out. She put it into the ignition at the bottom of the steering column.

"Here we go." When she pressed the ignition switch, though, nothing happened. Jude's spirits dropped. "What the fuck?" She pressed the button again. Still nothing. The dashboard lights and display were lit, but the engine didn't turn over. She slapped the handles. The Vespa started rolling away under her. "Whoa. Whoa." She grabbed the left handle and pressed the brake lever. The scooter came to a quick and jarring stop. "Okay."

The dashboard was lit. Her feet were firmly planted on the floor. She tried the Start button again. The engine puttered to life this time. Her hand was still on the brake. Duh. The brake had to be engaged so the scooter didn't surge forward once the engine started. She was such an idiot. Learn something new every day. The fact she had learned all sorts of new things in the last couple of days was not lost on her.

She took all of the other keys off the Vespa keyring, leaving only the one in the ignition and throwing the rest back into Mr. Emery's storage unit. She revved the right handle. Her feet slid across the concrete as Jude powered the scooter out of the storage area and into the main hallway toward the exit. Mr. Emery had done a great job setting the Vespa's idle. The scooter's motor purred and bubbled as she set it on its kickstand and moved to open the door. She looked through the mesh safety glass window. There was nothing prowling outside the immediate area.

"Nice bike."

Jude spun around. Two men—two live and non-flesh-eating men in their late teens or early twenties—stood behind the scooter. One was dark-haired with chiseled-jaw handsome looks on the verge of being a Ford model. The other one was nowhere close to being a male model. His hooded eyes darted around the corridor like he was trying to zero in on several imaginary gnats at once.

"Thanks," was all she could get out before she realized they both had one arm hiding something against the back of their thighs. Was it already too much to hope they weren't concealing weapons? "It's a Vespa."

"Can we take it for a spin?" the model asked.

"Sorry," Jude replied. "I need to get across town."

"How about just around the block, then?" the first man asked. "Frankie will stay with you."

"Why do you get to ride it, Hernan?" Frankie asked, his eyes settling on male model Hernan for a moment with his lips curling down at a severe angle.

"Because it was my idea, shit heel," Hernan told Frankie. He tapped his hand behind his leg a couple times with impatience. "You'll get your turn."

"I better." Frankie seemed mollified by Hernan's promise. As per usual, things were not going Jude's way. There was a palpable tension in the air, both between the two of them and toward her. They wanted the bike. She couldn't let them take it. Someone had already stolen her car. She had stolen the Vespa from a dead man fair and square. "Do you know what's going on out there? Is there any news? Have you seen any of the dead?"

Hernan thought through Jude's barrage of questions, nodding his head slightly and working his tongue through his mouth. Frankie

126

started to speak, but Hernan immediately talked over him. "It's a mess."

"What does that mean?"

"A mess! A fucking mess!" Frankie jumped in before Hernan could properly answer. His eyes darted around during his outburst, while a silly grin split his face open. His eyes scrunched up, making them into wrinkled pinpricks. He apparently found the whole conversation quite hilarious.

Hernan gave his partner a sideways glare that instantly popped Frankie's bubble of happiness. He cringed and looked away. Hernan continued. "A mess. Everyone's going crazy. Cellphones are useless or dead because of the outage. The other side of town is burning down. I mean, it's just a power outage and there are already those two goddamn jumpers splattered on the sidewalk out front, for Christ's sake."

"Splat!" Frankie's smile came roaring back to his face.

"Where?" Jude asked.

"I told you," Hernan spat back. "Out front on the sidewalk."

"No. Where is the town burning down?"

"Geez, bitch." Frankie took another shot at her, that stupid shit-eating grin plastered to his face. Jude was sure he was going to be trouble. "Clinton Street!" Hernan gave him another look. Frankie slumped his shoulders again, but didn't cringe as much as before.

Clinton Street? That was a few blocks from the apartment she had just plunked down first, last, and security. She had spent almost a year slaving away waitressing at the diner to save up enough in tip money to get out of her parent's apartment. God knew how many lewd comments and ass grabs she had endured with a smile to get the money she needed. Now, she had to endure an entitled pretty boy and a socially deficient mental case.

127

She really had to get out of here. Now.

With the door still closed, the fumes from the Vespa had started filling up the corridor. A slight haze had started to linger close to the low ceiling. The Beretta was still in the back of her jeans, mostly hidden by her shirt and the laden backpack. She assumed Hernan and Frankie hasn't noticed it. Otherwise, she might already be dead. Discretion is the better part of valor, Shakespeare had said.

"You wanna take her for a spin? We'd better hurry up, then, before the exhaust kills us." Jude pointed at the swirling smoke around the fluorescent lights and gave them a believable chuckle before backing into the latch bar on the door. The hallway was suddenly bathed in light as the door swung open. Jude stepped onto the concrete landing and held the door for her two new friends.

Hernan gave her a big smile and hopped onto the Vespa. He tucked whatever was in his hand into his back pocket. He revved the engine and popped the scooter off its kickstand. Releasing the brake, Hernan powered the bike forward up the long ramp to ground level. Frankie let out a whoop as he chased after his friend, oblivious of the fact Jude could clearly see the kitchen cleaver in his closed fist.

With the Vespa changing ownership, Jude was quickly forgotten. That was alright. She hadn't forgotten them. She followed them up the ramp in time to see Hernan driving the scooter in tight circles around the parking lot. The tires squeaked loudly on the asphalt.

"Oh, yeah!" Frankie yelled out as he swung the cleaver around his head. He stood in the middle with Hernan driving around him. He reached for the bike with his free hand. "My turn, bro! My turn!"

"Knock it off!" Hernan yelled at him.

Frankie swung the cleaver at Hernan menacingly. He was too far away to hit anything, but the gesture did let his partner know he seriously wanted his own turn on the scooter. Hernan braked the scooter and revved the engine, giving Frankie another one of those glares, before peeling away to the other end of the parking lot. This time, Frankie stood his ground with his fingers curling tight around the cleaver as Hernan rounded the center grass median and charged back at full speed. He nearly clipped Frankie as he came to a quick and awkward stop.

"I need my bike back," Jude insisted.

"No way!" Frankie yelled with the cleaver pointed at her. He turned to Hernan. "Give me the bike."

"No," Hernan answered simply. "Get your own."

"What?" Frankie screamed, his knuckles turning white and the vein in his temple throbbing. "My turn!"

Jude backed up a step.

"My turn!" To Hernan's complete surprise, Frankie's cleaver swung down and cut deep into his shoulder. Hernan couldn't turn his head as the blade had severed all of the muscles on that side of his neck. He stared at it out of the corner of his eyes with disbelief as blood sprayed out with high pressure. Frankie's scream was laced with a spray of spittle. "Give... me... the... bike!"

Hernan's eyes rolled to white as his hands slipped off the handles. The sputtering bike lurched forward and bucked his dying body off the back of it. Frankie caught the bike with both hands before it fell over, having to drop the cleaver in the process. He swung around and straddled the scooter. "My turn!" he yelled in triumph.

Jude pressed the barrel of the Beretta hard against Frankie's head above the ear, pushing his head to the side. She put her own hand on the brake handle.

"Wha..."

"Get the fuck off my bike," Jude whispered into his ear, hoping the gun barrel would improve both his hearing and cooperation. "You wouldn't be the first person I killed today." That statement came out as a growl from her throat, carrying with it a seriousness Frankie recognized instantly. He put his hands up and stepped off the Vespa on the far side. He glanced at his dying friend on the asphalt, then in the other direction to see how far the cleaver was.

Jude never let the Beretta's front sight drift away from Frankie's head as she mounted the bike. Matty had taught her well enough for her to know she couldn't miss at this range. She settled in and released the brake, using her legs to back up the bike to a reasonable distance between her and Frankie. He kept dimly calculating his odds of getting to the knife before he was gunned down. Knowing she would eventually have to put the gun away to drive, she took a chance to capitalize on her anger. "Go ahead, Frankie. Go for it and end up like Hernan. I dare you."

Frankie heard her tone. Her use of his name gave him pause. He licked his lips. But, with his hands still raised and a furrow in his brow, Frankie still dove for the cleaver.

Jude pulled the trigger.

His hand reached the cleaver, but his face slammed into the asphalt as he skidded to a stop. His hand flexed, then stilled. Two men lay in the parking lot in front of the sputtering Vespa, life draining from one of them and gone from the other because they thought the rules didn't apply to them. They thought they could take advantage of a seemingly defenseless woman.

The Beretta went back into her waistband. She revved the scooter, released the brake and buzzed through the parking lot. Hernan had claimed Clinton Street was burning. She guessed she would just have to follow the dark plumes of smoke to see just how hopeless things were.

**32**
## *Wild Ride*
+2 Days – 9:42am EST

Jude was breaking all manner of laws by not wearing a helmet or obeying the 25-mph speed limit where not otherwise posted. She saw a couple cars on the street and a few pedestrians on the sidewalks, but she focused solely on the road ahead. Someone tried to wave her down. She ignored him and sped away as fast as she dared, especially as he ran after her for a block and a half before giving up the chase. Her heart sank at her decision to not assist him, but her own safety was paramount—especially after her run-in with Hernan and Frankie.

At least, she was starting to see more living people.

True to Hernan's word, the skies to the east side of town were cloudy with the smoke of dark angry fires seemingly burning out of control. She saw a single fire truck matching her speed as it raced along a parallel boulevard, its sirens blaring and its warning squawks sounding before every intersection. More people were on the streets now, many carrying their own backpacks or rolling suitcases behind them. Jude imagined they were fleeing in all directions, like rats scurrying from a sinking ship.

Jude rode past another fire truck parked up on the curb with its flashers still spinning. She thought she saw a firefighter in his turnout gear sitting against the side of the truck's massive back wheel, but couldn't be sure... and wasn't going to slow down to make a positive identification.

Clinton street was up ahead. She braked and idled next to a stop sign at an intersection. The shops and the apartments in both directions were in flames, smoke billowing out from the windows. Jude heard screams. Someone was pleading for anyone to help find their kid. Another one was whistling for his dog.

A guy with slicked back black hair, cargo shorts and black T-shirt walked past her without even a glance. When he reached the opposite sidewalk, he grabbed a city garbage can and hurled it into the plate glass window of a department store with its second story windows licking flames against the interior glass. Air sucked deep into the store. The oxygen ignited. The front of the store exploded. It engulfed him with glass, debris, and shrapnel from the electronics he had been hoping to steal. A terrible scream pierced the air, coming from his melting lips and burning throat.

Jude yanked the handle and quickly revved away in a panic. Her heart raced. Her own throat burned, having sucked in hot smoke. The next block was even worse. There were no people on the street, but the screaming and moans persisted. The buzz of the Vespa was too quiet to drown out the sounds. She rode past burning shops and apartments—past fewer and fewer fleeing refugees dragging their worldly possessions behind them.

Finally, she arrived at the block where she had sunk all of her tips and savings. The building wasn't on fire, but flames were licking at its brick face from both of the adjoining apartment buildings. It was only a matter of time before it would join the others in burning solidarity. Now what? She had no more money. It had been all tied up in a studio apartment on the third floor of the ten-story building set in the middle of the block. The majority of her belongings were in the trunk of a stolen Toyota. A real and positive future had been so close for her. Now, her hope for a new lease on life was going up in flames. Story of her life.

She felt the heat billowing in the air all around her. She was in the middle of the intersection, but it felt like a convection oven set to high. The air was hot and dry, the toxic smoke driving her into a coughing fit. She pulled up the collar of her shirt to fend off possible lung damage. She took one more look at her lost future before driving away from it forever.

## 33
## *Bridge over Troubled Water*
+2 Days – 11:15am EST

The Vespa had been a smart choice. Jude weaved in and out of snarled traffic, revving the scooter up on the sidewalks when the cars were bumper to bumper in the streets. More and more people funneled out from the side streets, congesting the sidewalks and resembling a mass exodus of folk leaving the city via the bridge connecting the waterfront to a greenbelt in the next town. Cars and light duty trucks choked all lanes in both directions on the bridge. People were trying to get into town as much as others were trying to get out. That was a bad omen lost on the passengers driving away from the reflections in their rearview mirrors, but not paying any attention to the carnage apparent through their front windshields. The Vespa sputtered along the sidewalk next to the westbound lanes, Jude having to jockey around the slower—and more exhausted— foot traffic hefting their belongings with them.

"On your left," Jude called out to a group of women walking side-by-side. When her words didn't exact any results, she pressed her left thumb on the horn button. It blared, making the women scurry to one side. Mr. Emery had indeed put all of the bells and whistles into this bike. She zipped past the women. All of them glared at her. One of them went so far as to flip her off. Figured.

When she was halfway across the bridge—the point of no return—horns started blaring at the snarl of vehicular traffic in front of her. A murmur came from the people pressed into the pedestrian walkway trying to find their exit on the other end. Jude was forced to bring the Vespa to a full stop. She wasn't going to get through the rest of the crowd any time soon. Jude popped the kickstand and chanced standing up on the precarious seat for a few seconds. Men were yelling at someone to let them by. Women were pleading to let them and their children pass. People were being funneled through a series of steel fence barricades for inspection. The cars were being forced into coned lanes between parked police sedans for the same reason. Getting through this mess was going to take forever. She dropped back down to straddle her seat.

"Jesus Christ," a young brunette woman next to her said to herself. Jude looked over and caught the woman's attention. From the condition of her mascara, she had been crying. "Sorry. I wasn't referring to you. I'm just so done with this shit."

"I hear you. I'm Jude."

"Pam. What did you see on your lofty perch?"

"A cluster…"

"Fuck. Figures."

"Where you trying to get to?"

"To my boyfriend. He usually picks me up, but with this mess he's stuck on the other side. I figured I would be able to get across

134

a lot easier then him trying to come to my side. Hell, we all need a bit of exercise, right? How about you?"

Good question. Where was she trying to get to? There wasn't a chance in hell she would go back to her family's apartment. All that remained there was death. Her new apartment was mere hours from burning down. She really didn't have a clue as to her destination. Maria and Kenny lived in Maryland but, while they had always treated her like a daughter, trying to get to them seemed like an impossible task. Jude had zero idea of where she was going. Her Plan A had gone up in smoke. There hadn't been time to come up with a Plan B. All she could think to do was to keep moving forward. Like a shark. "Still figuring that out."

People pressed into them on both sides. The Vespa kept people from pushing her from behind, but Pam wasn't that lucky. She snapped her head around and glared at the immediate crowd of people surging behind her. "Damnit! Quit pushing! We ain't going anywhere!"

The crowd eased up, but it was a stop-gap measure, at best. Stopping the surge of this crowd was akin to trying to stop the rush of water from crashing up on shore using a plastic pail full of sand. The water would divert around the sand and, eventually, sweep right over it. Pam moved forward a few steps. I hopped off the kickstand and waddled the scooter forward alongside her.

"You have a place to go?" Pam asked, her eyes still sending daggers out to the people behind us.

Jude hoped Pam was offering her a place to crash, but ended up answering with a nervous teeter "I have no idea."

"Just keep moving, I guess?" Pam had Jude dead to rights.

"Yeah. Exactly."

135

"It's all good. Sometimes, any movement is progress. Doesn't matter if there is a destination in mind, or, even, if you're going in the right direction. Just keep dropping your feet one in front of the other." Jude didn't have time to answer as Pam spun around to a fat guy who had bumped into her from behind again. "You serious? You trying to trample me under you? Back the fuck off!"

One of the men behind us whispered, 'Sorry,' and tried to push the people behind him back a step or two. The look in his eyes was apologetic. There was a hint of fear there, as well. He seemed to be by himself. The others around him were not clinging to him or pressed into him for protection or support.

"What's your name?" Jude asked him.

"Timmy," he answered quickly.

"We'll get out of here soon, Timmy." Jude assured him.

He let out a ragged breath of relief—one he had apparently needed permission to exhale. He was alone against the tide of the crowd. Even though he was a hulking man in his thirties with tan skin and a square jaw good enough for any romance novel cover, he was as scared of the pressure of the crowds as Jude and Pam were. Now, he threw his lot in with Jude and her new gal-pal, Pam. "Thanks."

"Just stick with us, kid," Pam told him as they collectively took three steps forward. "We'll get you there."

Timmy, with Pam's words, puffed out his chest and straightened up to his full height. He was even more imposing when he had his confidence set to high. Yep. Jude hoped he would continue to ebb the flow of the tide… at least until they were past the checkpoint. Let him be the up-ended pail of beach sand for them.

**34**
## *A Bridge Too Far*
+2 Days – 12:37pm EST

"I'm so glad I left New York," Timmy grumbled with obvious sarcasm. "So much easier getting out of the city when things start going downhill."

"You from New York?" Pam asked.

"Not born or raised," Timmy corrected her. "But I spent quite a few years there for work. I wonder if they're going through the same thing right now."

Jude imagined escaping from New York would be comparable to clawing one's way out one of the circles of Hell from Dante's Inferno. Just reaching the barricade had taken an hour from the time they had introduced themselves to each other. She could finally see two officers and a sheriff from the police department, plus four Massachusetts National Guardsmen manning the pedestrian and vehicular checkpoints. One was patting pedestrians down, shining a light in their eyes and down their throats. The other three were slowing cars down for inspections in the vehicular lanes.

It was only then Jude noticed faint coughs coming from somewhere in the crowd behind them. Nothing serious about it. They were dry and intermittent, more likely from spring allergies than from some rampant contagion. But the military presence did little to quell the growing paranoia seeping its way from the seed in her brain to the churning acids in her stomach. She contemplated voicing her concerns to the others, but they looked frightened enough all on their own. They were probably thinking the same thing. Was it some epidemic making people come back to life?

"Come on," Timmy griped. "It can't be this serious, can it?"

137

"We're almost there," Pam said. "Won't be long now."

She was right. As they inched along the length of the bridge over the last hour, they had managed to slide their way to the railing. They had a spectacular view of the river and the land on both sides. The plumes of smoke from the east continued to rise from the buildings, more and more of the skyline behind them now in flames. There would be the blare of a fire engine every so often—giving way to an inkling of hope in Jude's heart—but then the sirens would stop altogether. All the while, the fire and smoke continued to spread.

The good news was the three of them were heading in a smoke-free direction and over land again. Although, still several stories above a scraggy shoreline, Jude could tell herself they had reached the other side.

"Awesome." Pam put a bright smile on her face. "I bet we'll be through in another ten minutes."

"Did you ever get through to your boyfriend?" Jude asked.

"I did before I left work. He'll be waiting in a park by the bridge. We agreed there was no way he was going to be able to get closer than that."

"True," Timmy agreed.

"How far?" Jude asked.

"About a mile, maybe," Pam answered.

Another mile? Ugh. At least Jude had the Vespa. It had been a Godsend for her. Pam might be able to climb on the back if she wore Jude's backpack. Then, she could hold on tighter. There was no way Timmy was going to fit as a passenger. Someone was going to be the odd man—or woman—out. And that person was not going to be her. Not after what she had already done to acquire it... and to keep it.

Pam looked at Jude's face and gauged her silence. "No worries, girl! I've been running on a treadmill for over a year since I got dumped by my last boyfriend. I'll jog next to you like I'm Secret Service."

Jude smiled thinly, knowing she wasn't that important.

"We'll get there," Timmy chimed in, repeating Pam's line. He looked like he worked out every day, too. Jude was woefully out of shape in comparison to either of them. She had kept her mouth shut about the cramps she was already getting in her legs from pushing the Vespa forward. Thank God it was a gentle downhill slope now and she could mostly use the brake to control her roll.

Pam smiled when, correct in her ten-minute prediction, they were only a few people away from the checkpoint. She was almost giddy about it. Jude figured she was less floored by her amazing predictive skills and more excited by the fact she was much closer to seeing her boyfriend again. Ah, young love… so shiny and new. Jude longed for something similar. Something new and filled with hope and longing. Something that wasn't inappropriate and taboo. Something that felt–

"What do you mean?" A man at the checkpoint, with a younger woman and two pre-teen kids, waved his hands in the air at the Guardsman. "Let us through!"

"Sir. Ma'am. You will have to stand to the side, please." One of the officers came over and put one gloved hand up to halt the man's progress through the checkpoint. He hadn't laid a hand on the pedestrian yet, but it seemed eminent. The officer's other hand was drifting slowly to the grip of his sidearm.

"We've waited two hours to get across this fucking bridge," the man yelled in the officer's face. "You assholes couldn't run a checkpoint if your lives depended on it!"

This guy's anger was dialed to eleven. He wasn't going to be talked down with diplomacy or common sense. The rest of the crowd between the checkpoint and Jude surged forward a step. It felt like a collective and aggressive gesture—an organic and angry mob mentality wanting either justice for the wronged family man or to grind the family into the pavement so they themselves could get through the checkpoint.

"Everyone! Calm down!" An authoritative voice on a bullhorn boomed out. Or was it called a megaphone? Jude couldn't remember. It took a few cranes and twists of her neck to see the sheriff where he was standing next to a police cruiser with the bullhorn in his grip. "We will get you through as quickly and safely as possible. Panic will do nothing but keep you here that much longer."

The crowd wavered and swayed on its feet. The push behind Jude, Pam and Timmy loosened a little bit again. It was still claustrophobic with people around them on three sides, but its oppressiveness had receded somewhat. The man and his wife at the checkpoint glared at the people in charge. The two kids with them just looked scared. The officer glared back, his fingers now around the grips of his sidearm. The angry man finally reigned in his anger when a second officer joined the others at the checkpoint.

Once the situation was mostly defused, the family was shepherded to a set of steel barricades to the right of the checkpoint by the two officers. Several other men and women had already been sent there to wait, as well. The wife—Jude assumed she was the wife by the way she complained to the blustering man—pulled at his sleeve and whispered a torrent of words in his ear.

"Almost there," Pam said hopefully.

The wife continued to talk in the man's ear. All the while, her husband shook his head.

"Nathan said he would be driving the Bronco," Pam continued. "Said it would fare better in case we needed to make a run north to the mountains for a bit."

The wife continued her tirade. A vein pulsed in his temple.

"How we gonna find your boyfriend in the park?" Timmy asked

"That's easy!" Pam answered cheerfully. "He got his Bronco painted custom cobalt blue. Blue with chrome trim. It's beautiful!"

"Nice," Timmy commented.

Three people were let through the checkpoint by the Guardsman. The wife in the quarantined area pointed at them and put more words into her husband's ear. The two preschoolers with them seemed all but forgotten. Jude felt for them. She knew the feeling of being forgotten all too well. The only way you knew the kids were with the parents was the fear in their eyes and how their tiny fists clung to the grown-up pant legs.

"Very excited! Only a few more people to go."

"Easy does it. Pam," Timmy said with a chuckle, already infected by her bubbly personality. She pulled out a water infuser and offered it to Timmy. "What's that?"

"Filtered tap water, cucumber and blueberries. The only way to go."

"Saving the earth from the bottled water conglomerates?"

"Hell, yeah!"

"Me, too!" Timmy took the water with a nod and took a quick swig. He offered it to Jude, who refused it. As usual, Jude's bladder felt full and she had the sensation of needing to pee again.

Another person was let through. The angry man corralled with his family started to nod in agreement to his wife's words.

"Can't wait to see Nathan," Pam said, taking her infused water back and taking a swig for herself. They were two people away from getting through the checkpoint. Minutes away until she could turn her Vespa back on and motor to the park Pam was so excited about.

"We met at that park," Pam told Timmy.

Timmy grinned. "Real–"

That's when all hell broke loose. As if the first several rings of Dante's Inferno hadn't been enough.

## 35
## *Love and Bullets*
+2 Days – 12:59pm EST

There was an echoing clap of thunder. Something hot misted across Jude's face. The man who had been next at the checkpoint dropped to his knees before falling into the open arms of the Guardsman. The report of a pistol shot—Jude realized the first clap hadn't been thunder at all and the mist on her face wasn't a burst of splattering rain—took the Guardsman down with a bullet ripping through his shoulder. He twisted and caved to the pavement, the checkpoint victim still in his arms.

Everyone had dropped to the walkway. That wasn't true. She was paralyzed, still straddling the Vespa. She had a great view over the prone pedestrians. The three National Guardsmen, the two officers and the sheriff were scanning for the shooter. In the quarantine area, the harangued man stood his ground with his arms at his side while his wife and kids were flat on the ground next to him. She was the one who had started this. She had poked the bear... and the bear had reared up.

The Guardsmen and officers should have easily spotted the only person still standing in the corral a few yards away from them. Instead, they rushed around, looking desperately through the crowd for the shooter. They scanned the mouth of the bridge and around the cars idling at the checkpoints. When the two officers turned toward the corral, the man shot twice more. The officers received bullets in the chest and went down hard to the roadway. The Guardsmen panicked and rushed to the fallen officers, ignoring—or forgetting—the immediate threat of the active shooter. The sheriff was not so easily distracted by the carnage. The look in his eyes spoke volumes about the shit he must have seen in his day. He rushed toward the checkpoint.

The corralled and haggard man raised his pistol.

A white panel truck with a huge red plus sign on the side had been parked between the sheriff's cruiser and the quarantine corral. He would never see the shooter in time. Jude went for her Beretta hidden in her waistband and drew it up. She heard Pam say something to her, but it was lost under the chorus of screams and the loud beating of her heart in her eardrums.

The sheriff's hard blue eyes met hers, raising his weapon as he rounded the front of the Red Cross truck's bumper. Shit! He thought she was the shooter. The real shooter was fifty feet to his left. Matty had never had her practice on targets much farther away than twenty feet—at a gun club owned by a Marine buddy of his. The idea of setting up old glass bottles or empty beer cans was something she had expected out of a movie, not in the reality of an urban cityscape. Jude shifted the sights to the shooter, anyway.

She didn't have a choice.

The sheriff hesitated, knowing something was off as the business end of Jude's Beretta pulled away from his direction. Did he think she had a death wish? Did he think she was going to shoot someone else instead? Was he going to shoot her?

The quarantined man tightened his grip, straightened his arm, and targeted the sheriff as he ran out into open ground. Jude continued her pivot and landed the Beretta's sights on the man in the corral. The sheriff realized Jude was not the real threat, finally spotting the quarantined man out of the corner of his eye. The sheriff twisted his body just as the man pulled the trigger. Jude squeezed the trigger of the Beretta with a long exhale. Multiple gunshots filled the air at the same moment.

The shooter went rigid before collapsing to the ground. Jude didn't see where she had shot him. The sheriff crashed to the asphalt. Jude was still straddling her bike. People were yelling, maybe shouting orders. Maybe they were giving her words of encouragement and congratulations. She had neutralized the threat. That was worth a few pats on the back, right? Saving the day deserved some validation, at the very least.

Through the din of screams and shouting rose up one voice more shrill than the others. The wife of the shooter stood up. She stepped away from her crying and cowering children. Her left cheek was covered in red. Jude suddenly wondered what her own face must look like.

The sheriff slowly got to his knees, just as the three Guardsmen fully abandoned their stations at the vehicular checkpoints. As they cleared the roadway, several cars took the opportunity to peel out and escape from between the orange cones. An SUV clipped one of the Guardsmen, sending him hard into the concrete guardrail. Shit! Pylons were crushed as more of the waiting cars sped away from the threat. The other two Guardsmen didn't even notice the hit-and-run.

The sheriff slowly stood and rolled his shoulders. He looked okay, probably taking the bullet in his vest.

"Murderers!" The wife of the shooter smeared blood across her face as she wrung her fingers through her hair. The kids were forgotten. The husband was forgotten. All that was left was fury... and her husband's gun in her hand.

## 36
# *Taming of the Shrew*
+2 Days – 1:13pm EST

Jude guessed she was in what her southern cousins—and Quentin Tarantino—would call a Mexican standoff. The Beretta was still in her hand, a slight tremor and the onset of isometric fatigue making the front sight waver away from her target. The same could not be said for the recovering sheriff. His weapon was rock steady in his capable hands. He shrugged his shoulder where he had been hit, trying to unknot the muscles that had taken the impact under his bullet-proof vest. The Guardsmen were not as steady as him, their rifles weaving and swaying with every step they took. All barrels—steady or not—were pointed in the direction of the shrew who had instigated this mess. She was running on pure hatred and adrenaline. Her children wailed, both having wrapped their arms around her knees. The husband lay dead in front of them, face down in an expanding pool of his own blood. Expanding pools... there seemed to be a lot of that these days.

The pedestrian and the checkpoint Guardsman continued to bleed out on the walkway. They were probably dead already. The hit-and-run Guardsman wasn't in view, hidden by the concrete divider. The officers had not gotten back to their feet like the sheriff had, but, at least, they were still moving.

"Get down," came a meek voice from beside Jude. Another voice, with deeper tone, joined in. She paid them no mind. The instructions were too far away. Hence, she couldn't be bothered to acknowledge them. She knew there was care in the voices, but she was kind of in the middle of something right now. Something tugged at her sleeve. Jude shrugged it off.

The corralled woman looked around with wide eyes. Usually, seeing that much white around the pupils was reserved for people diagnosed with Graves' Disease or, some say, one of the symptoms of the clinically insane. She waved her weapon between the sheriff and the two Guardsmen. Jude wasn't sure if the woman realized she also had a weapon—or that she had been the one responsible for killing her husband. "Murderers!" the wife screamed out again.

The mass of people on the pedestrian walkway were still as flat on the pavement as possible. Jude was surprised they fit on the ground, especially after being so pressed together when they had been standing up. The cars on the roadway were still zipping through the now non-existent checkpoints, the Guardsmen now otherwise occupied. Better to take their chances with fines and admonishments than to face another hail of bullets. Tensions and fear were at an all-time high.

"Drop the weapon," the sheriff ordered, his gun not wavering in the slightest. "Drop it!"

The Guardsmen fanned out to flank him. Smart. The shrew swung her husband's gun in a wider arc to keep the three of them at bay.

"Get down," came those annoying pleading whispers again.

Shut up! Couldn't everyone see she was dealing with pressing matters? Her finger was pressed against the trigger of an instrument able to swiftly mete out death. She tightened her grip, ignoring the voices and the tremor spreading up her arm to nest in her shoulder socket.

"Come on. Get down here." The voices still begged her.

"Shut the fuck up." Jude hissed back the words to the bodiless voices. She hadn't meant to sound so feral, but she didn't have the luxury of politeness at the moment. The voices stopped. Good.

A couple heads popped up to waist level in an effort to see if the coast was clear. Idiots. As if they couldn't hear the sheriff and the military guys ordering the woman to drop her weapon. Jude felt a wave of panic settling into the crowd—a wave ready to surge forward. The cars were quickly escaping off the bridge just a couple feet away. Why shouldn't the pedestrians try the same thing? Unfortunately, this particular wave would probably end up crashing into a barrage of gunfire.

The children in the corral wailed tears as they sat next to their dead dad and at the feet of their mom. The wife screamed her contempt at the people in charge. The sheriff ordered her again to drop her weapon.

A bead of salty sweat dripped from Jude's brow, stinging her eye. She tried to blink it away, only succeeding in blurring her vision further. Fuck! She should have listened to the voices. They'd had the right idea all along.

The shrew moved. She stepped over her husband's body, three steps closer to the sheriff. The kids had to get to their feet to do the same, their arms still clamped around their mom's legs. The terror in their eyes was genuine as they walked through their daddy's blood.

"Drop the weapon. I will shoot." The sheriff had also stepped forward. "Think about your kids, ma'am. They need their mother."

The woman paused—or seemed to—at his last words. Her gun didn't drop, but something changed. It was an almost unperceivable shift in muscles. Something in the stance? A slump in the shoulders? Jude couldn't tell what it was, other than to know something had happened. The sheriff knew, too. He took the opportunity to gain control of the situation.

"That's it," he said quietly, but loud enough for Jude to hear. "Easy does it. Let's talk this through. Let's get your kids to safety. They need their mom."

The Shrew bristled and tensed up. "These ain't my fucking kids, pig!"

Oh, shit.

The shrew fired.

The Guardsman to the sheriff's left howled in pain. The other Guardsman retaliated with three shots and a couple choice curse words. The crowd behind Jude pressed itself flatter into the ground again. No more crowd surging to worry about. The able-bodied Guardsman's shots missed completely. Maybe one of his downed friends had been the better marksman. The sheriff cursed, but took careful aim at the woman who was ready to take another shot of her own.

In the end, it didn't matter. The shot never blasted from either weapon. The kids screamed—not in terror, but in joy. That didn't seem right, did it? The shrew who wasn't a fit mother yelled out. Her gun dropped to her side. The husband got to his knees, pulling himself up by grabbing hold of the bottom hem of his 'new' wife's blouse. She was dragged down a bit by his weight, even as she tried to get her hands under his armpits. Once he staggered to his feet, he reached out to hug her. She did the same, crying in relief.

He bit into her exposed neck. The cries turned to ones of terror. When he pulled away, he took with him a tear of skin, muscle, and a section of her carotid artery. A look of shock crossed her face, now covered with both his drying gore and her own fresh and hot blood. Shit. Shit. Shit. Jude could see the same thoughts wash across the sheriff's face. The Guardsman who was still on his feet was mortified, his eyes darting from the bloody shrew to the sheriff to his downed partner and back again.

Before anyone could rationalize what to do about the man eating his wife, more screams erupted from the people behind Jude. She turned in time to see several people getting up from their prone positions. They tried to dance their way through the crowd of bodies still face down, a couple of them twisting their ankles in the tangle of limbs before falling down again. Two more gunshots. One of them sparked off the bridge support next to her. Any remaining adventurous members of the mob dropped to the deck again, this time laying on top of others already occupying those spaces.

The Guardsman who had been the victim of the hit-and-run was back on his feet. What the fuck? He was still alive? Damn, he was resilient. He definitely was in bad shape, though. His left leg dragged behind him and his left arm was pinned to his side. The marksman Guardsman who was, in actuality, a terrible shot realized Hit-and-Run was shambling toward him. Marksman's eyes went wide a moment before he fired his rifle wildly at him. Every shot went wide.

A man was eating his wife. Guardsman was shooting wildly at his teammate. The sheriff stood in the middle of it all trying to calculate what to deal with first. The children had crawled away to the barricades, cowering with the other quarantined people. All they could think to do was hug each other. Hit-and-Run continued to stalk Marksman, who was backing up toward the sheriff. The other Guardsmen were still on the ground, not moving. The officers had stopped moving, too.

The lull in the gunfire made the braver pedestrians poke their heads up yet again. Jude made out a few mutters from those who had been squished under the sudden jarring weight. A shout came from the roadway, snapping Jude's attention back to the people with the guns.

Marksman finally bumped into the sheriff, who grabbed him by the collar and held him at arm's length with his free hand. The husband had become disinterested with his wife's neck—since she was now a cooling corpse. The shrew dropped to the pavement, Jude no longer able to see her clearly through the crowd and barricades. The children's cries erupted into shrill screams. The people shielding them shouted for the father to stop. Hit-and-Run continued to limp toward his teammate.

The sheriff pushed the Marksman away. He widened his stance. And squeezed the trigger. The man who was father to two children and husband to a shrew stopped and dropped to the asphalt on top of his wife's body. Hit-and-Run clawed at his partner, only the stock of the rifle between them. The sheriff pivoted smoothly—it was amazing to see his skills in action—and fired again. Hit-and-Run went down, his shot missing Marksman altogether. They both went down to the pavement, Marksman's flak jacket snared by Hit-and-run's clutching fingers.

The sheriff moved to help. He was pushed to the ground from behind. The guardsman who had been shot in the shoulder by the shrew was on his feet again, his bloodshot eyes possessing a wide crazed look and his body ticking with riddled spasms. The sheriff rolled onto his back. He brought the gun up. The shot went into the reanimated guardsman's heart—center mass. The heart stopped. The guardsman did not. He was on the sheriff immediately, his weight pushing the sheriff to his back and pinning his arms to the ground.

Cars continued to whiz by. The ramp—having been blocked for so long—was an open and inviting road of escape. More yelling and movement came from the direction of the quarantine pen. Shouts rang out on the walkway. The crowd behind Jude was getting restless again. They couldn't see what she saw. If they could, they wouldn't be so eager to press forward toward the bullets and sudden conversions to cannibalism.

37
## *Right Between the Eyes*
+2 Days – 1:31pm EST

"Jude," a voice pleaded. "Please get down." The voice was whiney and small. It hadn't seen the things she had seen. That voice didn't know how the world had shaped up over the last couple of days.

"We're getting out of here." The voice coming from Jude's throat was gravelly and deep, filled with decisiveness and control. It was a voice she hadn't heard for a long, long time, if ever. The checkpoint was unattended. There were only three pedestrians between them and freedom… and they all cowered against the concrete guardrail separating the crowd from the roadway. The checkpoint Guardsman and the pedestrian the husband had shot were still down. It didn't look like they were going to come back from death any time soon. "Get up."

Pam and Timmy hugged each other as they pulled themselves to their feet. Pam had been crying, her eyes red and puffy. Timmy had held it together better, but not by much. Muscles didn't do much to hold down emotions, Jude reckoned. She stuck the Beretta in the front of her jeans, turned over the key in the ignition, and pressed the start button. The Vespa roared to life—well, as much as a scooter motor could, anyway. Pam got on the back, struggling to get herself situated behind Jude's filled backpack. Timmy ran forward and slid the barricade out of the way. Jude gunned the Vespa through the opening past the other pedestrians still too stunned to move, with Timmy running after them. He didn't fall too far behind, filling up the right-side mirror.

The sheriff was dead, his gun still in his hand. The Guardsman perked his head up to see what other tasty morsels were nearby. Shouting still came from the quarantine corral. The shrew had gotten to her feet and was growling at the others. Jude braked.

"What are you doing?" Pam cried out, grabbing Jude's backpack tighter. Timmy came to a stop next to the scooter. The crowd on the other side of the checkpoint was starting to get to its feet, watching and waiting to see what was going to happen next.

The Beretta was in Jude's hand again. One bullet went into the top of the flesh-eating Guardsman's head. He dropped on top of the sheriff. Jude pivoted, swinging the gun toward the corrals. The shrew was a couple feet from her step-children. The Beretta discharged with a boom. A new hole suddenly appeared next to the shrew's earlobe. She staggered a step before dropping like a sack of potatoes. Marksman was of little concern. He just stared at her with a blank and lost expression—a look all too familiar to one Jude had seen in the mirror on many occasions.

The sheriff started to wheeze under the weight of the newly dead Guardsman. He opened his eyes. The stark blue had dulled, mostly replaced by a muddy red and gold. He still held his revolver, but had no interest in it. Nor was he overly concerned about getting out from under the body seeping blood onto the side of his neck.

"We need to help him," Timmy offered, some of his backbone coming back to him.

"Sorry." Timmy frowned at Jude's apology. That was okay. The apology wasn't meant for him, anyway. Keeping her fingers wrapped around the brake handle, Jude rested the Beretta on her forearm. She exhaled. The world went out of focus. Only the sheriff remained. His formerly blue eyes were still bright and captivating in their own strange way. They stared at her with a different kind of intensity. When her bullet went through his forehead, even his undead intensity drained away.

"Shit!" Timmy exclaimed. That summed it up in a nutshell. Thanks, Tim. Pam hugged Jude's backpack tighter, as if she was trying to climb into it. Jude couldn't blame her. It was a dangerous world out here. The officers were still alive. Someone else could deal with whatever might happen next.

The crowd stared at her. She could feel their eyes on the back of her head, even with the backpack and Pam serving as shields between them. It only took one look in the side mirror not blocked by Tim's massive frame to confirm it. They stood at the checkpoint, not advancing but not retreating, either. Some glared at her with anger and exasperation, others with fear and loathing. All feelings she was comfortable with; all feelings she had already learned to endure under the Sawyer roof.

"Try to keep up, Tim," Jude ordered, revving the engine. "It ain't going to get any easier out there."

"Lead the way," Timmy replied with a grim nod.

Good boy, Timmy. There was hope for him yet.


38
## *The Grass is Always Greener*
+2 Days – 1:59pm EST

Jude didn't know where that saying had come from. The grass was never greener on the other side. This side of the bridge, while not on fire, was still in turmoil. Cars were abandoned or crashed in the middle of the street. Jude navigated the Vespa easily around the shiny discarded hulks of metal, knowing many of them still had plenty of finance payments left to go. Timmy kept up, jogging behind the scooter. When the streets clogged enough to force Jude to putter the Vespa up onto the sidewalk, it gave Timmy time to catch his breath.

"How far is the park?" Jude asked Pam. She didn't reply, still more interested in hugging the backpack as fiercely as her muscles would allow. Jude wasn't even sure if she had lifted her head from the top of the pack since they left the carnage of the bridge behind. "Tim, do you know?"

Tim shrugged as he looked at the street signs at the upcoming intersection. He started to shake his head, but pointed at another sign halfway down the next block. A decorative painted wood sign hung from one of the streetlamps. It had a silhouette of a maple tree, with a knockout relief of a river beside it and the span of a bridge behind it. At the bottom was a bent arrow. "Right at the next block."

"Good job, eagle eyes." Jude nodded. There were still people on the street, but they didn't look like they would have been very accommodating if asked for directions. A couple of them eyed her Vespa in the same way Hernan and Frankie had in the apartment basement. She appreciated the weight of the Beretta against her belly, even if it dug into her stomach muscles.

"They don't have power here, either," Tim said. "I was hoping it was only on the other side of the bridge."

Hunkering down until the power came back on was the typical course of action in these situations. There were people inside the shops and buildings from what Jude could see through the plate glass windows. It wasn't business as usual, but it wasn't yet full-fledged panic. Just like on the bridge, the standard method of operation was to wait and see.

They turned at the corner like the sign had advised them. The empty street rose up at a steady incline. No cars were abandoned in the middle of the street, although the curbs were lined with them.

"You're going to need to get off, Pam," Jude ordered, not sure if her extra weight would let the Vespa get up the hill. "Tim, help her." Tim took Pam by the waist and practically lifted her off the scooter. It took a little pulling to tear her fingers away from the nylon of the backpack. When her feet touched pavement, her legs threatened to collapse under her own weight. Tim held her up, his own tired muscles straining.

"Stand up, Pam," Jude ordered. "Tim isn't going to carry you." Her words sounded pointed and far away when she spoke them, but she appreciated she was able to find them within her. Now was not the time to pussy-foot around.

"We're here!" she practically squealed as she stood up straighter, finally taking in her surroundings. That was when she ran up the hill toward the park without them.

"Are you fucking kidding me right now?" Jude shook her head. "You can't make this shit up."

"That's what I was going to say," Tim said with a chuckle, still looking a bit whipped.

Ah, love at first quip. She pointed at the Vespa. "You wanna trade?"

"No. I'm good." Such the gentleman.

"You want the gun?"

He looked at Jude, then at the Beretta in her waistband.

"Nah. You're way deadlier with it than I would be."

"More reason to trade so I have my hands free."

"Let's get up to the park first. Then we can talk trade."

Pam had practically sprinted halfway up the block while Jude and Tim had exchanged their pleasantries. Jude revved forward and Tim jogged alongside her. She did, indeed, look like a madam president going out for a ride with her casually dressed secret service detail next to her. The thought made her smile. The two of them reached Pam just as she crossed the next intersection into the entrance to the park. She didn't use any discretion as she yelled her boyfriend's name and ran deeper into the park. "Nathan!"

"Shouldn't she keep quiet?" Tim asked.

"As long as she's motivated," Jude said, "she can scream her bloody head off." At that, Jude and Tim shrugged to each other and started their slow chase after their lovesick friend.

## 39
# *A Day in the Park*
+2 Days – 2:28pm EST

The park was decidedly cooler than the city and the open expanse of the bridge. The canopy of trees covered much of the jogging paths and curving asphalt roadways. Exercise stations had been erected every fifty feet or so for those who had such interests. For others, pet stations had been added, supplying both poop bags and waste receptacles. No excuses for pet owners to not pick up after their animals. In the distance, the treeline gave way to a grassy field and a promenade bordering the river, offering the best photo opportunities of the bridge and the water under it.

"Nathan!" Pam continued at a steady pace along the gravelly edge of the roadway in search of her boyfriend and his Bronco. She stumbled over the edge of a concrete pad where a water fountain was located, catching herself before face planting into the dirt beyond it. "Nathan!"

The park seemed devoid of cars, but not of life. A few cyclists rode on the roadway. A man and his dog walked along the same path, keeping close to the trees and grass for the black lab to investigate. These were the people who thrived in life without the shackles of electricity. Jude wasn't sure they were completely off the grid, though. One of the bike riders had his earbuds in. The dog walker was swiping the surface of his Galaxy smartphone. Jude wasn't sure what the man was looking at, but he didn't seem annoyed.

"Nathan!"

The dog walker looked up from his phone. The dog looked up as well. "You looking for someone?"

No shit, Sherlock.

"My boyfriend," Pam said, the words coming out a bit winded. "I'm supposed to meet him here."

"Try the far end in the south parking lot," the man said. The dog, knowing his owner was pre-occupied, sat down and waited. "I've been here for a while. Some park rangers have been coming around and telling people they can't park on the roadway. Of course, I don't see the rangers around anywhere now…"

Pam took off in a southerly direction without another word, picking up her pace with the fuel of the dog walker's information.

"Thank you," Tim said, covering for Pam's social faux pas. "We appreciate it."

The man nodded and made a clicking noise with his mouth. The dog stood and waited patiently to see which direction they were going to go.

"Pretty dog," Jude said. "Well behaved."

"Thanks. He's my little fur baby."

"Welcome." Jude let out an embarrassing laugh before turning her head and puttering away on the scooter. Tim resumed his pace, his eyes on her. "Not a word."

"Who? Me? Never!" Tim let out his own hearty laugh. "A giggling girl with a gun. What's funny about that?"

"Keep poking me and you'll find out!" Jude revved the scooter faster, forcing Tim to quicken his pace to keep abreast of her. That would teach him to mock her.

Travel quickly became more treacherous for them as they cut through an open field to follow Pam. There were no paths or roadways so the Vespa was forced to go off-roading through the grass. It was fairly smooth, other than a few sunken boggy patches wanting to suck her tires down into their mire. Once she manhandled the scooter through the mud, she rewarded herself by racing over the pitcher's mounds of both of the baseball diamonds at the end of the field before the grass changed over to the concrete and asphalt of the south parking lot.

Pam stopped at the raised curb for exactly one second before she squealed and raced across the blacktop toward one of the few vehicles in the lot. The cobalt blue of the Ford Bronco was almost iridescent, shimmering in the bright mid-afternoon sun. The chrome dazzled, almost painful to look at from certain angles. The tires were oversized, sitting on an aftermarket raised suspension system. Nathan certainly loved this truck. The windows were tinted dark enough to keep them from knowing for sure if anyone was inside the cab.

Disappearing to the driver's side, Pam started rapping her knuckles on the front fender and door. Tim and Jude swung around the front bumper as Pam climbed up the foot step and tried to look inside with one cupped hand. "He ain't in there." She hopped down and did a full turn. Her eyes were wide with worry and her breath was ragged from running through the park. She was making Jude dizzy with her frantic spinning.

"Maybe he's by the water," Tim offered.

Pam snapped her head in that direction and, in spite of her tired muscles, ran off to the paths leading to a landscaped promenade.

"Glad I'm riding the Vespa," Jude said. "I'm exhausted just watching her.

"It's good exercise, though." Timmy trotted after Pam, leaving Jude to make a wide circle on the scooter in order to face the same direction as her nimble and quick friends. Once she got the Vespa oriented, she buzzed after them in the continuing search for Nathan.

**40**
## *Body Counts*
+2 Days – 2:44pm EST

Jude hadn't been on this side of the bridge before. The city had put their tax dollars to work in a productive way gentrifying the riverbank around the park. The pathway from the parking lot wound between two raised mulched beds, the landscaping filled with colorful impatiens and tall yellow-and-green grasses. As the path curved to the right, it opened up to a promenade and a spectacular view of the river with the bridge looking like an alabaster skeleton above it.

Jude wondered if Nathan would have heard any of the gunshots from earlier, some of them discharged from her own weapon. Benches faced the water. One of them had a dusty suitcase slid under it. The next one had several sheets of cardboard between the bench and the steel garbage can next to it. Obviously, the groundskeepers hadn't been around this morning to pick up the trash. And, in Jude's opinion, it probably wasn't a great idea to have a waste receptacle so close to a park bench. The flies, bees, and wasps would be an instant deterrent to her wanting to sit there. That was for damn sure.

"Nathan!" Pam called out again.

Jude parked the bike. It seemed a waste of fuel—and lazy—to keep puttering along on a scooter when Pam and Tim were probably exhausted. He looked at her pensively.

"What?" Jude said, instantly bristled and on the defensive.

"Are you okay?" Tim asked. She must have had a strange blank expression on her face, her eyes searching his for meaning. "You had to shoot those soldiers. That must be tearing you up."

Tim surprised her by caring enough to ask about how she was holding up. That was something she wasn't used to, instantly making her suspicious. Yes, she had shot the man in the holding pen. She had shot the National Guardsman. She had shot the sheriff, a man of the law who, in any other circumstances, would have been the leader of this little survivors' party. She looked at Tim with as earnest an expression as she could. "I had to kill my own parents and my brother yesterday, Tim. I guarantee you I'm not feeling much of anything right now."

Tim took a step back and swallowed hard. Jude bet he hadn't expected to hear those words come out of her mouth. She kept to herself the fate of Mr. Emery and the would-be Vespa thieves. She figured Tim wouldn't be able to handle much more. He was trying to muster up the right words in this situation. She appreciated his efforts, but she was fairly certain there wasn't a Hallmark card that dealt with the aftermath of killing one's undead family. *Roses are red. Violets are blue. You killed most of your own family, and now there's only you.* Suck on that, American Greeting Cards.

"Are *you* okay?" When he didn't respond, she started to defend her actions. "They had already... changed. I wouldn't have killed them otherwise."

"I... I'm sure," Tim said, reaching out to the railing for support. "I can't believe you had to do all that."

Jude didn't know how to make what she had done sound more rational. All she could come up with was an old standard people told other people out of sheer desire to smooth things over. "It'll be okay. Everything will be okay." Those words were laced with steaming bullshit! Her parents were dead. Her brothers were dead. Mr. Emery, the lecherous asshole he had been, was dead. She had killed a few more in the span of a few hours. Things were not going to be okay.

Tim was placated, though. He stood up straighter, his resolve buttressed a bit by her words. Maybe, all he needed was someone to verbalize the unrealistic fantasy of a world not falling into chaos. If that's all he needed, she would play along for as long as it lasted. Of course, that was when the screaming started.

41
## The Old Adage
+2 Days – 3:03pm EST

Pam was not yelling for Nathan anymore. Instead, she was screaming bloody murder. Tim and Jude raced along the curve of the boardwalk in the direction of her wails. It was less than a hundred feet before the lush landscape and the bend in the Riverwalk gave way to Pam on her hands and knees.

A man sat on a park bench in front of her. He was in his late twenties or early thirties—probably close to Pam's age. Sporting what Jude considered the start of a hipster beard with the hair on the top of his head buzzed close on the sides and spikey on top. He looked out onto the water, not giving Pam a second glance. His distressed gray T-shirt with the Journey beetle from the Escape album cover—yeah, her dad had been sure to expose her to all sorts of classic rock music—was covered in dark drying blood from the massive tear in his neck and shoulder. He must have died quickly. His arms were draped over the top of the bench and his expression was one of contentment.

Tim went to Pam, kneeling down and hugging her. He was smart enough to use his body to shield her from seeing any more of her boyfriend than necessary. She fought against him, not wanting to lose sight of Nathan. Luckily, he was much stronger and able to bear the brunt of her flailing arms and twisting body. Jude brought out the Beretta. Her experience so far told her Nathan would probably not look out at the water for much longer. Although, Michael hadn't turned.

"Don't you hurt him," Pam yelled at Jude. "You leave Nathan alone."

Tim tried to console her and keep her in his arms, but, in the end, she proved too slippery for him. Maybe, all that running *had* worn him down. Pam escaped and practically fell across her boyfriend's lap, her arms extended out in front of her in a warding off gesture. She was now between the business end of the Beretta and her boyfriend.

"He's going to turn into one of those things, Pam," Jude told her as evenly as possible. "You need to get away from him."

"No!" Pam cried.

"Tim," Jude ordered, glancing in his direction, "get her away from him."

Tim nodded and got back to his feet.

Pam screamed. Both Tim and Jude snapped their attention back to her. Nathan's arms were wrapped around her, his teeth deep into the back of her shoulder. Tim rushed to her.

"No!" Jude shouted. Goddamn it! Now, Tim was in the way of a clean shot. Jude flanked to the edge of the bench. Clear shot. She fired. Tim recoiled from the blast and the spray of blood and gray matter cast off from Nathan's head. The former boyfriend slumped forward over the still sobbing Pam. The tension in Tim's body made it look like he was still determined to get her away from the now dead man. "Tim, stay away. There's nothing you can do. She's going turn into one of those things. She's going to end up like Nathan. Guaranteed."

Tim finally listened to her and backed away, his want to be a Boy Scout dimming against his need for self-preservation. Good boy. Pam was still alive, in spite of the volume of blood spilling out of her shoulder. She looked at Jude, her eyes silently begging her to make life different. Begging Jude to make her reunion with Nathan better... something more romantic... something more like a fairytale.

It was something, alright... a nightmare.

"It'll be okay, Pam." Jude managed to say the words without choking on them. Pam tilted her head down with the slightest of nods, closing her eyes and squeezing more tears out. Her breathing slowed, her chest rising and falling faintly.

"What do we do?" Tim asked, trying hard to keep his shit together. His arms were crossed and his fingers were digging into his biceps. Jude shrugged her shoulders and stepped toward the bench. She knelt at Pam's side and swept away a stray lock of hair plastered to her sweaty forehead. There was no glimmer of life left in Pam's eyes, a hardened glaze forming content to stare into the abyss of what was to come after. Jude wondered if the white light supposedly accompanying death and the afterlife was even a real thing. If it was, did the soul chase after it even now, or would the spirit be forever trapped in an animated rotting body?

It didn't change what Jude needed to do. She pressed the barrel of the Beretta to the hollow of Pam's throat, looked away and pulled the trigger. The blast was muffled, but the report was still loud. Jude didn't look at the carnage of the exit wound, figuring the bullet had probably spun out of the back of Pam's head and into Nathan's belly.

Something caught Jude's attention. A black spherical object lay under the bench. Blood dripped from the underside of the bench, narrowing missing it. The widening pool of Nathan's blood threatened to overtake it in another minute or two, especially with the added drainage from Pam's head wound. Jude swiped it off the pavement. It was a set of two keys connected with a chrome chain to a floating encased compass ball. She pocketed them, careful to point the keys downward as to not have them poking into her hip if she bent over.

"We should cover them," Tim said.

"With what?" Jude shot back. "We don't have anything to cover them with." She didn't mean to snap at him. She knew he was just trying to show respect for the dead... to show respect for his new friend. Jude would want him to show her the same courtesy when her time came. Several yards away, a swatch of blue suddenly flapped against the warm breeze. "There."

Tim looked where she was pointing and nodded, trotting over to the tarp covering a pile of mulch. As he busied himself with untying the ropes holding it down, Jude took a moment to look at Pam. They had not known each other long—only a few hours—but their bond had been forged in the fires of duress. The entry wound in her throat was a darkening red, a black circle burned into her skin around it. It hadn't been fair Pam had seen her boyfriend torn open. Jude squeezed her forearm and muttered a half-remembered prayer from her youth in Catholic school.

"Run!" Tim yelled.

Jude looked up in time to see him racing toward her, no tarp in hand. What the fuck? Behind him were several lumbering and growling people. They looked homeless, their clothing dirty and in tatters—and several layers deep. The layers of clothing didn't slow them down or bind up their movements. Each time Tim stumbled—either from fear or fatigue—it seemed the homeless park-things had an opportunity to descend upon him.

Jude fired into the crowd, making sure she fired away from Tim. While one bullet caught one of the homeless-things in the arm, all of her other shots missed. She squared off her stance and fired again, this time catching one of the bums in the face. He slid onto the ground face first. She exhaled and fired again. Another homeless-thing felt to the pavement. Another squeeze of the trigger. Another bum dropped to the concrete.

Tim ran past her. "Come on!"

Jude squeezed the trigger again. Nothing happened. The slide was locked open. Fuck! The magazine was empty. The other magazines and boxes of rounds were in her pack strapped to her back. She would never be able to pull any of it out of the pack before the homeless-things descended on her. Tim didn't need to be fast... just faster than her.

## 42
## *Transmission*
+2 Days – 3:19pm EST

Jude easily caught up to the heavily panting Tim, her legs well rested from the miles traveled on the Vespa. The Beretta was still in her right hand, heavily swinging back and forth with every pump of her arm. The laden backpack was throwing off her center of balance.

"Shit!" Timmy hissed out the word under his breath.

'Shit', was right. The winding path onto the promenade was teeming with the animated dead. Access to the path and the waiting

Vespa was out of the question. Tim cut behind her and hurdled over the bench where she had seen the luggage, landing in one of the raised flowerbeds edging the parking lot. Jude followed around the bench, taking one last look at Mr. Emery's Vespa. It would always only be a partial apology for him being such a skeevy creep.

The homeless-things changed course as they reacted to Tim and Jude's zig-zagging movements. They wanted warm flesh, but were stymied by the knee-high brick and stone borders. Since they couldn't get to them in a straight line, they simply stood at the low wall groaning.

Tim and Jude made it through the bushes of the berm and stopped. The landscaping sloped gently into the grass and sidewalk. A few large boulders had been strategically placed along the edge, but they weren't meant to serve as barriers for a defendable position. The homeless-things would easily be able to reach them once they flanked around to the parking lot side. Other undead had appeared in the parking lot from elsewhere in the park, enough of a threat to make Jude pause and wonder how in the hell they were going to get out. They had probably been attracted to the shots.

She shrugged out of the backpack and quickly unzipped the main pocket. The sound was loud in her ears. She let the magazine fall out of the Beretta's grip into the open backpack and replaced it with a full one.

She squatted down lower when one of the things wandered into view from the pathway. Ouch! The compass keyring keys dug into her thigh. She fished them out as quietly as possible, careful not to make any sudden movements. The bum with a missing cheek and too many layers of clothes turned his head their way but hadn't noticed them… and she meant to keep it that way.

The keys jangled.

167

Fuck. Jude took in a hiss of a breath. She froze until the bum changed direction and wandered away. Once he was out of sight, Jude exhaled and tapped Tim on the leg to show him the keys. While there was nothing distinguishing about the compass keyring, the keys themselves spoke volumes. The bow was square with rounded corners and the name Ford embossed on both sides.

"Seems logical," Jude whispered as she nodded toward the cobalt blue Bronco. Tim looked down at the keys turning over in Jude's fingers. His eyes were wide, but Jude didn't think he was actually seeing the keys like she was. He nodded at her, anyway. She put a hand on the inside of his bicep and pressed against him. "We make a run for the truck. Okay?"

He nodded again.

Backing away from Tim, Jude flexed her grip on both the Beretta and the keys. The run to the truck was only fifty yards or so. Six of the homeless-things shuffled around the parking lot between them and their goal. If they ran fast enough—and in an erratic manner—they should reach the truck before the undead could descend upon them.

"Ready?" Jude asked.

Tim shook his head, but said, "Ready."

They practically exploded from between the bushes, trampling several tulips in the soft dirt as they ran across the sidewalk to the parking lot. Their sneakers slapped loudly against the pavement. Yellow lines on a sea of fresh black whizzed by as they cut right to stay out of the reaching hands of the closest homeless-thing. Another zag left allowed them to slip between two more. Jude's heart was pounding in her ears, drowning out her ragged exhales from her already taxed lungs. Damn, she was out of shape.

The bums were slow to react. As Tim and Jude raced to the Bronco, though, all of the dead slowly started to adjust their shambling pursuit. Being faster and more agile wasn't going to be an asset in another couple of seconds. She awkwardly swapped the keys into her right hand, her left hand unfamiliar with what to do with the gun. Of course, her right hand didn't seem to know how to manage the keys on its own, either. Instead, she resorted to using her teeth to straighten them out. The keys were metallic tasting—obviously—and had an added seasoning of oil and copper. Jude stopped thinking about what was coated on those keys and focused on getting the right one in the door lock. She turned the key to the left, locking all of the doors. Sonofabitch!

"Hurry up," Tim whined. "They're coming."

Jude chanced a look over her shoulder. The homeless-things were much closer than expected. How much time had she spent locking the unlocked doors? Another ten or twelve feet and the bums would be on top of them. She twisted the key again and watched the door locks pop up. She fumbled with the handle. The raised suspension and the Beretta in her hand made opening the door near impossible.

"Tim! Open the door!" She backed up and switched the Beretta into her right hand again. Tim rushed forward, slamming into the side of the truck and trying to get his fingers on the handle at the same time. It didn't work as his weight was keeping the door closed.

One of the homeless-things reached for her. The Beretta was pressed against his grimy forehead before she even realized it, keeping his arms out of reach of her neck. He must not have been too bright in life since he could have clawed her arms a dozen times over. It didn't matter. The muzzle shot was muffled. His greasy gray hair flapped back, now also coated in a dark red. He dropped at her feet. Three more bums closed in.

What the fuck? Had a goddamn bum tent city been zoned for the park? She shot an elderly black woman in her gaping mouth, the spine at her neck severing instantly. A slovenly white-haired man behind her fell dead on top of her. The same bullet had tumbled through his eye. Shit! She was like a modern-day Annie Oakley! A sour stench puffed up from where it had been trapped between their layers of clothes. Jude wrinkled up her nose.

"Jude!"

She quickly backed away from the gunned-down bodies. The Bronco's door was wide open, as evidenced by the fact her head bumped off it. She hissed from the impact, knowing there would be a knot on the back of her noggin with Tim's name on it in a few hours.

She swung around the door and hopped up into the waiting cab. Just as she reached for the door, one more homeless man reached in and grabbed her wrist. Jude screamed in surprise, recoiling into the seat. The bum growled at her with a mostly toothless grin. It only took a couple teeth to bite into the skin and she wasn't going out like that. No fucking way! Tim pulled her away from the door. She thrust out her leg. The sole of her sneaker caught the man square in the face under the nose. His septum broke and dark blood gushed from his nostrils and mouth. He staggered back. Jude lunged forward, grabbed the inside door handle, and slammed it closed. The homeless-thing recovered and slapped at the door. Jude was fine with that.

"Take that, asshole!" Her words came out in ragged bursts. She slid around to face front. She put her fingers tightly around the steering wheel—the right hand still holding the Beretta with two fingers and her thumb—hoping Tim wouldn't notice how badly her hands were shaking. "That was fucked up."

"You okay?"

Her nerves weren't shot yet, but the adrenaline was starting to dissipate. Matty had told her adrenaline was an amazing part of the body's ability to survive. He also told her it left the body a shocky, tired mess. "We need to hydrate. Take my pack and get out the Gatorade."

She slumped her shoulders in an effort to help Tim get the pack off. He put it between them on the bench, unzipped the main pocket, and fished around until he found one of the sealed bottles under a pair of her clean undies. Of course, the neck of the bottle caught on the leg hole of the pink VS panties when he brought the bottle out of the pack. She swiped it away and stuffed it back into her pack before he could get as flustered and embarrassed as she already was. How mortifying!

After he broke the seal and each of them took two or three long swigs, the Beretta moved from her fingers to her lap. She held her now free hand out. "Okay. Hand them over."

Tim looked at her open palm with a strange stare as he put the bottle back in the pack and zipped it up again. "Hand what over?"

"The keys." She tried to use a civil tone, knowing it still had an edge of 'what the fuck is wrong with you, are you an idiot?' lilt.

"They were in the lock," Tim said in his defense. "I only opened the door like you told me."

She opened her mouth to chew him out for being such a dimwit, but quickly snapped her teeth together again when she realized he was right. *She* was the dimwit. She had left the keys in the door. She peered out the driver's side window. Yep. The compass was dangling from the chain where the key was turned in the lock. The bum slapped against the door, hopelessly too short to reach up to the window. By now, several more of the shuffling undead park residents had arrived. They set up around the perimeter of the Bronco, slapping and clawing at the beautiful custom cobalt blue paintjob.

Three others had cozied up to Bum #1 at the door. Their reach wasn't any better than his, but having so many flailing arms wouldn't make things any easier. Without the keys, she couldn't power down the window. Going through the cab's back sliding window was out since she was way too wide to fit through it. Fuck! She tapped her fingers on the steering wheel for a few seconds before declaring, "I'm going to have to open the door."

"No way!" Tim exclaimed, suddenly very protective of her.

Sweat had started to form on her neck. She wiped it with her hand and held it up. "See this? If we don't get the truck started, we are going to die like abandoned dogs in here with the temperature rising as quick as it is."

"It's dangerous."

"Yeah? Ya think?" The sarcasm was evident. "Listen… I fucked up. I forgot the keys. We need to get moving before all these… things choke us in. Okay?"

He nodded, but she could see he wasn't fully on board with the plan. What plan? Beyond the obvious 'get the keys' part, she had no defined plan at all. Seemed simple enough. Open door. Get keys. Close door. KISS—keep it simple, stupid.

Before she had a chance to procrastinate more, she grabbed the gun in her right hand and unlatched the door with her left. The bums' weight was against it, keeping it closed. She pushed her shoulder into the tan leather panel. The door opened enough for her to slip her left hand out. It was also open enough for Bum #1 to wriggle his arm into the cab through the same gap.

His fingers scraped against her jeans. Her fingers searched for the keychain. Her middle finger, appropriately enough, grabbed the compass ball and wriggled the rest of the keychain into her grip. She turned the key. The door locks engaged. The scraping on her jeans grew louder. His face pressed into the crack. His teeth snapped open and closed. She blindly tried to wiggle the key out of the lock.

"Come on," Jude muttered. "Come on."

The Bum moaned at her, seemingly just as frustrated.

She jiggled the key in the lock. Sweat poured down her face. Tim started slapping at his own window and yelling some choice expletives. She couldn't concentrate on what the fuck he was doing. She had enough to deal with at the moment with the chomping homeless-thing and her fingers' inability to extract car keys by muscle memory. Damn it!

The bum jumped up and tried to snap his jaws at her forearm. She rested the Beretta in the crook of her arm and took aim at his smile. The sound of its retort filled her ears. Tim fell silent. The echo of the gunshot was replaced by a loud and steady ringing tone. The Bum dropped away from the opening. The door cracked open wider without his weight pressing against it. Jude swung out onto the truck's climb-up step amid several dead people. She pulled the key out and slipped back into the cab before any of the remaining undead had time to get past Bum #1. The door slammed. Or, at least, she thought she heard the door slam. The ringing in her ears hadn't abated, so she couldn't be sure of anything.

Jude spun back around to face the steering wheel. The Beretta went into her lap between her legs again. The barrel felt warm against her left thigh. She jammed the key into the ignition and turned it over. Nothing happened. She turned the ignition over again. Nothing. "What the fuck?"

"...press down..."

"What?" Jude yelled. She still couldn't hear shit due to the ringing. It wasn't really a ringing. More like the tone from the Emergency Broadcast System on television. If it had been an actual emergency...? Well, this was an actual emergency of the highest order, and she hadn't heard one peep from the EMS before the power went out. Civil defense services were great in theory.

""...clutch.." Tim was pointing to the floor under her sneakers. "...engage the clutch."

Jude darted her eyes to the tall stalk with the ball on the top of it. She finally realized she needed to have her left foot on the clutch and her right foot on the brake pedal. She was sitting in the drivers' seat of a truck with a standard transmission. This day just went from bad to worse.

## 43
# *Murder in the First*
+2 Days – 3:42pm EST

Jude stared at the tall black shifter. It had been her nemesis ever since she had learned to drive a car. Forget the growing crowd of homeless undead hordes outside the cab who were hungry for her flesh. Forget the slapping and clawing against the truck's cobalt blue. The manual transmission in front of her was the most terrifying of monsters. First gear was a terror she had never vanquished. Period.

"You put your foot on the clutch," Tim instructed.

"Shut up."

"But," Tim said, pointing at the footwell, "the truck won't–"

"I said to shut it. I know how to drive." She snapped at him, not wanting him to know how shitty a driver she was of anything with three pedals. Her answer was to jam the clutch pedal all the way to the floor, do the same with her other foot on the brake, and grab the shifter like she was squeezing a man's balls to within an inch of their usefulness. She glared at Tim until he sat back and buckled in. His eyes darting to the Beretta in her lap probably helped to cow him a bit. She had certainly proven she, at least, knew how to use something with proficiency.

She turned the key over in the ignition. The Bronco roared to life. The reanimated dead growled at the front grille, lunging at the bumper. She took her foot off the brake and tapped the accelerator. It roared with enthusiasm. She smiled. "That's more like it."

She feathered her foot off the clutch and onto the accelerator in equal measure. The ratio must have been off. The Bronco's grille surged itself into the undead. They launched off their feet and ended up under the front bumper before the engine stalled. "Shut up," Jude warned Tim before he had a chance to speak. She went through the same motions, changing the amount of pressure she gave the gas pedal before fully releasing the clutch. The Bronco surged forward again, the oversized tires riding over the bodies like small speed bumps. She swallowed hard at the thought of them bursting apart under the heavy rubber treads.

Tim breathed heavily through his nose.

She pulled the wheel to the right, clipping a few more undead vagrants. They fell under the tires, too. Jude drove by the promenade's entrance. The Vespa sat on the wide concrete walkway where she had left it. A dozen walkers milled around it. *Thank you for getting me here.* Maybe, someone else would be able to use it to escape this craziness. Jude stomped the accelerator and jetted across the parking lot teeming with undead.

"You got–" Tim said meekly as the transmission started to whine.

"I got it!" Jude engaged the clutch, released the gas pedal, and jammed the shifter into second gear. The transmission growled when she released the clutch, making her wonder how successful she had been with finding second gear. She tried again. This time, the Bronco surged forward. Success!

More shuffling undead streamed out from the wooded areas around the parking lot. Jude swerved out of their way, but many were too close to avoid. The weight of the Bronco dealt with them handily with sickening thumps. She counted at least twenty bodies in the side mirror by the time they exited the wide paved area.

Once they were out of the parking lot and heading toward the exit, Jude found third gear and relaxed a little. The trees swished by on both sides, the branches and leaves a canopy of shade. She felt calmer as she navigated the lazy curves of the roadway. The park engineers had known what they had been doing.

The feeling of relief ended a minute later when she saw a familiar Labrador Retriever racing across the road, his extendable leash still attached and bouncing along behind him. As Jude slammed on the brakes and watched the dog high tail it into the bushes, she could have sworn the dog's slick red coat had been lighter the first time she had seen him.

## 44
# *Congested Conversation*
+2 Days – 4:03pm EST

Jude stayed on the side streets for as long as she could. The traffic was lighter, although just as frantic as everywhere else in the city. Horns blared loudly and tempers flared hot. Several people on the sidewalk rolled along with hard shell suitcases or hiked up backpacks more designed for deep woods camping than for college life. The pedestrians mingled with the cars in the street, most times moving faster than their metal counterparts.

"We're going to be caught up in the traffic just like everybody else," Tim announced from the passenger seat.

"You're welcome to walk with the rest of them." Jude pointed out the windshield. She was also on the lookout for any of the undead who may have followed them out of the park.

"Are you going to shoot me if I do?" Tim asked, his eye again glancing to the Beretta under her thigh. "Or, maybe you'll shoot me if I don't?"

"I'll shoot you if you don't stop being a turd about our situation. How about that? Is that a good enough compromise for ya?"

Tim didn't reply. Probably a good thing. Jude was dealing with a gnarl of traffic in front of her, in addition to her disgruntled passenger beside her. She didn't want to think about the carnage she left in her wake. Dead parents. Dead brothers. A father with a spiteful new wife and two small children from a previous mother; an officer of the law who probably had his own family—both gunned down by her hand. Jude couldn't forget about the busload of homeless park dwellers crushed under the massive knobby wheels of the Bronco. They had lost Pam… and her boyfriend, Nathan.

177

And, while she hadn't seen it, she knew the owner of the black Labrador Retriever had succumbed to the craziness of the day, too. Her heart felt heavy—it was heavy. Her muscles felt like they were laced with concrete. She was tired. In a soft voice, she assured him with, "It's going to be okay, Tim. We just need to get away from this congestion."

He shrugged his shoulders heavily. They slumped quickly after using the energy to convey his passive-aggressive frustration. While the traffic was slowly moving in front of her, Jude wondered why people weren't more panicked. What she and Tim had witnessed in the park would have turned a normal crowd into a hysterical mob. She had seen too much in the past twenty-four hours. Hadn't everyone else seen their own friends, family, or people on the street turned into flesh-eaters?

Right in front of them, two drivers got out of their respective cars and came together between their bumpers. The front guy was dressed in a snappy gray suit. The man from the second car—who had tapped Mr. Gray's bumper—wore a flannel shirt and jeans. They spoke to each other with a measure of civility, using their arms in wide gestures and slight smiles to let the other know everything was going to be okay—they were just cars, anyway. Maybe Jude should have used a smile with Tim—a gesture to pull him out of his defeatist mood.

"What's with this bullshit?" Jude asked. Ahead of Mr. Gray and Mr. Flannel, more people were starting to gather in the intersection under the dark streetlights. They pointed beyond the next intersection, some shaking their heads. She shouted as she slapped the steering wheel. "This ain't helping with the traffic, people!"

Before long, the people started to retreat toward the Bronco. The two men discussing their fender-bender had to sidestep between their cars to keep from being trampled. Jude and Tim followed their migration from the side mirrors. Objects were closer than they appeared according to the mirror, but those people were still getter tinier with every step. When the crowd reached the next intersection, Jude abandoned the mirror and returned her gaze to the line of vehicles waiting at the street signals in front of them.

Another parade of people moved at a leisurely pace along the sidewalks and between the cars toward them. Some stopped to check on people still in their cars; others continued to make their way through the intersection. A tall blond man with a swelling knot on his head, wearing a purple Polo shirt with its collar turned up, and khaki pants, approached Mr. Gray and Mr. Flannel.

They stopped chatting and waved him over. Preppy quickened his pace. Mr. Gray put out his hand to shake his hand. Instead of the typical greeting, Preppy lurched forward at Mr. Gray. He caught Preppy by the arms, but not in time to keep Preppy's teeth from digging into his flesh. Mr. Gray screamed.

"Shit. Shit. Shit." Jude locked the doors.

Mr. Flannel tried to pull Preppy off his new friend. While the three of them grappled, Jude could see the top of Preppy's head was a bloody mess.

"Did a brick fall on his head?" Tim asked.

Jude looked past blond Preppy. There were others just like Preppy walking toward them. Shrill screams and angry shouts started filling the air, easily heard over the blow of cool air from the vents. "I don't think so."

Jude's heart raced. Without even thinking about it, she put the Bronco into first gear, spun the steering wheel hard to the right and revved the engine. The Bronco slammed into Mr. Flannel's car. He glared at Jude, his attentions divided between trying to pull Preppy off Mr. Gray and the worsening condition of his own vehicle. That made it all the easier for Preppy to twist around and bite into him. Mr. Flannel gurgled as a chunk of skin and muscle was peeled away from his neck by Preppy's teeth.

"Sorry. Sorry. Sorry" Jude's heart dropped as yet another person was going to be killed because of her actions. She had to save herself. "Shit. Shit. Shit."

Jude put the truck into Reverse and jammed the accelerator. The Bronco's tires squealed and created white smoke as the rubber spun into the asphalt. She hit something hard, causing an abrupt thump and the sound of scraping metal and tinkle of broken headlights. Slamming the shifter into first gear, Jude demanded the Bronco forward again. She cleared the bumper of Mr. Flannel's car. There was no other lane. Jude was aiming for the sidewalk.

"Watch out! Christ! Look out!" Tim yelled, holding onto the handle at the edge of the door frame.

Trash cans, café furniture, assorted potted plants... all of it got pushed out of the way by the Bronco's front bumper. Jude hoped it was equipped to withstand repeatedly smashing into structural elements of building entrances.

"I'm looking!" Jude gritted her teeth. The sidewalk opened up enough to allow a clear shot to the intersection. She almost hit a bolted down USPS mailbox, but pulled the steering wheel right enough to shoot between the blue box and a gray lamp post onto the side street. The main road they had been on had been backed up for several blocks—and was at a standstill for several blocks more beyond. The reason was easy to see. The undead had taken over the road and sidewalks, either trapping the people inside their cars or attacking those escaping on foot. Either way, there was no way those cars were going to be moving to let her and Tim get out of the city.

She floored the accelerator, the Bronco's motor growling and its tires gripping the pavement with authority. The torque of the truck threatened to fish-tail the rear end into a parked car, but Jude was finally able to get the Bronco under control again. Luckily, there wasn't anyone on the side street to get in the way.

"What do we do now?"

"How should I know?" Jude snapped back at him. "This ain't my city. I have no idea where we're going. All I know is we need to keep moving and keep ahead of those things!"

"That," Tim acknowledged, his grip on the handle not loosening at all, "is the best plan I've heard."


**45**
## *Putting on the Ritz*
+2 Days – 7:58pm EST


Jude and Tim didn't make it nearly as far out of the city as they had hoped, barely managing to keep ahead of the biggest threats on their list of threats—traffic jams and the undead. Where the river had cut diagonally to the northwest—the traffic was the lightest they had faced. North of the downtown, the area was predominantly high-end residential suburbia, most of the houses sitting on more than an acre. As a result, there weren't many cars on the road or people milling about. And, because of that—and because most of the houses were on gated properties—the influx of wandering undead was also very light.

They had argued about going across the river again. Tim told her it would eventually lead them out of the city and toward the Interstate. Jude told him no-flat out. She should have countered with

181

her fear of being stuck on the middle of a bridge with no way to turn around or move forward if things got harried. But, she had just said no and silently challenged him to go against her. She won the non-argument—probably because she was the one driving and was the current owner of the only handgun.

As a compromise, Jude had ended up parking the Bronco on the roof level of a five-story parking garage attached to a movie theater. They stared out their respective side windows without a word to each other. As evening descended, the unencumbered building fires across the river glowed brighter. The smoke was black and gray, filling the skyline with a thick and hazy exhaust. Jude wondered if Los Angeles smog looked like. She would probably never know for sure, especially if she had to walk from coast to coast to find out.

Jude glanced at Tim. He was wholly turned toward the passenger window. All she could see was his tensed-up broad shoulders and the back of his hair. She sighed quietly, cursed at herself for being so difficult, and silently vowed to be a better person from this point forward. She screwed up a bit of courage and spoke up, "Tim."

He didn't answer. Instead, he curled up his body, the muscles in his shoulders flexing so he could wrap his arms tighter across his chest.

"Tim," Jude said again. She didn't really know what to say to him. She hardly knew him. He barely knew her. Well, except the fact she seemed to have a short temper and loved to shoot people. Pulling the trigger seemed way easier than dealing with people without the handgun. She feared pulling the trigger would continue for the foreseeable future. It was dog-eat-dog out there... and she, for sure, was not going to be the neck at the end of another's muzzle.

She swallowed her pride and said two words she never liked to utter aloud. "I'm sorry." He still didn't say anything, but his shoulders loosened a bit. That was a start. "I didn't mean to snap at you. And, I didn't mean to sound like I was ignoring your feedback. I just couldn't bear to be caught on another bridge. Not with what happened to that guy in quarantine or the cops. I didn't want to have to shoot our way out of a bad situation again." Now that she was talking, it seemed like she couldn't stop the floodgates. "I had to kill too many people today, as it is. That's not how I want to be. It's getting too easy to pull the trigger. It's getting harder to think of other ways to get out of a sticky situation, you know? Is this what life is going to be now? Having to dodge these walking dead things every hour of every day?" Her words were cracking, starting to fill in with a wash of sadness, fear, and exhaustion.

Tim turned to her, his eyes glazed with wetness. "We'll figure it out. There has to be a safe place. Heck, this parking garage was a great idea, for starters. That was all you. Thank you. I'm just being a bitch because I'm not the guy saving the day, I guess."

Jude chuckled, but the laugh quickly drained of any of its mirth. "I didn't save the day. I couldn't save Pam. Or Nathan."

"That may be," Tim agreed. Why did he have to agree with her? She didn't need unwavering support to know when she fucked up! "You did save me today. I'm grateful. Maybe, I'll be able to return the favor one day."

Jude nodded and gave him a thin smile. She figured there was going to be plenty of opportunities for them to one-up each other in the 'save the day' department. She just hoped it wouldn't become a long tally sheet.

Suddenly, her stomach growled loud enough that Tim looked at her belly and laughed. She clasped her hands over her middle and grinned. "I guess it's time to dig into the pack and see what I brought."

They did just that, unzipping the pack and pulling out the flavored crackers and packaged string cheese. They gobbled down a few of the crackers and followed it up with a couple more swigs of the Gatorade. With crumbs all over her shirt, Jude checked the side mirrors before opening the driver's door and sliding down to the pavement. Tim sent her a worried look, but after checking his own mirror and cracking the door slowly, he joined her at the chest-high concrete wall. She swept a hand over her shirt, loosening up the crumbs rooted in there.

Evening was quickly giving way to night. Even the blaze across the river couldn't keep the darkness at bay. It enveloped the parking garage and the man and woman standing on its roof. The street was deserted. Across the street loomed a luxury apartment building. No candlelight flickered a yellow cast and no battery-powered lanterns cast a soft white light from behind the edges of any of the curtains. It seemed it was just the two of them tonight. They stood there at the railing for some time, just taking in the crisp night air and the quiet. Jude had just started to let in the belief the last few days had just been an extremely bad dream when harsh reality returned in the form of a gunshot. When that died down, a shrieking wail replaced it for some time. When Jude and Tim couldn't bear to listen to the sounds of chaos any longer, they returned to the truck. The heavy doors and windows of the Bronco muffled the noises enough to let them drift off to sleep.

**46**
# *Goodnight, Moon*
+3 Days – 3:22am EST

*Jude pretended to sleep. She knew her father would come into her room soon—as he always did before work. Her sleeping theatrics had always been her best defense. She always played possum, taking measured breaths and closing her eyes tight when she felt his stares from the doorway, and during the eventual too-familiar and too-long caress across her cheek. She just had to endure it for a few minutes. He wouldn't be late for work. Just like his proclivity for unwarranted advances toward his daughter, Jude's father was engrained with the need to be punctual for whatever job he was performing.*

*Tonight was no different. She felt him at the doorway, staring at her. She could even hear his tongue running over his dry cracked lips. She breathed in a regular and deep rhythm, never wanting to let on she was awake... and terrified. He closed the distance across the bedroom. His shadow fell over her, blocking out the butterfly nightlight. She could feel the heat from his hand as it closed in on her cheek. His hand didn't caress her there this time. Instead, her covers were pulled back. Twitching fingers groped the top of her breast.*

*His breathing was no longer regular. She opened her eyes to slits, hoping the darkness would keep her acting from being discovered. Her father's decaying face was inches from her. His split lips peeled back. White teeth were made whiter by his blackened gums. She couldn't move. He snapped his teeth. His eyes were milky, but they still focused on her—right through her. He plunged forward, his teeth finding her neck. Her blood pounded*

185

*loudly in her head, throbbing through her carotid. The skin tore away. The artery was laid open. Her body and clothes were drenched in a spray of hot blood.*

Jude snapped awake. Her hand knocked into the driver's window, making her knuckles throb from the impact. She cradled it against her chest until the pain went away. She looked over at Tim. He was still out cold. The stress of the previous day had hit them both hard. It was just an unfortunate fact of life. Jude suffered with poor sleeping rhythms. Of course, being unable to sleep into the morning hours since she was twelve-years-old because of her father might have had something to do with that. Her father having taken such an expressed interest in her after that birthday definitely had something to do with it. Her father was dead now. She had no reason to wake up in the wee hours to defend herself against him anymore. Now, she had the opportunity to wake up to more terrifying threats. It was ironic she had jumped from one terrible thing to wake up to straight into another.

Fuck her life.

The rooftop was quiet. No new cars had arrived. No walking dead had found their way up to the top level, maybe not even into the parking garage at all. That was a good thing. She and Tim were still alone. At least for the moment. She exited the truck and slipped down to the pavement, closing the driver's door with a soft click as to not wake her slumbering passenger.

Since her phone had died—and because she had stopped wearing a watch years ago—she had no idea what time it was. It was still the middle of the night, though. She also knew she had to pee again. Ugh! She shouldn't have chugged so much Gatorade before going to sleep. The rooftop was barren of anything except the same cars there when they had pulled in. Thank God for those cars because they provided cover while she dropped her jeans and squatted to pee. Roadside peeing was an art form, requiring practice and the proper angles to keep from pissing all over one's self. She had luckily practiced in preparation of a long road trip with Ginnie a few years back, knowing there would be stretches of road where formal bathrooms were going to be non-existent. Now, she did her business without incident and quickly left where she had marked her territory in favor of the safety of the Bronco.

There were flickers from the fires, but the horizon had taken on a deeper glowing orange instead of the intense yellows of the previous day. The city where she had grown up seemed to be a hotbed of embers, still smoldering with heat but slowly dying. Maybe, the fires had been a blessing, cleansing the city of those undead things. She could only hope the living had been able to escape before the fires had consumed everything. She knew her wish was naïve, but she vowed to hope and believed the good had been spared.

She walked to the chest-high edge and leaned on the top of the steel-tube railing. As her eyes adjusted back to the darkness, she could see the street below. Something rumbled from a line of garbage cans at the corner. A lid popped off one of the cans. It made a startling racket as it hit the sidewalk and spun on its edge for a few seconds before settling flat on the street. Jude's hand eased off the grip of the Beretta when she realized two stray cats were rummaging through the wonderful delicacies that humans were too stupid to keep for themselves.

In spite of the racket the cats were making, the streets remained empty. Nobody pulled the curtains back from any of the apartment windows. Of course, at this late hour—or early hour, if that was your preference—the odds of seeing any lights would be minimal. Where was everyone? Yes, she had been part of the mass exodus from the bridge. Yes, she had seen plenty of people trying to get away from those dead-things. It just seemed strange only she and Tim had managed to have found a safe haven for the night.

Something suddenly moved.

Jude thought she saw a curtain pull back on the corner third-floor apartment. She stared at it, willing the curtain to sway again. She didn't want it to be a trick of her mind. She wanted there to be more people out there. There! The curtain moved again. A hand appeared at the glass between two folds of drapery. Then, another hand. A young girl of maybe six or seven bumped her forehead into the window before pressing her hands against the glass. Jude's muscles tensed to wave. The girl stared down at the street for a moment, maybe looking for the cats. Then, she turned around, the curtain shifting with her movements. She stopped, facing the curtain and a room she couldn't see into. It reminded Jude of playing hide-and-seek in their apartment. Jude was always able to see his feet poking out from the bottom hem of the curtain whenever he tried hiding at the windows.

She never finished her wave. In fact, her arm recoiled back to her chest. The young girl's nightshirt had been ripped open, blood darkening the light cotton in an umbra pattern below the tears. The skin was flayed down through the muscles, white poking through. Was that her spine? Was Jude looking at slices of the back of her ribcage? She wanted to turn away, but her curiosity won out over her revulsion. It was easier when one was safe on a rooftop. The girl was behind glass, in an apartment on the third floor. Many locked doors separated them. Plus, she had the Beretta. Always the trump card if all other things started falling out of her favor.

The girl didn't move. Her back—a ruined mess—still faced the window. How did she get like that? Had her own father gotten infected with whatever was going around and clawed the meat off her bones while she slept? Jude hoped this little girl hadn't needed to pretend sleep to get safely through the night. Of course, sleeping peacefully hadn't saved her either, had it? Not this time.

Jude mourned for her. She lamented for the innocence lost. She tried to console herself in the knowledge the little girl would never know a world as it truly was—hard and relentless, and fueled by greed, self-interest, and any combination of the seven Deadly Sins. It was better to be driven by mindless hunger than to have a mind filled with all the rot and corruption in the world. Maybe, that was what the planet was doing. Maybe, the undead were scavengers, sent to eat away all of the rotten meat and pungent entrails of the world. Being so deep in her own thoughts about the mechanisms of Mother Earth, she never sensed the approaching person until fingers dug into her shoulders.

47
## *Hide and Seek*
+3 Days – 3:35am EST

She didn't scream.

Instead, she used her suddenly electrified tendons to duck and spin out from underneath the grasp on her shoulder. She swung her arm up and reached for the Beretta at the back of her waistband. The rooftop-thing was massive, even as its arms flailed from her counterattack. She kicked the lumpy form in the chest. The gun finally came up from behind her. The rooftop-thing let out a grunt as it hit the chrome grille guard of the truck.

"Oww!" The rooftop-thing spoke. That was a new skill she hadn't encountered yet when facing the undead. "Chill, Jude."

It knew her name.

"Don't fucking shoot me, okay?"

The Beretta was pointed center mass at the thing's chest. Even with the burst of adrenaline, her hand was steady. It was then the moon decided to make a surprise appearance. Reflected light bathed the top deck of the parking garage in a wash of soft white. It wasn't enough to define a full spectrum of color, but enough for Jude to realize it had been Tim who had snuck up on her.

"You wanna put that gun away?" Tim asked, his arms still up at chest level.

"Depends," Jude considered. "You going to sneak up on me again?"

"Definitely not! Can I put my hands down?"

"I should make you hold them up for another hour, but I'm too tired. Lucky you."

"Yeah," Tim agreed. "Lucky me. Sorry."

"Just use your head next time."

"Okay." Tim sounded a bit defeated, but wiser for the experience. "Anything good out there?"

She thought about the dead girl playing hide-and-seek behind the curtains, wondering if there were any other family members in the apartment still alive... still alive and completely oblivious to the fact one of their loved ones had turned into a flesh-rending machine. Should they help them? Should Jude elicit help from Tim and put their lives on the line on the off-chance someone might still be alive in the apartment across the street? "Not really. Just trying to clear my head."

"I hear that. Me, too."

"Glad you approve of my methods." Jude's face lightened a little bit. She batted her eyelashes at him, the moon still out enough to get her playful point across. "That means the world to me."

"Weirdo."

"Maybe. You'll never know."

"I already know."

"Yeah. You may have me on that one." Tim chuckled back at her comment, thankfully still leaning against the grille. She didn't want the lightness of the conversation to darken. A little normalcy wasn't too much to ask, was it? If he saw the dead girl, the direction of the discussion would quickly descend into talk of death and survival.

"Should we get on the road again? We can't stay here forever, unfortunately."

Jude guessed normalcy was too much to ask. "We need food before we get too far. Plus, we have no idea where we're going."

"I don't know the streets here," Tim said, "but I know once we get on the interstate, I can get us to my brother's farm."

"A farm? You've had a farm in your back pocket this whole time?"

"Yeah," Tim shrugged. "But, it's over a hundred miles away. It didn't seem like a realistic idea while we were trying to stay away from the undead."

Jude tried to think of other alternatives. Going back home was a useless gesture. She didn't know this town very well, either. She and Tim shared in that ignorance. They would be able to grab a few things easily enough to make the trip. It was just a matter of getting to the Interstate. Who knew what barricades or police presence would keep them inside the city limits? Maybe they could get some protection by someone in a position of authority, "We going north or south?"

"West, actually. We'd take Route 128 to Route 2 past Fitchburg."

"That's a ways away."

"Told ya."

"Alright, then. Let's get some Twinkies and get on the road."

"Perfect traveling snack."

"Damn right!" Jude grinned at Tim, taking one last look at the empty street and one more glance at the little dead girl with her perfect hiding spot behind the curtain. Whoever found her would be very surprised. Her grin faded, but she was happy to have a plan and a destination charted.


**48**
## *Pantry Raid*
+3 Days – 4:01am EST


Jude's idea to ransack one of the waterfront estates was met with skepticism by Tim, but he didn't try to stop her from trying. What finally stopped her was the twelve-foot brick spear-topped stone walls surrounding the estate. She had stared at the wall, thinking she could've backed the Bronco up to it and climbed over from its roof. The problem was she would never have been able to get back over afterward. Fine, she sighed to herself as she drove the empty side streets. It probably wasn't one of her best ideas.

"Where are the people?" Tim said as he stared out the front windshield.

"Everyone is probably hunkered down. I wouldn't want to be out on the streets with those things."

"Except for the fact we are."

"We have the Bronco. It's done pretty well against them so far. Although my back is not a fan of climbing in and out whenever we stop."

"And, by the way," Tim asked, "why do you get to drive all the time?"

"Because," Jude answered simply. He didn't need to know she needed all of the practice she could in this rolling Detroit steel.

"Well, that's one answer." Tim looked out the side window for a while, taking in the view of the deserted street they had decided was probably the easiest way out of the city. Fewer houses and industry up here as far as they could tell. She knew she had hurt his feelings again. He was so goddamn sensitive. He would definitely have being crushed under the Sawyer roof.

"You don't have a phone, do you?" Jude asked, trying to change the subject and engage him in conversation again and press back down her thoughts of family.

"Yep. It's been dead since yesterday. Battery life sucks on those things."

"Don't I know it." Had she not been half out of her mind at the onset, she would have retrieved her phone from the gutter or gone back to the apartment to get Michael's. Had she not been a victim of her car being stolen, she would have had a car charger. While the electricity continued to be out wherever they drove, the Bronco still had a cigarette lighter port. A car charger was a stupid thing not to have.

"There," Tim called out. His finger was pressed solidly on the side window glass.

In the gloom of the pre-dawn, sitting in a sea of concrete, was a Quick Stop convenience store. It didn't have electricity either. The street lights were extinguished and the front of the store looked as dead as everything else they had encountered since escaping across the water. There was little way to tell if there were people moving around inside in spite of the lack of fluorescent lights. Various posters describing how tasty their hot dogs were or how delicious their "freshly made every twenty minutes" coffee was covered the majority of the available glass window real estate. Jude pulled into the lot and parked in the blue-lined handicap parking space in front of the entrance. The wash from the Broncos headlights lit up the front doors and part of the center aisle inside the store.

Jude slipped out the Beretta's magazine. Fourteen rounds. She cocked the hammer, peeled her finger away from the trigger, and pulled back the slide to check the ejection port. There was a round in the chamber. A flick of her thumb on the decocker lever slapped the hammer home again. Timmy cringed at the sound. She slapped the magazine back home in the gun's grip and put her free hand on the door handle. Timmy hadn't made his own move toward his door. Jude didn't think he had been ready for an early morning convenience store raid even before she had parked, in spite of his eagle eyes. Now, he watched her check the Beretta, his face paling even more. She caught him staring at the gun out of the corner of her eye.

"You ready, Freddy?"

Suddenly, his stomach growled in a long, drawn-out gurgle. The alluring food posters must have put his belly over the top. He finally nodded and grabbed at his door handle. They both slipped out at the same time, softly clicking the doors closed. They needed to make this quick. While the Bronco's battery was doing fine for the headlights, Jude didn't want to drain it unnecessarily without the engine running to recharge it.

Tim squatted down and picked up a palm-sized rock from the next parking spot, hefting it in his hand. He was, of course, entitled to a weapon, too. When he hurled said stone at the glass pane of the right-side door and shattered it, she gave him a glare and threw up her hands.

"Shit!" Jude exclaimed. "A little warning next time, huh?"

"Sorry," Tim answered sheepishly.

Jude reached for the door handle. She gave Tim a sideways glance as she pulled it open without having to unlock it from the inside. "Open twenty-four hours, bro. Remember for next time."

She didn't wait for another apology, walking into the store with her shoes crunching over the crumble of glass. Her shadow from the light of the Bronco extended deep into the bowels of the store, casting her as a hulking shape on the back wall. She didn't feel intimidating… more the opposite. Regardless, she let the Beretta lead the way—always the equalizer.

She reached over the register counter and grabbed a couple plastic bags, handing one to Tim. He steered between the window and the first set of shelves. Jude wasn't sure he would find anything edible in an aisle loaded with batteries, dish detergent and charcoal, but left him to make her way to the back wall to a deli counter. Without refrigeration, the meats, cheeses, and salads were starting to turn. The smell wasn't bad yet, just a bit stronger. Given another few days, that aroma would drastically become more pungent.

The rustling of Tim's plastic bag and the clinking of metal hitting metal was evident from the aisle he was plundering. "Finding anything good?"

"We'll see," Jude answered. She turned and grabbed two small boxes of White Cheddar Cheez-Its. She was more of an original cheese flavor fan, but this store was not stocked with her favorite crackers. She grabbed a red can of Pringles from the end cap before moving to the side wall and the beverage refrigeration units. Obviously, without power, the soda and beer were warming up as fast as the deli meats and cheeses. She grabbed a couple more Gatorades and added them to the bag draped on her forearm. Tim was adding bottled water to his own bag from a newly delivered stack on a small pallet.

"You ready?" Jude asked.

"Yeah. I think we have enough to get us where we're going. I know Sal usually has his pantries well stocked year-round."

"Cool," Jude answered. "Then let's get out of here before we're arrested."

Glass shattered in the last aisle. Jude stepped closer to Tim. The bag on his arm was still swaying, even though he wasn't. The Gatorades in her bag weighed down her hand, making it near impossible to raise her gun hand to defend them. Stupid. She let the bag slide to the floor. It sounded like the Pringles can had been crushed by the bottles. She was sure the chips would be tiny shards. If she ever had a chance to open the top.

"Stay here," she ordered Timmy.

Jude made her way down the second aisle—the candy aisle. It was empty of threats. This aisle was where Tim should have started his quest for supplies. There were still plenty of King-Sized Snickers to choose from. Jude loved them. They had always left her satisfied. Focus! No time for that now.

Another sound of glass shattering on the tiles came from the back of the store, this time a softer jingle of glass. When she slipped into the main aisle, where the lights from the Bronco were bright and strong, Jude made sure to not look directly at the beams. The last thing she needed was to be blinded to whatever was deeper inside the convenience store. She passed the bread aisle and the bagged salty snacks. More bad food she loved. Canned goods and cereals were also there. Damn, she was hungrier than she thought. She took a deep breath and hurried around the endcap of stale doughnuts.

Something moved at the far end of the aisle.

"Whoa!" Tim yelled. He stood in front of the wall of refrigerators with his hands up.

"Goddamnit!" Jude said with a shaky exhale. "I almost shot you."

"Sorry." He was full of apologies lately. Jude hoped that this wasn't an indication of the days to come. If so, she needed to start keeping company with people who had thicker skin and a backbone.

There was no deli-thing lurking about. There was, however, a jar of Prego spaghetti sauce with its red innards spreading across the floor. Next to it was a glass jar of peanut butter. It was still mostly intact—due mostly to the sticky texture of the PB inside—but it had shattered across the bottom, giving it a strange lopsided appearance of sinking into the floor itself. Jude checked over the deli counter. Nobody was there. The door next to the counter was sturdily locked, so nobody had used that exit.

"Maybe they just slipped off the shelf," Timmy wondered out loud.

"Maybe," Jude answered, not so sure the jars had magically ejected from the safety of their assigned perches.

A dark blob oozed to the floor left of the peanut butter with a soft thump. Jude spun around. She got a bead on it with the Beretta's front sight. It slithered a foot across the aisle before stopping and rising up. Tim stared at something behind the counter, completely oblivious of what Jude was tracking across the floor.

She put pressure on the Beretta's trigger. The blob chuckled as it scurried into the light of the main aisle. It raised its tiny black hands in surrender, a smattering of spaghetti sauce on them. It was a bandit of the highest genus. The raccoon took a long look at Jude and the barrel of her gun. She stared right back at it. Eventually, Tim looked down at the raccoon and yipped. The furry rodent spun around and gave him a hiss before it hightailed it—literally—up the aisle and through the broken front door like a thief in the night.

Another moment passed before Jude burst out in laughter. She let it go on until it started to sound a bit maniacal. That's when she reeled the laughter back in. Even Tim had a smile on his face. "What the fuck was that noise coming out your mouth?" Jude asked. "Was that a yip?"

"Shut up," Tim mumbled, his tentative smile fading into a grimace. "I didn't know it was a raccoon."

"Okay. Okay." She looked around. Tim went back to the middle aisles to fetch the dropped bags. Jude shadowed him along the main aisle. There wasn't anything more sinister than the raccoon in the store. Well, that wasn't necessarily true. She took the recovered Pringles bag from Tim and filled it with the tray of Snickers bars. When she realized she still had room in the bag, she did the same for the tray of Reeses' Peanut Butter Cups. That damn rodent had got her thinking about peanut butter.

"Damn! You have a sweet tooth!" Tim asked, ready to be done with this raid. "Can we go now?"

"Yeah," Jude said as she walked out of the candy aisle. She realized she had been lying when she stopped at the endcap and added several resealable bags of beef jerky to her loot. "Now. Now, we're ready to go."

It was only then they followed the raccoon's example and headed to the entrance. There was a spinning rack of phone chargers at the register counter.

"What's your phone?" Jude asked.

"Samsung Galaxy."

Most of the chargers were USB types one would plug into the wall. The few that were old-style cigarette lighter car chargers were for Apple products. "No luck."

Jude took one more look around the store. She knew other people would need supplies. As long as they didn't have a hankering for the same stuff she had just commandeered, they would be happy with what they found. She wondered if she should have left a few dollars by the register. In the end, she knew she didn't have nearly enough to pay for the food and drinks, let alone the shattered door.

**49**
## *Questionable Classifications*
+3 Days – 4:16am EST

Jude drove the Bronco steadily away from the city. The route Tim had suggested ended up being clear of snarled traffic or guarded blockades. At times, Jude had to steer the massive 4x4 off the pavement to skirt around accidents, but, otherwise, escaping past the city limits was relatively easy. It had almost been too easy, as countless movie antagonists had uttered before she had ever had the thought to say it, too. *Having it easy* was not a phrase typically accepted or adapted into her vernacular. She thought back to the last twenty-four hours. It had not been easy—not at all. Maybe she should just be grateful she was finally catching a break.

The developed sprawl of suburbia suddenly gave way to an increasing plateau of countryside. While she drove, she satiated her own rumbling tummy with two of the Snickers bars, almost a full bottle of Gatorade, and her surprisingly intact potato chips. Tim guzzled down one of the flavored bottled waters—something flowery, maybe a berry flavor—before he had started on one of the bags of jerky. *You're welcome.* They drove in comfortable silence for a handful of miles before an itch started at the base of Jude's brain. Once the itch took hold, it became incessant until she couldn't take it anymore. Maybe the reason this new notion was so intense was because her brain didn't want to think about other things that had a right to boil over to her consciousness.

"Is a raccoon a rodent?" she burst out.

"What?" Tim asked sleepily, surprised by the question. "Is a what a what?"

"A raccoon," Jude repeated. "Is a raccoon a rodent?"

Tim wiped his sleepy beef-jerky-induced eyes with the palm of his hand and sat up straighter in his seat. He looked out the side window for a second, Jude assumed to see if he missed any eye boogers. When he looked back at her, his face had a strange glowing quality courtesy of the green of the dashboard light. He looked half angelic, half alien. Besides that, he was all serious. "I think a raccoon is a bear."

200

"A bear?" Jude asked in exasperation. "How the fuck is a raccoon a bear?"

"That's what I remember reading. I know it's not a rodent or a rat."

"A bear? Come on. You expect me to believe that? Why you messing with me? I'm being serious, here."

"Hey. You asked me."

"Where's Google when you really need it?"

"Ain't that the truth."

"Why do we need to know shit when Google has always been the answer to any question?"

"Especially the question of whether raccoons are rodents. Of all the questions needing answers, that's certainly one of the most pressing."

"Well... yeah!" Jude mocked.

"Not how to build a fire or survive the apocalypse, but... raccoons."

"Don't harsh my mellow, bro. You're ruining my Snickers high."

"We wouldn't want that." Tim curled up a bit smaller with his arms folded across his chest. He closed his eyes and let out a deep exhale through his nose. "Just keep going until you get to Route 2. Then, go west."

"Sir. Yes, sir."

"Raccoons." Tim chuckled. He turned toward the passenger window again, the highway signs and telephone poles blurring together as they whizzed by in the dark. There was just enough pre-dawn light to see beyond the graveled soft shoulder into the corn fields and grassy meadows. Tim's breathing deepened, a random nasal snort giving way to a steady low snore. Great. He got to sleep while she was doing all the driving. She would have to let him know she was finally okay with him driving a little. She was sure she had gotten enough practice at this point.

"Bears," Jude said slowly out loud, shaking her head. "Fucking bears."

## 50
# *Mad Skills*
+3 Days – 4:49am EST

Finding Route 2 had been easy. Finding a way to get on Route 2 proved more challenging. Tim was still sleeping. She thought to wake him up, but figured he deserved a bit of rest. Pretty soon, it would be time for him to direct them the last bunch of miles to his brother's place. Maybe, he could do the last bit of driving. For now, she knew she could figure out how to get onto Route 2 by herself.

The scene at the interchange was surreal. Each of the ramps was barricaded by a single police cruiser. Leading up the off-ramp, over a dozen cars and trucks were lined up on the shoulders or in the middle of the road. One of the two bubble flashers on the cruiser sitting at the top at the off-ramp was still spinning. Only one. The other looked like it had taken a few cracks from a baseball bat.

A light fog clung to the edges of the grass. A thin film of condensation lay on the cars, beading up more so on the newer models. From where she was sitting, Jude was almost positive the cruisers were abandoned. The lack of living authority figures made it easier for Jude to decide to do what she did next. Making sure Tim still had his seatbelt on, she passed under the interchange and slowly swung the Bronco around in a wide circle. The on-ramp wasn't congested since the barricade hadn't allowed anyone onto Route 128 from Route 2, anyway. Jude accelerated the Bronco up the ramp, aiming it for an open slot between the cruiser's rear bumper and an outcropping of rocks. Incredibly, she managed to slip through without so much as a scratch on either side of the truck.

"Woot!" she exclaimed to herself at her obvious extreme-driving prowess. Tim was fast asleep, having missed her amazing display of newly-honed driving chops. His loss. Being excited for herself, though, without Tim to show his appreciation, ended up a bit hollow. Oh well. She knew she did an awesome job. The proof was she was now heading west on Route 2. Before she revved across the overpass, Jude noticed an officer sleeping inside the State Police cruiser. It was early in the morning, but she figured he should have been standing at his post until relieved by another officer. She understood, though, people were dead tired—no pun intended—and this had already been an exhausting day or two for everyone.

Eventually, she would have to wake Tim up to get directions to the cabin from Route 2. For now, she was content with her achievements, the quiet and empty road, and the sliver of cold orange coming up from the horizon in her rearview mirror. Death was behind her and, even though she was chasing the darkness to the west, she knew there had to be something better ahead.

## 51
## *Bench Warrant*
+3 Days – 5:31am EST

Jude tapped her fingers on the steering wheel of the idling truck, its engine purring softly. Route 2 had been an easy ride up to now.

She hadn't passed a single car on the road in either direction. That wasn't entirely true. There had been a few cars on the soft shoulders. Some of them had been quietly parked in the gravel, while others had careened into the ditch in the high grasses. The skidding rubber marks burned into the road had hinted at some more elaborate vehicular drama at play.

That had been the story of the last dozen or so miles. Now, she idled the Bronco as she looked in both directions at the powerless, but slowly swaying, yellow/orange colored traffic light of whatever one-light town they had entered. Two abandoned cars were lined up in the lane in front of her. Another hunk of quiet steel faced her from across the intersection. The lane to the right was clear at the corner, a few cars parked in the diagonal spots in front of a row of storefronts a couple hundred feet away.

Jude tapped her index finger in the steering wheel, followed with her ring finger and thumb whenever they felt like joining in on the nervous rhythm she was creating. She glanced over at Tim. Thankfully, his snoring had stopped a while ago. There was only so much snoring a waking person could endure in an enclosed environment. Regardless of how deep he might be sleeping, now was time for directions.

"Tim," she said quietly. "Tim, wake up."

He didn't even twitch from the sound of her voice.

"Tim," she said louder. Still nothing. She put a hand on his shoulder and shook him. He didn't stir, but did slide into the window face first with a light thunk. "Oops. Sorry."

She put the Bronco in Park and watched his chest. It wasn't moving. Shit. The sobriety coin in her father's curling hand flashed across her mind. She pulled the Beretta, inching herself closer to the driver's door while she held the barrel on him. Her free hand searched for the door latch, slapping across the door's plastic and upholstery until her fingers found the cool chrome-covered handle. She never took her eyes off Tim, even as she swung her door open.

Slipping to the road, Jude closed the door with a light click and made her way around the front of the truck. The shining chrome and glittering paint had been marred somewhat by the goop included with the splattering of various-sized flying insects against a fast-moving object. She had always theorized bugs should just slide into the slipstream and drift right over cars when at a high rate of speed. Looking at the Bronco's grille, that theory would obviously never be approved by her peers in any scientific journals. Of course, the added gore from the park-things to the bumper didn't help her case any.

She exhaled nervously as she reached the passenger's side door. Wrapping her fingers around the door handle, she yanked the door open and brought up the Beretta. One empty water bottle fell to the pavement, making her hop back a step. A second half-filled bottle was slower to escape the cab, finally rolling from the bench and landing upright in the street. Tim slumped toward her, the seat belt keeping him in the truck. His head lopped sideways and his arm dangled toward her.

Jude wasn't going to touch him. She knew he was dead. A constricting pain squeezed her chest almost to the point where she couldn't breathe. He was dead and she couldn't imagine his heart had just given out. He had survived a three-mile jog, a sprint away from a horde of homeless undead, and a confrontation with a furry bandit. Her driving hadn't been that terrible. Okay, bad joke.

The seatbelt kept him in place, even in death. There wasn't going to be any way for him to get at her when he reanimated while he was strapped in. Jude went back around to the driver's side, reached in, and pulled the key from the ignition. She wanted to conserve on gas. She dropped the keyring onto the bench. Without the engine running, the quiet of the morning enveloped her. No dogs barked in the distance. No cicadas, frogs or crickets chirped away in the pre-dawn hours. And, even though she was in the middle of a one-stop light town, there was no whoosh of traffic or quiet murmuring of people milling about on the street.

Tim hadn't reanimated. He hadn't stirred to fight against his seatbelt. Not yet, anyway. There was no way she was going to keep driving while he was in the passenger seat. She didn't need him reanimating and grabbing at her while she was barreling down the highway at sixty miles per hour. There was just no fucking way she was going to let that happen. Jude stepped over to the passenger side again, watching Timmy through the windshield. He didn't twitch a muscle. Of course, her father hadn't twitched either—until he did. Tim could come back any moment.

She swung around the open passenger door and pressed the Beretta into his lopped head, tilting it in a more downward angle for the best trajectory for the bullet to do its work. She tried to squeeze the trigger—but couldn't. She exhaled loudly and pressed the Beretta's barrel against Tim's temple again. She gritted her teeth and willed herself to tighten her index finger against the trigger. A whimper escaped her throat at the same time a single hot tear fell down her cheek. Unless he did something to give her a reason to, Jude just couldn't shoot him.

Fuck. Come on!

There was a bench behind her, set up in front of a barber shop. The striped pole on the brick wall couldn't spin without electricity, making it strange to not see the white, red, and blue stripes slowly making their way to the top. She would put Timmy on the bench.

Reaching in with just her arms, Jude tried to unlock Tim's safety belt. The button release was just out of reach. She climbed up on the foot step and stretched her arm. Her fingers were just able to touch the release mechanism. She hesitated and stepped down to the pavement. What if he re-animated when he was slumped over her—the safety belt no longer restraining him? She would be trapped under him, effectively pinned across his lap.

He hadn't moved.

Come on, Jude! Get your shit together. She would have to chance it. Hopping up again on the foot step, she felt for the release button for what seemed like a tense eternity, pressed it and dropped back to the street. The nylon of the safety belt zipped back into its housing, catching under Tim's armpit.

Jude grabbed his shirt and pulled. He tilted off the bench, falling toward her. Oh, shit! His elbow caught the safely belt at the last second, spinning him around and slowing his descent enough for Jude to jump back to the safety of the curb. He crashed to the pavement. Step one complete.

Now to drag his ass to the bench. She tried to pull him, but needed two hands to do so. She tossed the Beretta onto the bench and grabbed him under his armpits. Her thighs strained to get Tim oriented in a straight line toward the bench. She worked up a head of steam and powered him across the sidewalk, mentally cursing herself for this stupid plan. Tim outweighed her by a hundred pounds of muscle. It would take a miracle to lift him onto the green painted slats of the bench seat, even though she knew the wrought iron frame would hold him.

Dead weight was no joke. She sat him up by pushing on his back with her hands and knees. Before he slumped too far forward, Jude wrapped her arms around his chest, braced her legs on either side of

207

him and attempted the dead lift of her life. Her muscles strained as she made a sustained grunting noise to get his ass even with the seat. Jude twisted and practically dropped him on the bench, the wood creaking from his weight and the iron thumping from his flopping limbs.

Jude stepped back, her heart racing from the exertion. Her legs didn't feel so good. She straightened up and pressed both her hands into the small of her back. Tim sat there, leaning against the arm of the bench looking very relaxed. The pain coursing through her back reminded her she was still alive. At least that was what she was going to tell herself later when she was begging for an Advil or three. She wasn't sure who she going to be begging to when that happened, but she was hopeful there were still others out there who had survived overnight.

She grabbed the water bottle still sitting in the street. Some water sounded really good at the moment. She unscrewed the top and looked at the resting Tim.

"Sorry." It didn't say much, but it meant many things. She was sorry he had died. She was sorry she hadn't been nicer to him. She was sorry she couldn't have done anything to save him. She raised the water bottle to her lips.

The Bronco's engine suddenly roared to life. A door slammed. Jude spun around just in time to see the truck peel off around the line of cars waiting at the intersection.

"Hey!"

The passenger door swung closed from the rapid acceleration. She dropped the water and went for her Beretta at the back of her waistband. The Beretta was gone, sitting in the passenger side of the Bronco's bench. Her backpack was tucked into the footwell next to the shifter. The only thing left behind with her… was Tim. Even the water bottle had decided to not repeat its feat of remaining upright this time, its flavored contents spilling across the asphalt and heading to the gutter as quickly as her hopes for a better tomorrow… or today.

"Fuck!"

## 52
# *Ties That Bind*
+3 Days – 6:00am EST

"Can you believe that shit?" Jude asked. "Is the world already so fucked up that people have been reduced to stealing other people's cars? Again? Fuck my life." Jude didn't wait for an answer. "I know. I know we took Nathan's truck." She chewed on the inside of her cheek for a second. "But, he was dead. They were dead. We had to get away from those homeless park people…" She paused again. "…or, we would be dead, too. There weren't any fucking dead bodies around here when that asshole stole our ride."

Jude looked at Tim. She had propped him up better on the bench. Luckily, she had been able to find twine from a left-out display in front of a hardware store three doors down. One of his wrists was tied to the arm of the bench while the other was draped over the back rest with the arm strapped through the top horizontal slat. If someone was to pass them on the street, it would look like he was just taking a quick nap while she waited next to him.

"What am I supposed to do now?" Jude asked, knowing there wouldn't be an answer. If he came back to life, he still wouldn't have an answer for her. Her father laid in bed for hours before he had turned into a snapping, gurgling monster. Who knew just how long it had taken Dad to die during that night before he had come back during her final visit with him. "You should have written down the directions to your brother's place. Probably still too far away to get there on foot."

The street was quiet, just like it had been when she had contemplated which way to turn at the intersection. She could use a drink right now, regretting having left the gun, backpack, and keys in the truck. Such an idiot. Just when she thought she had everything under control, the entire world got pulled out from under her. It was just the way her life went. Just the way it had always gone—which was to say, it had not gone her way.

Why would someone steal the truck instead of trying to talk with her? "Maybe they didn't want to be seen with a dead person. You were pretty floppy back there. No offense." Tim didn't seem to mind. His head was still resting on his chest, not a care in the world. "I miss Floopy."

Jude was suddenly sad and tired. Either from the driving or from the stress of the last few days, all she wanted to do was to curl her legs up under her, fold her arms and close her eyes. Just for a little while. Tim was secure. He wouldn't be a problem if he turned. She didn't have anything of value. So, she didn't need to concern herself about that, either. She wouldn't let herself fall asleep. She just needed to rest her eyes for a few minutes.

## 53
### *If That Black Bird Don't Sing*
+3 Days – 9:13am EST

From very far off came a squawking caw. It was the first bird she had heard in a few days. Maybe they hadn't all disappeared. It sounded like a crow or raven. Like the bird Uncle Billy owned in that old Jimmy Stewart movie about Christmas—the one that wasn't about Christmas, at all, if you ready thought about it. The movie's title escaped her, but she could see the bird as clear as day. The caw came out of the darkness again. This time, it sounded much closer. What was the name of that movie? There was an old Savings and Loan building in it. And, Old Man Potter. Jude remembered that old scurvy spider as clear as day. The bird's cry insisted she pay attention to it, practically squawking against her ear.

She opened her eyes. The bird was a raven. A symbol of ill omens and death. It sat on the back of the bench, walking across the top of the wood and hopping up onto Tim's arm. The bird was not alone. Another of its flock had landed on Tim's other arm, using it as an armrest—no pun intended. It flexed its wings and dug into its breast with its beak, scratching away at whatever itch had pulled away its attention. Another caw. A third black bird stood on the sidewalk at her feet, tilting its neck in different directions as its eyes stared at her.

The bird on the back of the bench called out several times, extending its neck and throat to get the most out of its vocalization. It blinked at her as it clicked its talons into the wood. Jude was unable to tear her gaze away. There was something hypnotic about the way the bird moved across the top of the bench. Something about the way it bobbed its neck and tilted its head at an angle a human could only dream of achieving.

As the bird crawled across Tim's arm and perched on his shoulder, she didn't look away. As it pecked at his hair to see if he would react, she couldn't look away. As beads of dark thick blood dribbled from his hairline, she should have looked away. When the black bird impaled its beak into Tim's left eye and the other birds cawed their enthusiasm and support, Jude stared. She couldn't look away... but she was able to scream.


## 54
# *Happy Camper*
+3 Days – 9:13am EST

Jude screamed.

She screamed until she squeezed tears from her eyes and felt the hot wetness down both cheeks. She was frozen to the left side of the bench, unable to get a message to her brain to escape from the atrocities of the black birds. When the screams tapered off to a throat-torn mewing sound, Jude realized the birds were gone. Tim was on the bench—still strapped in and dead. There was no blood seeping from his scalp and he still had both of his eyes.

She let out a ragged exhale. "Come on, Jude. Get a grip. Fucking dreams." She put her fingers through her tangled curly hair. She needed a shower. Her hair needed a bit of love with shampoo, conditioner and a brush. "Talking to yourself is the first sign of craziness." She looked at Tim. "Maybe that's why I've been sitting here with you. Can't use an earbud anymore to make people believe I'm talking to someone."

Jude laughed a little at the visual, but quickly tightened her lips into a grimace. She knew she had to get up from this bench and leave Tim behind. She had to get to her feet and start creating distance. As to where she was supposed to be heading, that was still a mystery. What wasn't a mystery was the symbolism of the dream's ravens. Tim was a rotting dead end. They had wanted her to see that—to understand. Pecking eyeballs out tended to get that point across.

Jude stood, surprised to find she had the strength in her legs to do so. Will wonders never cease? She touched her fingers to Tim's outstretch, but bound, wrist. "Thank you. Tim. Thank you for everything. Sorry I didn't treat you better. Sorry we couldn't make it farther together. It's probably better for you this way."

She didn't know what else to say. Even though they had just met, he had been a steadfast friend. That was probably because he didn't have any real notion of what she was like in real life. All he could have figured out about her in the past several hours was she was a gun-crazy lunatic with a quick temper. She let her fingers linger on his outstretched arms for a moment more before she turned away for good.

She needed supplies. Jude had to replace the food and the other necessities she had lost from the carjacking. The odds of finding a new Beretta and ammunition would be a longshot, but the rest should be easy enough to acquire. She walked to the intersection and turned right. There was a Chase Bank ATM set into a brick wall. Past that was a bridal boutique and a store with a dozen wicker baskets of varying sizes filled with paper and felt crafts. She wasn't wearing a wedding dress for the foreseeable future, both from a marital and a practical perspective. The baskets might be useful for Dorothy Gale to carry Toto around the yellow brick roads of Oz, but wouldn't be of any use to her. She walked toward the third storefront—its window filled with camping gear and, somehow, a kayak tipped up on an angle. It would probably have what she needed.

The door was locked. Jude made easy work of the barrier by employing the Tim's Stone Method of Unlawful Entry. The glass shattered. Jude made her way inside, careful not to let herself get snagged on any shards left in the frame. The front of the store had two round aluminum racks filled with thermal shirts and something called trekking pants. She quickly grabbed a couple of each in her size and tossed them on the counter next to the register. Next to go on the pile was a six-pack of white cotton tube socks. She also swapped out her ratty sneakers for a pair of hiking boots that actually fit. Huh... go figure.

Going behind the counter, she grabbed one of the backpacks from the hooks on the wall. She didn't want one with a frame, so she went with one similar to her old one. The clothes and her worn sneakers went into the main zippered pouch, the sneakers put in first to keep from dirtying the rest. Jude spied a display of CLIF protein bars. She dumped the entire tray in the pack. Yeah, she tended to go big or go home with trays of packaged snack food.

There were several knives in the counter display case. She tried to slide the back panel to the left. It was locked. She slipped her fingers behind it and gave it a hard yank. She slammed against the opposite wall, the dislodged panel still in her hands. The backpacks swayed above her, but didn't fall down on her head.

She set the panel aside and looked at the knives through the countertop glass. The first knife was a Swiss Army multi-tool. She put it on the counter. The next knife looked like a folded-up hacksaw, having a heavy handle and a serrated blade. The last knife she grabbed was nasty looking. It had an ergonomic grip and a loop for the forefinger. The end of the handle had a compass that unscrewed from the base. Inside were matches and a few band aids. The blade itself was serrated on the top edge, with a wicked curved edge for whatever may come her way. She pulled the sheath out and unbuckled her belt to slide it on. Once she buckled up again, she dropped the knife smoothly into its home.

She was as ready as she was going to be.

Wait. Not yet.

Under the register was a six-pack ring of bottled water. They had been there awhile, with only one bottle missing and the remaining five sealed. The water was nothing fancy. No flavors or carbonation added. They went into the top of the pack and the zipper was closed. She shrugged into the pack and was suddenly weighed down as she walked out from behind the counter. Yet, somehow, she felt lighter.

Her new socks and hiking boots crunched on the glass. Before leaving the store, she stopped suddenly and grabbed an Australian Outback style hat from a rack stationed beside the store window display. She set the hat on her head and looked in the attached rack mirror.

"It'll do," she said to herself. With a nod and a glance back at the ransacked store, Jude stepped out of the outfitter's store. She paused when she hit the sidewalk, letting her feet get comfortable in her new boots. "Which way, feet? Left or right?"

In the end, Jude didn't go in either direction. Instead, she crossed the empty street in pursuit of something else she had always been interested in.

**55**

## *You Better Put a Ring on It*

+3 Days – 9:29am EST

Jude wiggled her fingers. The warming sun flashed silver off four of them. Mom had never let her wear rings, having said they were too ostentatious—that she didn't want Jude to attract the wrong sort of attention. That had never stopped her father from checking in on her each morning. Jude doubted adding rings to the mix would have changed anything.

She shook her head of the thoughts and looked at the rings on her fingers. The cheap sterling silver bands made her happy. She didn't really know why, but they did. She liked the way the rings looked. She liked the way they felt. Their weight was almost non-existent, but strangely comforting. Maybe she would find more along the way.

Standing across the street from the outfitters store, she could see the broken glass door. She was leaving a trail of property damage in her wake. While she had been cursing out the person who had stolen her Bronco—correction, Nathan's Bronco—Jude had shown little compunction about tossing a rock through a store window to get what she wanted. She could always say she learned it from watching Tim. He had definitely been a bad influence on her. Although she shouldn't speak ill of the dead. Jude wondered if he was still dead... and if the bindings would hold. She hoped so because she wasn't going to go to the corner to find out.

She couldn't stay here, having already smashed through two storefronts to take stuff that didn't belong to her. She could spin it any way she wanted, but, in reality, she would be judged as a common thief. The odds the owners wouldn't bother to check in on their store or, better yet, be completely understanding about her breaking in were slim to none. Mostly, none. Shame and guilt flooded in. She was no better than those people she always judged as destructive and malicious.

She looked at her rings, tempted to take them off and toss them into the gutter. Instead, she hiked up her newly stolen backpack and moved away from Tim and the scene of the crimes. Only an idiot would stick around until the police arrived. They might not be as effective these days as they used to be, but Jude wasn't going to end up in a jail cell on the off-chance a cruiser decided to roll up next to her.

The retail block ended after four more stores. The cross street was a single lane road, curving into more wooded areas in both directions. The little downtown abruptly stopped; as if the shops were just movie set dressing set on a studio backlot. A hundred yards away from the winding road to her left, someone meandered toward her listing to one side with what looked like a club foot. The well-built man was not a movie extra. Jude knew better than to believe that, so she moved down the sidewalk in the opposite direction to a narrow alleyway behind the shops. She pulled out her newly found tactical knife from its scabbard and gripped it tight. Her muscles sang from the tension of waiting for the shambling thing to get to her.

For him to limp the length of a football field seemed to take forever. Finally, though, Jude heard his low growl. Then came the smell. Apparently, he hadn't been holed up in a curtain-drawn room waiting for the perfect time to reanimate. The air was filled with the rot of his sliced-open entrails and evacuated bowels. It smelled like an open cesspool on a hot day.

She covered her mouth and nose just as he came around the corner. He had caught her scent amidst his own odors. He snarled at her, blocking her only way of escape. She wasn't sure what her plan had been when she had ducked into the alley, even with the knife firmly in her hand.

The hulking muscular man lumbered toward her and she backed up a step to maintain a safe distance. He reached out with bare muddy arms. Her thigh hit an empty garbage can. It fell over, the lid popping off and clattering on the ground. As the noise distracted him, Jude drove the knife into his chest. It was as high as she could reach with any leverage. He wasn't distracted anymore. It was odd he didn't look at where the knife blade went in. Instead, he stared at her, gurgling and swiping his arms in front of him. Jude backed up, the knife now stuck between his ribs.

Fuck.

She turned and ran down the alley. The back doors to the shops were to her right. She didn't bother to try any of them. They were undoubtedly locked and wouldn't be opened by a simple rock's throw. The alley ended in a blank ten-foot tall brick wall. Who designed this place? All of the garbage cans were behind her... and behind Muscle Man. Jude grabbed a pallet leaning against a shop wall and dragged it to the end wall. It would make a good step ladder.

She scurried up the slats, her heart beating fast in her chest. As her right foot reached the top edge of the makeshift ladder, the weight in her pack counterbalanced and pull her backward. Jude found herself in midair. She landed hard, but not as hard as she thought. Muscle Man was under her, pinned by her weight. Ragged fingers scratched against the nylon of her pack. He had been the one who pulled at the backpack, causing her to fall.

Rolling off him was actually easier with the pack because her center of mass was higher. Jude managed to get her legs under her and pulled the knife out with her left hand at the same time. Sweet! She switched it to her right and, before she gave it any thought, drove the blade straight into Muscle Man's gaping mouth. He stopped floundering on the alley floor, his teeth settling against the blade with a click.

Jude dragged herself away and leaned against the angled pallet. She stared at Muscle Man for a while. The knife was still in his mouth. His limbs had stopped twitching. It would be easy enough to skirt past his body. Easy to escape to the entrance of the alley and to the rural road beyond. But, the same fatigue she had felt sitting on the park bench next to Tim—a lifetime ago—set into her bones again, making her eyelids too heavy to keep open. Maybe, if she was careful, she could just recharge here for a while on the pallet in the relative hidden safety of the alley. What was the chance another of these dead walkers would hap–

## 56
# *Blind Alley*
+3 Days – 10:23am EST

–sun had risen higher in the sky. It barreled straight through her eyelids, forcing Jude to squint away the spots from her vision. She reminded herself she would have to find a pair of sunglasses. *Find* was the operative word, since breaking into more shops wasn't sit well with her. It didn't matter if it was easier to steal what she needed from the closed stores. She needed to be a better person. Even if the world was descending into anarchy, she could, at least, ride up on the crest of a wave of morality on the incoming tide. It didn't change the fact she was still a hypocrite. Almost everything she owned was stolen. The only things she hadn't shattered glass to obtain had been taken from her anyway—the Bronco and the Vespa. Someone had stolen her Corolla when she needed it most. She was just returning the favor. Actually, if she still had her beater of a car, she might have never gotten off the bridge out of the city at all.

She didn't want to wake up. She just wanted a couple more minutes to shake the cobwebs out of her head. The nylon of the backpack felt comfortable against her cheek. She just wished people would stop kicking the bottom of her boots to wake her up.

She opened her eyes to thin slits, making sure she didn't blind herself in the sun. A woman crouched at her feet chewing on the leather of her boot tips. She tensed up her leg, ready to kick the woman away. She didn't follow through, though, because three men stood around the muscular man with the knife in his mouth. It was obvious they were dead—from the blood on their clothes to the massive tears in their skin and muscle. The blackened gums, red and cloudy eyes, and strange noises were also dead giveaways. No pun intended, again.

The woman was content to gnaw on the steel toe of Jude's hiking boot, not noticing Jude tensing up. The others didn't seem to realize Jude was there. Or, maybe, they were too pre-occupied with the blood pooling at their feet to be drawn away by her living flesh.

Story of her life.

Here she was, being slowly eaten by another woman, three brooding and unpredictable men standing behind her. Somehow, it was a ghoulish parallel to a college party she had gone to a few years ago. She had been told she couldn't go, but that hadn't stopped her. How she had extracted herself from that situation had involved patience and an overabundance of alcohol consumption. Jude doubted either of those would help her here. Patience would only allow this attentive woman more time to rend through the tip of her boot, and, perhaps, the others to notice her. Alcohol. Well, alcohol wasn't ever going to slow these things down.

What to do?

The long-haired brunette inched a hand up her pant leg. Yep. Just like at the college party. There was nothing within reach to defend herself with. She had her new backpack and the pallet. The knife was still in Muscle Man's mouth. She had nothing else to—

Idiot! She still had two more knives in the pack. The Swiss Army knife was a useful tool but wouldn't be effective against the four undead. The hacksaw would work much better... if she could get at it before the things started paying closer attention to her.

Jude never took her eyes off her new friends as she slipped her hand across the nylon. She felt around for the zipper to the main pocket, got her thumb and middle finger around the tab, placed her index finger against the teeth, and pulled. She did her best to muffle the noise coming from the moving zippers. Science and technology had yet to come up with a sound-proof design. The woman continued her tough meal. The men swayed and stared at each other. The pack opened one set of zipper teeth at a time, each one a booming click in Jude's ears.

After an eternity of clicking zipper teeth and watching the others click their own, Jude finally made a six-inch opening in the pack. She slipped her hand inside in search of the saw. She suddenly regretted packing the food and water on top. She slithered her fingers past the plastic and crinkling food wrappers.

The quartet of undead were starting to become more animated.

Finally, she felt the metal handle of the saw. Eureka! She grabbed it tightly and slipped it out through the opening. She was just in time, too, as the male alley-things had shuffled a couple feet toward her.

It didn't matter. Jude grinned as she held it in front of her as if it was Excalibur of King Arthur. Her sense of triumph faded when she couldn't flip open the foldable blade. She chanced a look down. There was a ring of plastic looped through the handle and blade to keep it from being opened before purchase.

"Shit," she whispered. She needed the army knife to unlock her saw. The woman looked up with cloudy eyes. Maybe, she didn't approve of Jude's choice of expletives. Her clothes were modest— long sleeved top and calf-length skirt—if that was any indication of her demeanor. Many times, the clothes did make the person. Everyone knew that. The modest woman was now focusing her eyes on Jude's. The others ventured another step toward her.

Her scary knife was down a dead corpse's throat. The Swiss Army knife was probably deep at the bottom of the backpack. The saw in her hand wouldn't be able to cut anyone.

She didn't have a plan. She needed a plan. What was the plan?

The alley-things moved closer. The female put her probing fingers on the interior of her left thigh. Anger bubbled up from somewhere deep inside, forcing Jude to let out a primal yell. The woman snarled back. Jude braced herself against the pallet and brought up both legs. The dead woman's fingers slid off the denim and slapped onto the alley floor, leaving her to look up at Jude. A second later, she caught the bottom of two boot treads in her face for her trouble. Her head snapped back at an obscene angle. There was a rubbery twang before the woman's face dropped to the asphalt.

Like Jimmy. Jude swallowed hard to keep her stomach contents where they were supposed to be. That was not the thought she wanted to focus on at the moment.

The remaining trio roared their venom for their two lost comrades and advanced on her. They blamed her for the bodies in the alley. Jude flung the backpack between the outstretched arms of the closest alley-thing. He was the tallest of the three and seemed to be their leader. It slapped him in the face and caught on one of his arms. He stopped. Jude didn't. She swung the folded saw at the man-bunned alley-thing to the right of the leader. She connected hard with the side of his face, but the blow only managed to stagger him sideways a step or two. The third and smallest walker was now blocked behind the other two. That wasn't the plan, but she'd take any advantage. Duck and weave. Attack and evade. Jude ran, but only after she stooped down to extract the big knife from Muscle Man's mouth.

They turned to give chase. The backpack dropped to the ground. The men were awkward in their muscle movements, but, like greyhounds chasing after the motorized rabbit, closed the distance behind her too quickly. Jude stuffed the saw into her back pocket. She pulled three stacked pallets down across the alleyway. Then, she turned around to face her pursuers. Just her and her big knife, a hat perfect for an Australian Outback movie, and a folded-up saw hanging comically from her back pocket.

The backpack sat in the middle of the alley behind the undead men lumbering toward her. It sat upright—in spite of the food and water being packed at the top—but leaned to one side in a sad and abandoned way. She decided she wasn't leaving it behind.

The strewn pallets were enough to force the walkers to a halt to figure out how to climb over the uneven wood slats. Apparently, memory and coordination weren't absolutes after death. Maybe they just needed incentive. "Come on, if you're coming."

They renewed their focus on her, climbing over the pallets without thought. Chief quickly dropped a foot between the slats. He twisted his ankle and fell forward to his hands and knees. Jude drove the big blade into the base of his neck before Chief had a chance to get up again. She gave the knife a quick twist before pulling it out in case the initial stab hadn't been enough.

"See?" She said to the remaining two, the blade dripping with dark, almost black, blood. "Easy."

Man-Bun stepped up onto the one level pallet. He was way more agile than Chief. Shit! Jude grabbed the handle of a nearby garbage can. Thank God it was empty. She swung it side-armed into the walker's head and shoulder. He stumbled into the wall, his foot now stuck between two of the pallet slats, as well. She swung the garbage can into the thing's head repeatedly. The aluminum twisted, denting more out of shape with each strike. She only stopped when she heard a noise to her right. The smallest one—the quiet one—had snuck up beside her before letting his position be known with an involuntary groan. She swung the aluminum can around square into the top of his head, making a funny thumming sound. Jude tossed the can back at Man-Bun before slitting the throat of Church Mouse.

"That'll teach you to sneak up on a girl!"

She kicked him in the chest, sending him into the white rear door to the outfitters' store. Before he could regain his balance, Jude drove the blade into his face, slitting his face in half from above the cupid's bow to below the bridge of the nose. He slid down the door.

"Hold on," Jude told him. "Wait. I need that." She wriggled the blade out of his face as he fell, straining her biceps and shoulders to extract the knife before Church Mouse hit the ground. "Damn. My back ain't up for all this strenuous shit. You know what I mean?" He didn't answer her, sliding to his side against the wall.

She looked at her handiwork. Chief and Church Mouse were no longer a problem. Man-Bun—the recipient of the repeated blows from the garbage can—stirred. His face was a bloody mess, his eyes not properly aligned anymore. He somehow still knew she was close. He swept out his arms in front of him, snapping his teeth and making a moaning noise that made her break out in goosebumps.

The backpack was several stores away. She walked down the alleyway to retrieve it. She shrugged into the pack once she put the saw back and zippered it closed. The woman was still face down, her skirt hitched up to her thighs. Oh, the scandal!

She returned to the barricade of pallets and bodies. Before she climbed over the wood, she paused long enough to push the Man-Bun's head forward and slip the blade into his neck. When his moaning stopped, she withdrew the blade, and wiped it on one of the only clean spots of his t-shirt. Once the blade was shiny again and back in its scabbard, she easily climbed over the pallets. "See?" she pointed out. "That's how you do it."

Jude wasn't tired anymore. She felt energized. Since she didn't know how long the feeling would last, she figured she better make the most of it. She exited the altogether too-crowded alley and turned left onto the narrow side road. She didn't have a new plan, but figured one would present itself when the time was right.

## 57
## *Inexpensive Luxury Cars*
+3 Days – 3:56pm EST

Jude's decision ended up being a time suck and a dead end. The road had ended in a cul-de-sac with three modest houses built around it. The Muscle Man had been walking from that direction so there wasn't a reason to believe the others couldn't have come from there, too. But, all of the houses had been locked up tight, so the odds were she was wrong about that assumption, too.

She had then returned to Route 2 and walked in a westerly direction, not seeing any other people—alive or undead. It was disconcerting she was on a highway without coming across at least one other person. She had dispatched the four undead things in the alley, but that had been hours ago. Apparently, the only other living person had been the Bronco thief. Just her luck.

Massachusetts Route 2 had become George W. Stanton Highway somewhere along the way. It was as barren of life as the town where she had left Tim bound to the bench. There were cars and trucks on the road to prove there had been life there before now. Most of them were parked on the soft shoulders. The rest were left in the middle of the lanes. A few of them were completely abandoned and left open. There were people inside all of the others. They all looked like they were sleeping. She had checked on several of them, tapping on the windows in an attempt to get the occupants' attention. But, they weren't sleeping. They were dead, just like Tim had been dead.

Entire families—with roof racks, trunks, and back seats full of supplies, survival gear and empty water bottles. They had packed all of the precious memories too heavy to carry on one's back if on foot.

226

Every one of them were slumped against the door frames or head rests as if they had all just been too tired to drive even just one more minute.

She stopped on the side of the westbound lanes. A somewhat hidden elevated sign had an Olive Garden emblem—where she bet they used to treat people like family. Under that was a Best Buy sign and, most importantly, a Dick's Sporting Goods. She stepped between the bumpers of two cars and ended up tapping her fingers on the guardrail. The parking lots were difficult to see through the tree line, but there was plenty of empty blacktop still visible.

Did she need to go down there? What was she in search of? People? More supplies? Another mode of transportation? She looked through the windshield of the Lincoln Town Car to her right. The man behind the tinted glass in the driver's seat had his hands on the top of the steering wheel with his head leaning on them. He didn't have any answers for her, either. Nobody seemed to have any answers these days.

She turned around and sat on the guardrail. She leaned forward so the weight of the pack didn't overbalance her and send her careening backward into the brush and gravel. Her hands dropped between her legs, suddenly too heavy to be of much use. Hours had passed and she had forced herself to keep up a healthy walking pace along the way. She felt how the man in the Lincoln looked.

Why had she walked the whole way? There had to be better ways to travel. Of course, knowing where she was supposed to be going probably would have helped, too. It wasn't as if Tim's brother's place would have a highway sign with an arrow leading to it. But, somehow, the idea there was a well-provisioned remote farm somewhere had kept her going. If she stayed on the highway going west, she was going to end up in the middle of downtown Fitchburg.

227

That was going to be anything but remote. Towns meant people. People meant undead people.

The man in the Lincoln kept drawing her attention. Maybe it was the way he looked as sleepy as she felt. She tapped her fingers together before rocking back to her feet. The pins and needles in her butt and thighs were an indication she needed to keep moving.

Jude walked over to the driver's door of the sedan, pulled the knife with one hand and grabbed the handle with the other. She took a deep breath and opened it. The driver lunged out of the car at her as soon as the door was opened. She jumped back in surprise as he fell to the pavement. He hadn't been wearing his seatbelt. He wasn't undead—just dead.

The smell assaulting her from the car was almost worse than the dead driver at her feet. It was a thick flowery scent, invading her mouth and nose every time she inhaled. The overpowering lavender tones became a taste as it stuck to her tongue and coated her throat. She exhaled sharply through her nose, but the lavender had already taken up residence in her sinus cavities. Jude gagged and stepped away from the Lincoln, unable to take in any fresh air. Her stomach clenched. Retreating to the inside median, Jude hunched over the guardrail and retched into the gravel. Chunks of half-digested granola and drooling streams of energy drink mixed with the stones. Purple spittle clung from her lips. She spat out what she could before wiping her lips and chin with her sleeve.

Jude chanced a look over her shoulder. Lincoln Man was still laying on the road. He hadn't become one of the reanimated dead things. Tim hadn't turned into one of those things, either. Nor had so many of the people in their steel coffins along Route 2. Jude spat once more before straightening up and walking back to the Lincoln. The flowery smell had dissipated, but still lingered in the air around the black sedan. Jude sheathed the knife before pulling the driver back past the trunk.

She returned to the open door, pulled her shirt collar over her mouth and nose, and dropped onto the plush leather bucket seat. There were no keys in this expensive model, replaced by a push-start button. She took a chance and pressed it. Nothing happened. She pressed the button again. Still nothing. The disappointment of the Lincoln not starting—plus the near-overpowering smell of flowers still getting through the fabric of her shirt—clouded her vision with fresh tears. Cars are not this fucking difficult to start!

Getting out of the car, Jude pulled down the collar and let out a yell of frustration. She kicked the back tire. Ouch! Fucking Lincoln driver. She kicked him in the ass, instead.

Chink.

Jude pulled back for another anger-filled hit, but hesitated. Chink? What made that sound? Coins and keys did. He still had the keys in his pocket. She was so stupid! Ugh!

She crouched down and fished through his front pockets, trying not to think about anything else in there. Is that a banana in your pocket? She didn't think rigor mortis included such things, but she hurriedly found the Lincoln's fob amid spare change and some breath mints without having to make excuses for anything else her finger brushed against.

Gripping the fob tight, Jude returned to the driver's seat and hopped in, tossing her pack onto the passenger's side amid several empty bottles of flavored water. Maybe one of them had spilled. She pressed the ignition button again. Still nothing! What the fuck? She took a deep flowery breath—which almost made her gag again—and tried to think. Who did she know with a car with a push start ignition? Nobody, that's who.

Think!

She had to keep one foot on the clutch and the other on the brake when she started the Bronco. Her hand had to be on the brake lever on the Vespa. There was no clutch in this Lincoln. Maybe, she needed to have a foot on the brake here, too, even if it was in Park. She tested the theory and pushed her right foot on the left pedal. When she pressed the ignition button, the car came to life. The luxury-level motor purred and the dash display lit up with wonderful blue and orange colors. She powered down the windows before closing the driver's door. It was almost an instinct to grip the leather steering wheel as tightly as she did. Her lips pulled up on one side of her mouth in a satisfied smirk.

She was ready to make up some miles.

She backed up a couple feet in order to pull out without bumping into the station wagon parked in front of her. Suddenly, a large, loud and bright blue vehicle roared past. The cobalt paint and chrome sparkled in a brilliant high-definition blur in the afternoon sun as the vehicle drove at a recklessly high rate of speed west on the highway.

Nathan's Bronco! She had the quickly-receding truck in her sights. She slammed the shifter into Drive and pressed the accelerator. Gravel under the tires pinged off the grille of the car behind her. The front bumper screeched off of the station wagon's bumper. It didn't matter. Catching the car thief was top on her list of to-dos. In fact, it was the only thing on her list.

**58**
## *A Merry Chase*
+3 Days – 4:19pm EST

The Lincoln had amazing acceleration and horsepower. And, it was all at Jude's disposal. She was lucky the highway was relatively clear. At her current rate of speed, if any vehicles were angled out too far from the shoulder she knew she didn't have the driving skills to avoid clipping them and careening out of control. She clicked in her seat belt with one hand as a precaution, not taking her eyes off the blue truck a mile ahead of her.

Trees blurred by her on the shoulder and from the center median. Green and brown foothills rose up from the plains in the distance, the Bronco still a blue dot in front of her. Three exits for Leominster were coming up. The Bronco never wavered from the dotted white line between lanes. It swerved once to keep from hitting a Volkswagen Beetle broken down in the left lane. The shoulder was narrow there. The blur of green from the grassy median disappeared on the left side, replaced with gray concrete and closer eastbound lanes. The Lincoln's dashboard speedometer clocked Jude going 90mph. The Bronco was going just as fast... or faster. The carjacker couldn't be aware of her chasing them, or they would have tried harder to evade her. Just wait until she got her hands on them.

"You'll be sorry you ever stole from me, muthafucka." Her heart seethed with anger and her brain filled with all of the atrocities perpetrated on her. This was just the latest in a long list of shit she had survived. The rational part of her brain was carted away in chains to the back of her mind. Getting to the Bronco was her only focus.

George W. Stanton Highway merged with Interstate 190. The Bronco jetted through the interchanges. Jude pressed the accelerator to the floorboard, the numbers on the dash cycling through the 90s and low 100s. A beautiful blue reservoir popped up and stretched out on the left. A huge park or greenbelt could be seen through the trees on the right. The highway crossed a river.

Suddenly, the Bronco slammed on its brakes and skidded to the right as it reached the next exit. Its oversized tires squealed again as it drifted through the bottom of the ramp, skidding right as it turned left under the highway. Ironically, it had led them back to Main Street—the same street in just a different town. It accelerated again past several houses until it braked and slid left onto a side street out of sight. Jude heard a choppy noise as the knobby tires skipped across the asphalt.

The Bronco disappeared for a frantic moment until Jude accelerated to narrow the distance and turned onto the side street. The truck passed several cross streets with interconnected grassy areas filled with stones. At the last cross street, the truck skidded to a bumpy stop in the grass filled with smaller stones. The other side of the field was lined with thick copses of trees forming a dense rounded perimeter. Someone fell out of the Bronco before they picked themselves up and retreated away from the vehicle and into the grass.

Now was her chance. She wasn't going to let this asshole get away again. No fucking way! Jude braked the Lincoln to a sliding stop behind the Bronco. She got out and zeroed in on the stumbling and retreating thief as he weaved his way through lines of tall granite markers. She suddenly stopped to take in her surroundings, finally realizing their chase had led them into a cemetery.

Fuck it. She had dealt with enough death over the last few days. What was a few hundred more dead bodies going to do to change that? She pulled her knife and chased after the thief, hell-bent on getting vindication in spite of being in a field of the dead.

## 59
# *Plots*
+3 Days – 4:34pm EST

The thief staggered through the headstones toward a massive tree standing in the middle of this section of grass. The plots had been lined up around it years ago. He grabbed a few of the larger granite markers to keep his balance as he plodded toward it. Jude slowed down, easily able to walk faster than the thief was staggering about on his own. This was going to be too easy. He didn't even realize she had pursued him. A knife to the throat and he would quickly give up the keys to the Bronco.

The thief was definitely a male. His broad shoulders on his slight frame gave it away. He wore a ball cap and an oversized hoodie. The gray track pants were too big on him. He bunched them up with one fist to keep them from falling down.

Suddenly, he dropped to the ground in front of a granite marker with a cross carved out of its top. He crawled the last couple of feet to a dried-up bouquet of flowers set into a bronze vase on a placard at the base of the gravestone. Jude slowly approached. She made sure to leave at least one row of markers between them, while still being able to hear him.

"...leave without saying goodbye," he muttered, his hand outstretched toward the marker. He couldn't quite reach the stone, waving his fingers in an effort to close the distance. "Jacob and Annabel are with you now. Take care of them... like you always did." He coughed several times. It was a wet cough, filled with phlegm from the bottom in his lungs.

Jude stepped between two headstones to get a better view of what he was doing. He lay there, still reaching out for the marker. *Here lies Amanda Ritchie*, was carved on the face of the granite. *Beloved wife taken too soon*, the carving continued on a second line, with *Mother of two beautiful children* on a final third row. Jude swallowed hard, her throat closing up a bit and her stomach churning. The dates on the marker made Amanda Ritchie twenty-seven at the time of her death last year. Her grip may have slackened on the knife, but only a little.

"I tried to protect them, Mandy," the thief said. "I could... couldn't get away in time... time to get back to them. To get them to you. But... they're with you... now they are."

He turned over on his back. The front of his hoodie was covered in mud and drying blood. He hadn't been trying to keep his sweatpants up, but was trying to keep his exposed guts inside. He looked up at the sky, his eyes darting between the shapes of the white puffy clouds. Jude approached with purpose, the knife at her side with a renewed grip. This asshole had stolen from her, after all.

She stopped when he glanced over at her. If he had registered her, it was only for a moment because he quickly returned his gaze up at the sky. "I couldn't make it in time." Jude wasn't sure if he was talking to her or not, so she remained where she was with ten feet between them. His breathing became more labored and wheezy. "I tried. You know?"

Jude crouched down, deciding to lean against the back of an adjacent marker. He blinked away the glaze over his eyes and let the tears fall into the grass. Jude rested her arms and the knife on her bent knees. The anger fueling her during her high-speed pursuit was slowly dissipating. Instead, all that was left was a smattering of sympathy slowly mixing into the kettle pot of pity. She was sad for his loss. She could empathize for the loss of his wife and children. He had needed to protect himself and his family? She had done too many questionable things to judge what he had done. Her anger had fueled her through her long walk, the high-speed car chase, and the stumbling pursuit through this cemetery. Now, she was just tired again. Jude vowed to Amanda Ritchie, beloved wife and mother of two beautiful children, that she would take care of Mr. Ritchie when the time came.

## 60
## *Final Words*
+3 Days – 6:41pm EST

The sun was skirting the tops of the trees on the other side of the cemetery. Mr. Ritchie's breathing remained labored and he, at times, forgot she was there at all. Her ass had fallen asleep, the backs of her thighs regaling her with sharp needles every time she shifted her position against the back of the head stone. The knife never left her hand, her fingers being another part of her body that had cramped up some time ago.

"Did you see it?" Mr. Ritchie asked nobody in particular. Jude didn't reply, his ramblings to the sky having caught her embarrassingly answering his rhetorical questions a couple times already. He took in a ragged breath in and turned his head toward her. Their eyes met.

235

"Did you see it start?" His brows furrowed and he swallowed hard. While his mouth moved, nothing else came out. He cleared the phlegm from his throat and worked it down. A wet cough resulted, causing him to grimace and clench at his belly.

"Not long now," Jude told him in a whisper. Jude flexed her fingers around the knife handle.

"I know," he replied to her.

"You see me?"

"Yes." He blinked, nodding his head in a very deliberate manner. "Did you see?"

"See what?" Jude asked. At least she could distract from his physical misery.

"The end." The words drifted off and he chuckled painfully at the sound of them. Maybe, he liked the way they rolled off the tongue.

"We lost power and, eventually, phones," Jude told him. "People started dying... and coming back." The words flowed out of her like the powder of a bitter pill. She had seen so much death. She had caused so much death. God knows what Mr. Ritchie had seen.

He nodded and squeezed his eyes tight, tears sliding down his cheek. His arms flopped to the grass. Jude sat up straighter. She gripped her knife tight. Her muscles were not happy with her inactivity for the past couple of hours, but this might be the moment she had been waiting for. Finally, his fingers gripped a handful of grass. "Same... for me and the kids."

She barely comprehended what she had endured at home with her parents and brothers. To have two smaller children going through the same... to live through the loss of their mother and then die in what Jude assumed had been a terrible manner? She shook the thought of Mr. Ritchie's kids away quickly as it tried to congeal into a terribly graphic fantasy in her head. Instead, she tried to console him with one of the typical tropes. "They're in a better place."

"With mom."

"Yeah." Jude didn't tell him her thoughts on the practicality of an afterlife. Sure, she had been raised Catholic, but organized religion had done little to salve the wounds caused by her struggles in life. She still believed in a power greater than herself, but it certainly wasn't the Christian God. In death, maybe all the gods would end up being the same, regardless of what people called them. "They are in a better place, for sure." And, better off to exit a world where the dead had come back to life to eat them.

He didn't reply, going back to shallow breathing in an effort to stave off his body giving out on him. It might still be a while before he died, as the human body was an amazing engine of survival. Now, though, her adrenaline had all but bled off, leaving her shocky and bone-weary. At some point, Jude would have to get up. She didn't want her circulation to be pooling in the wrong places and her limbs asleep when Mr. Ritchie finally did decide to leave this mortal coil.

## 61
### *Graveside Chat*
+3 Days – 8:58pm EST

Mr. Ritchie expired a couple hours ago by her calculation. She hasn't been able to bring herself to put a blade in his head on top of where his wife was laid to rest. The sun disappeared a while ago, leaving the grass a deep forest green minutes away from becoming a bruised purple. In contract, the headstones were near luminous,

237

their carved stone bodies glowing bone white like teeth out of blackened gums.

She figured Mr. Ritchie would turn. It was a strange feeling, but he had a different aura— akin to a low hum from a power transformer —about him. She didn't prescribe to the mumbo jumbo of Dionne Warwick's Psychic Friends Network commercials or the *Long Island Medium* program Mom had enjoyed watching. It was just like Tim had felt. An empty husk—dead weight to rot away on a sidewalk bench. Mr. Ritchie, though, still had a strange crackle about him as he lay there with his eyes glazed over and locked onto the night sky.

"Stars are starting to come out." A familiar gravelly voice broke the silence of the night. Jude didn't like its familiarity. It filled her with both love and dread.

"It's going to be a beautiful night. A great night for flying. Remember when we went up that one night. Boy, Clinton sure got mad when we added another half hour to the flight time. Remember?"

She glanced to her left. A younger version of her Dad sat against the next headstone, his knees bent up to his chest and his hands folded on top of them. He wasn't the father-thing she had put down a couple days ago. He was the dad she had loved from his days of sobriety. "I remember, Dad."

He looked up at the sky, his eyes darting to the different constellations glowing brighter by the minute. He did finally shift his gaze to her. "I'm sorry."

"For what?" Jude swallowed hard, sudden emotions bubbling up in her throat.

"For being a terrible father." He kept looking at the sky, his head resting against the stone. "I could give you a ton of excuses about

why I am the way I am… about why I acted the way I did, but…"
He shook his head. "I tried to be better… tried to wrestle the demons
inside me. It was just too easy to fall back to earth with clipped
wings than to scratch and claw my way back to the clouds."

"An angel? You think you're ever close to heaven?" Jude's
voice betrayed her seething venom. "Ever?"

Jude's father smiled, but it wasn't one of scoff or mirth. The
upturned corners of his lips were laden with the weight of an
immense sadness. His eyes showed his understanding of his
ignorance and lack of self-control which had both caused her much
pain. "Maybe once… a long time ago."

"Before I came around," Jude spat out. "That's for sure."

"That's not true," her father said. "I loved you with all my
heart."

"You sure had a fucked-up way of showing it, didn't ya?"

He pondered her comment in silence while her ire boiled hotter
with each passing second. Her heart thumped in her ears. Her skin
tingled with a rekindled hatred. She was just about to unload a few
choice expletives about his parental behavior when he finally spoke
up again.

"Right actions in the future are the best apologies for bad
behaviors in the past, right?" He stopped a moment to compose
himself. "Tryon Edwards said that. Not sure where I read it." He
shrugged. "I don't have a future left to make up for what I did to
you, Jude. I can only hope for your understanding that I did the best
I could in this body." He held out his rough calloused hands, palms
up, and looked at them. "I was never perfect."

"Not even close," Jude said, her own eyes gazing at the stars her
dad had taught her about as a kid.

He looked from his hands to her face, slowly getting his large frame up on his knees to face her. He held out his hands to her. The sobriety coin glimmered in his right hand. "Please remember the times when I tried the hardest to be the father you deserved."

Jude's anger fell away when she saw the coin again, sinking into the hallowed earth. She hoped those at rest under her would finally leech the hatred away for good. She went to him. The hug she gave him was strong and tight—filled with the right kind of love between a parent and a child. He hugged her back just as tight and didn't let her go.

## 62
# *Reunions*
+3 Days – 9:11pm EST

She felt comforted by her dad's hug and apology. She leaned her head on his shoulder. His breath wasn't laced with alcohol. His flannel shirt didn't stink like it had been left overnight at the rim of a sooty chimney. Instead, he smelled of cedar chips and a hint of mint. Maybe, that's what the afterlife smelled like. She finally broke free from her side of the hug. Her dad continued to hold her tight.

"Okay, Dad," Jude said, patting him on the back. "Time to let me breathe. Okay?"

He paid her no mind.

"Come on, Dad." He wouldn't let her go. "I said to let go!"

She pulled back from her father. It wasn't her father anymore. She should have known better! She should have realized the aroma of cedar and mint would never be her father's scent. But, it was probably a smell Amanda Ritchie had become accustomed to when she was alive and happily married.

While she had been dozing and reconnecting with her dead father, Mr. Ritchie had come back from the dead. He chomped toward her neck, still too uncoordinated and clumsy to have a handle on his newly activated body. His head lopped to one side, his teeth missing her skin by mere inches.

She pushed her hands against his chest, managing to get a few more inches between them. His grip was painfully strong as his fingers dug into her back. She arched back as far as she could. Mr. Ritchie eyed her bare wrist. He snapped at it, his neck unable to bend that far.

He had at least twenty pounds on her and an endless, tireless undead strength. Hers was already flagging. She was quickly eating through her reserves. Her heart raged in her ears as the last of her available adrenaline pumped through her veins, but her muscles were quickly tiring.

Jude managed to get a foot under her. His hug was still a vise grip; his arms like unbendable steel as he dragged to his own feet. His still white teeth were getting closer to her face. Saliva shined off them. Or, maybe they looked whiter because his gums were getting darker? A gravelly purr vibrated from his throat. His red and golden-flecked eyes darted wildly at all the exposed parts of her body.

"My eyes are up here, asshole," she growled back at him. She gritted her teeth and shoved him. Even her anger-fueled muscles didn't budge him. Their embrace became a stiff-armed tug-of-war. The tendons in her neck stood out as they danced. Her legs tried for leverage, but she couldn't get a solid purchase on the grass and dirt. She felt the rock under the tread of her boot a split-second before she slipped on it and fell backward. Mr. Ritchie pitched forward at the waist, snapping at her face and biting down.

She crashed hard to the ground. Turning her aching head and feeling a shooting pain all the way down her spine, Jude's nose almost touched the edge of one of the headstones. Mr. Ritchie's fingers loosened. He had indeed bitten down hard, but not into her. The angle of the fall had sent him careening off target. He was still above her, but his teeth had been broken off on a protruding cherub carved on the granite marker next to her. His back arched back up in such a way the baby angel was the only thing holding him up. He had *curbed* himself—essentially killing himself by inadvertently driving his teeth into his brain.

Jude slipped out from under him, not wanting to touch him any more than she had to. She crawled away to the next headstone and leaned against it to catch her breath. She thumped her head against the cold stone, silently cursing herself for falling asleep and failing in her promise to Mr. Ritchie. Based on the grossly flexible man hanging lifeless by his mouth on the head of a baby angel, Jude could still argue she had fulfilled her promise to him, anyway. Next time around, she wouldn't hesitate or become distracted. Patting the knife in its scabbard at her hip, she promised herself she would make sure the dead didn't get have a chance to get up again.

She needed to get a grip. She needed to get her sleeping patterns in order. Yeah, she had walked a long way. True, she had held vigil over Mr. Ritchie for a few more hours on top of that. Her physical and mental stress levels had reached an all-time high. For the last few days, Jude had been skating by and staying alive on luck she didn't believe she had. Her alleged luck wouldn't last forever.

**63**
## *Laughter is the Best Medicine*
+3 Days – 9:34pm EST

Jude left Mr. Ritchie the way he was. She couldn't bring herself to pull him off and drag him over to his wife's grave to pay proper respects. She had had enough of dealing with the frailty between life and death for one day. Instead, she wandered away between the headstones. She reached her fingertips out to touch the cold marble and granite, lightly brushing against the stone markers standing as testaments to how families chose to immortalize their departed kin. She wondered whether the people buried under the tombstones had been deserving of the carved praise. Jude was sure Mom would have asked to have her father's headstone carved with all sorts of lofty platitudes. She couldn't think of any at the moment except, *Did the best he could in the body he was given.* Otherwise, her head was too foggy to think about anything more than putting one foot in front of the other.

The black Lincoln was right where she had left it, the driver's door wide open. The interior was dark, but the luxury-class driver's bucket seat was like a siren's song beckoning her to sit in it. The support it gave her aching butt muscles and throbbing lower back when she did so was heavenly. So much better than trying to climb up into the Bronco's cab. Grappling with the undead after sitting against an unyielding chunk of granite definitely wasn't conducive to proper spinal alignment. She would have to keep that in mind for future reference—if she found herself in a similar situation.

Jude chuckled as she thought about the absurdity of the last few days. It was an uncomfortable and strange sound in her ears, but she couldn't stop once she started. She covered her mouth to stifle the teetering laughter, her fingers unable to contain it. So, she stopped trying. The laughter caught a jagged edge and turned to wails. Hot tears streamed down her face. A snot bubble popped in her nostril, oozing to her upper lip. She didn't care. She had been through worse than runaway emotions since the start of the week.

The brother she loved was dead in the apartment. Her entire family was dead in the apartment. Even though she had been on the verge of moving out from under the tyrannical jack heel of her parents, her entire life had revolved around them. She had been teased as an outcast at school, never truly having found a circle of friends to rally behind her. She had been cruelly teased about having a crippled brother. She had been the butt of jokes about her early and lanky growth spurts. Nobody had talked or acted the way she did. But, she had been part of a family. She was a Sawyer. Now, she was the last Sawyer.

Jude was free now… free from the rules of her parents… free from her father's advances and her mother's blind eye. She could completely reinvent herself… and the idea of it scared the shit out of her. The idea of steering her own course terrified her. There would be nobody to catch her when she fell. There would be nobody to correct her mistakes or bail her out of jams. She would be responsible for every decision and have to take responsibility for the consequences of her actions. The weight of all of it made her all the more weary and exhausted.

With only the light from the rising moon to illuminate the top of the dashboard, Jude wondered if she had the strength in her to go on. Crickets and frogs in the wooded areas around the cemetery started up their own songs of survival, filling the night with something more uplifting than the quiet and indecisive voices battling in her head.

Silence was only golden when one wasn't constantly being betrayed by one's own mind.

Ironically, even the crickets and frogs' songs became too loud before long, forcing Jude to close the door to muffle them in favor of the lingering scent of lavender. The questioning voices in her head could be heard over nature's din, again. Jude knew she needed something else to distract her brain, so she stepped on the brake pedal and pressed the ignition button.

The Lincoln did not respond. She patted her pockets. The key fob was still there. She hadn't lost it in all of the commotion. She made sure the car was in Park. Yep. She stepped on the brake pedal. Check. She pressed the ignition button again. Check. The Lincoln failed to comply. No check. The Lincoln didn't bother to give her any indication of why it was being an asshole. No faint dinging or clicking noises. No flickering dashboard warning lights. Jude cracked open the door. The dome light didn't come on. Fuck! She had drained the already taxed battery by leaving the door open for however many hours she had been with the Ritchie family.

She let out a tired sigh, getting out of the sedan and walked over to the truck—Nathan's trusty cobalt blue and chrome-lined Bronco. As she got to within ten feet of the truck, she noticed the smell of gas. She couldn't see it, but it was heavy enough in the air for her to almost choke on the fumes. Jude crouched down to look at the undercarriage. She didn't need to be a car care professional to note Mr. Ritchie had driven up and over several short grave markers, ripping a long tear into the bottom of the gas tank. Great. One car with no battery life and a truck with no gas. Stepping away from the cloying gas fumes, Jude returned to the Lincoln.

What to do? Sleep. First on the list. She couldn't think much farther than that. As soon as she zeroed onto the idea of shutting down, her body ached for it. Sleep was such a welcoming concept. She would get some rest in the comfy interior of the Town Car and figure everything out in the morning.

Tackle the battery swapping in the morning. It should be easy. Ford and Lincoln were the same car company. A good night's sleep, some morning sunlight, and a fresh perspective would be just what she needed to get back on track. Everything would be better in the morning.

## 64
# *Famous Last Words*
+4 Days – 6:46am EST

The hope for a better day once the sun had come up again was quickly squashed. The batteries looked like they would be compatible, but it was hard to tell since getting them swapped was going to be near impossible in the current situation. It had been easy enough for Jude to get under both hoods and wriggle her fingers to the terminals of both batteries. The problem was neither vehicle had any tools helpful to scrape out all of the built-up corrosion around each post or, even, pop off the terminals themselves. Not even a flathead screwdriver in the center console, glove compartment, or trunk. She had even looked around for any tools a Neanderthal would have found useful for dealing with their own car trouble, but broken headstones and dry twigs weren't going to get the job done.

Sunlight and sleep. What bullshit to think the passage of time and a bright morning sky would give her the answers on a silver platter. She was still exhausted. Her broken sleep and the stress of having to do something she was unfamiliar with had made her focus a bit dull. She knew she could figure it out, but her brain had always been her worst enemy. Maybe, she had more of her father in her than she wanted to admit. She tapped her fingers on the radiator of the Lincoln, racking her brain for a magical solution to her dilemma. She guessed she could use the tactical—

A growl came from her left. Jude peeked around the edge of the raised car hood. A new member of the undead club bumped off one of the tall granite stones, spinning a little bit before he found his balance again. He craned his head. Did he just sniff the air? He looked straight at her, his eyes a milky gray. Yep. He was hunting her down like a coon dog. She pulled her shirt up to her nose and sniffed it and the musk coming off her skin. Yeah, she could definitely use a shower.

The man approached, decked out in work boots, coveralls, and a T-shirt boasting both yellow sweat stains and a patch of blood from a slash in the throat. When he staggered against the front passenger door, Jude moved right. The raised hood blocked his view. He seemed confused when he reached the front bumper and didn't find her standing there. At least, that was the impression Jude got as she crept around the back of the sedan and rushed along the passenger side.

She pulled the tactical knife and launched herself around the front bumper. The blade led the way, gleaming as the sun reflected off its edge. It was a pretty image ruined when the knife point careened off one of his vertebrae and came out through the existing gash in his neck. He turned and snarled, swiping her with his left hand. Jude was overbalanced from her attack, smacking into the grille and flailing across the cold and useless engine. The knife bounced off the top of the motor head, but she gripped it tight. She wasn't going to lose it again. The gardener-thing grabbed at her, his hands snagging on the side of her shirt. Her knuckles had gone white from holding the knife. The adrenaline was flowing again. She swung the blade around with surprisingly perfect timing. The gardener-thing had been rearing up, trying to pull her up with him. The blade impaled him through his right ear. All the way to the hilt. Damn. That was a lot of blade in there.

He fell backward from his own momentum. His weight pulled her square on her feet, but her grip on the knife threatened to drag her down on top of him. She grabbed the edge of the car frame. Now, she was the proverbial rope in a game of tug-o-war between the car and the knife blade in the gardener-thing's head. Finally, her grip prevailed as the blade slid out. She held the weapon up in triumph.

"Take that, sucka! Yeah!" She gyrated in a strange imitation of a victory dance, gloating over another dead body. She even pointed the knife at the gardener-thing, daring him to get up for another round against her. Jude guessed the joy of survival and the pumping of fresh adrenaline sometimes did strange things to a person. After her dance ran its course, she looked around her to make sure there weren't more ambulatory dead people around. She was in a cemetery. What better place to find dead people, right?

Luckily, she was alone again. She exhaled and leaned against the grille. Just her and another dead body at her feet. Just her and two non-functioning vehicles that would work great if she had the tools to swap engine accessories. Just her and a knife still dripping with some near-black goo she assumed was blood. She stared at it. The goo was pretty gross. Without thinking, she crouched down and wiped both sides of the knife on the gardener-thing's overalls, making the blade shine before balancing it between the top of the radiator and the fan housing.

She was the only living person in a field of the dead, both above and below the earth. The gasoline smell in the air closer to the ground was still potent, reminding her the vehicles were dead—worthless hunks of metal, plastic and rubber. The smell was nauseating. Her heartbeat was echoing in her eardrums. She couldn't quite catch her breath. Her hands were shaking. She needed to get away.

She rushed out to the road, the cracks in the asphalt too dark and too deep. The stray gravel seemed like boulders to be climbed over. The gasoline smell was not as strong here, so she kept walking away from the vehicles with the hope the nausea would go away. She was wrong. She bent over a tombstone on the other side of the road and dry-heaved. All that came out was a mewing cry and long strings of drool. She retched again, nothing coming up since she hadn't eaten solid food in a while. The dry-heaving left her with a pounding headache, dizziness added to it when she tried to stand again.

Fuck. She felt like shit warmed over—again.

Jude hadn't noticed any buildings on the grounds when she and the late Mr. Ritchie drove in—raced in, actually. She hadn't even realized they had been in a cemetery at all until she'd practically slammed into a headstone following Mr. Ritchie.

She peered across the lawns. Two white buildings were nestled in a crescent-shaped line of trees on the far end of the property—close to where they had entered from the main road. One had a portico and a set of double doors. She figured one was the office. Right of the office was a flat-roofed, white-painted concrete block workshop. It lacked any design esthetic other than being a box with a roll-up door on one side and a windowless door on another. There weren't even any bushes around it to give it curb appeal—or, at the very least, landscaping to camouflage it from view.

The smell of gasoline from the Bronco carried over to her on a puff of breeze, sending her into another fit of dry-heaves. She tried to gulp in fresh air after her stomach settled again, her belly desperately clenching from the fumes. She shuffled across the road to put more distance between her and the pool of slowly evaporating fuel.

The garage would definitely have the tools she needed to get the batteries swapped. Something sharp to scrape the corrosion off the terminals. Something with a long metal edge to pry the terminals up to be able to haul the battery out. Maybe, she would even find a filtered face mask.

She followed the road toward the buildings, leaving her saliva to dry at the base of the tombstone. The gravel on the road's shoulder crushed under her boots. It had a nice rhythmic sound to it, similar to walking on the frozen top crust of freshly fallen snow. The sound calmed her. The crunch reminded her of a time in her life as white as the buildings slowly getting bigger in the distance, the sound flooding her brain with a lost-forgotten memory of simpler days... better days.

## 65
# *One Horse Open Sleigh*
January - Sometime long ago

*"You okay back there?"*

*Jude held on for dear life, her little hands gripping the big side rails of the sled. It was hard to hold on. The mittens her mommy made her wear kept slipping and the stretchy clips to her sleeves made her look dorky. Her back pressed into the seat back of the sled, causing her legs to flop around. Her hand-me-down boy boots from Andy were too big for her feet. They weren't great for snow, either. Mommy made her wear stupid bread bags over her socks so her feet didn't get wet. Another reason to feel dumb. The rope at the front lifted higher, making the sled do a wheelie.*

*"Wee!" Jude giggled. She looked up at the hulk of a man pulling her around in the snow. His feet made a silly crunching sound. He was probably stomping around in the snow banks on purpose. He was covered head-to-toe in the tan puffy coveralls he always wore to work. His body was so wide, his shoulders just as wide.*

*He wore a knit hat Mommy had made for him. He wasn't really a fan of it. He had told her that once and made her swear to keep it a secret. But he always told Mommy how nice it looked and how happy it made him. Each time, if Jude was around, he'd tell Mommy these things and then give Jude a smile and a wink when Mommy's back was turned. She would always giggle.*

*"Hold on!" Daddy turned his head so Jude could see that same wink and smile. She gave him a big grin back. Daddy couldn't see it because he had bundled her scarf tight around her head and over her mouth and nose. But she bet Daddy could see she was happy, anyway. He must know.*

*Daddy's smile got wider before he turned back around front to watch where he was going, almost slipping on a patch of ice. He dug a foot in the snow and bolted across the white lawn with her in tow, crunching through the crust of the snow with every step. She couldn't help but squeal at the top of her tiny little lungs. This was a great day!*

## 66
# *Better Homes and Gardens*
+4 Days – 7:03am EST

Jude smiled. The memory of her and her dad on that snowy January afternoon was a good one. She wondered how she had forgotten about it. It had been after the New Year. It had been before she had started kindergarten. So, she must have been five or six-years-old. That had been a good day—just her and her dad out in the snow. It was a moment—a moment much older than Dad's attempt at sobriety—where she had been an innocent child and he had been an innocent parent.

What she hadn't expected were the tears. They streamed down her face, rolling over her sore muscles already fatiguing from her grin. Jude had read somewhere smells and sounds were greater cues for retrieving memories than sight. In this case, the stark white of the buildings and the sound of the gravel under her feet must have done the trick.

She went up the three steps between the well-manicured hedges to the double doors under the portico. The interior was too dark to casually see into so she cupped her hands against the glass for a better view. From what she could make out, the inside was carpeted with several plush armchairs and a reception desk placed in front of a hallway leading deeper into what must be the administrator's offices.

She pulled the door handle, but it held firm. Someone must have locked the doors before running off to their families or to a more secure location. Jude imagined hearing people coming back from the dead would make cemetery employees decide pretty damn quick if staying where a thousand dead were buried was the smartest place to hole up.

Jude tried the doors again. Since the convenience store, she figured she'd make sure she hadn't just pulled at the wrong door handle. After a couple seconds of rattling the handles, she was confident the offices were permanently closed for the end of days. She scanned the grounds behind her. Nothing was out there except stone monuments to those who had lived and died before her. A thousand lifetimes lie rotting under the earth. Maybe she should start—

Glass rattled behind her, the door banging at the end of its hardware. A snarl followed. Jude spun around. A faint rot assaulted her nostrils. Heat billowed across her bare arms. A female office worker stood on the porch with her. She had an ugly cut across her left wrist, starting at the base of the palm and ending at mid-forearm. She shuffled forward a step, her black pencil skirt restricting her gait and her pink blouse pulled loose to show more undergarment than it should have. The door was just swinging shut behind her, a paddle handle on the inside frame having allowed the office-thing to get out.

Fuck!

Jude backed up. Her boots wavered on the top edge of the portico porch before she found herself in midair. Her arms pinwheeled, doing nothing to help her regain her balance. Her back fixed her right up, though, slamming into the sidewalk in front of the steps. Her head hit a second later. The proverbial stars exploded in her eyes. Fuck. She didn't have the backpack to cushion her fall this time.

The office-thing toppled off the top step and landed between her spread legs. She reached for the knife. The sheath was empty.

Double fuck! Jude crawled away, looking around the sidewalk for the knife. She hadn't heard it skitter away. It wasn't on the concrete. It wasn't in the grass or the mulched flowerbeds. The office-thing crawled forward. A scrape on the office-thing's chin bled freely and left black drops on the sidewalk. Jude scrambled away in a painful reverse crabwalk, still looking for the goddamn knife.

The formerly striking woman pawed at Jude's legs above the knees. Next, her hands scraped against a thigh. Why were reanimated dead women violating her? Jude kicked the office-thing in the face. The front two top teeth disappeared down her throat. Jude rolled left, her back none too happy with her gymnastics. She got to her feet, and slipped a few steps before sprinting all out to the other building. The small of her back ached with every footfall.

By the time she rounded the corner and pressed herself against the wall, her lungs were burning. She panted, trying to recover her breath. Her heart was thumping way too fast and loud. She edged to the corner and peeked around it. The office-thing had made it to her feet and was now shambling toward the maintenance building.

There was a windowless door to Jude's left, centered in the wall. She retreated to it and tried the knob. It banged open. Shit! Jude hesitated from going inside. Her choice was to face the office-thing or the dark unknown interior of the maintenance garage. Her brain stalled in making any decision until the left foot of the office-thing came around the corner. Jude instinctively slipped inside the garage and pulled the door closed behind her.

The darkness was complete—she was effectively blind. Ventilation was for shit in here. The smell of cut grass and heavy motor oil filled her nostrils, her nausea creeping up her throat again. Slapping sounds came from the other side of the door. She felt for the inside knob and turned the lock. The last thing she needed was for the office-thing to Houdini herself into the garage by more sheer dumb luck. Her slaps turned more insistent, becoming fisted poundings upon the door.

Groans came from the other side of the garage. More than one. Jude slipped down into a crouch, making herself as small a target as possible against the wall beside the office-thing's slams. Turning her head and tucking her hair behind her ear, Jude could hear them. There were two of them, maybe three—shuffling from her right.

*How about some luck for Team Jude, huh? Keep the sides even for a bit? Come on, God! Hook a girl up, would ya?*

Jude duck-waddled ten steps to her left. The office-thing was just outside, still pounding on the door. Jude's eyes finally adjusted enough to see three dark shapes lumbering toward her from the other side of a workbench. They hadn't seen her yet. The office-thing's knocks on the door were keeping them distracted.

*Who is it? Candy-Gram.*

Jude was losing it. She lowered her squat even more, finding herself at the end of the work bench. Bang! Bang! The garage-things sniffed at the door and responded with soft moans to the office-thing demanding to be let inside. The bench was several feet long, filled with what felt like wooden stakes and metal slats. The stakes were too flimsy, the slats too unwieldy to help her. She bumped her hand against a bolted down vise and moved it over other small tools. A typical workshop—one Dad would have appreciated.

Jude pivoted and felt out to the wall. She could feel the wooden or metal handles of several garden tools. The moans grew louder at the door on both sides. The acoustics of the building made their gurgles sound like they were breathing directly beside her. Suddenly, the slapping and moaning stopped.

Oh, shit.

255

Jude's leg cramped up. Her back throbbed with a sharp pain starting at her tailbone and darted all the way up to the base of her neck. She shifted her weight, her boot squeaking loudly on the epoxied floor. The dead started up their growls again. Jude stood up quickly, the soles of her boots making more untimely noise.

The dark forms of the garage-things hurried toward her, their arms reaching out wildly and their throats emitting gurgling warbles. Jude grabbed the closest tool on the wall. A flowerbed shovel? What the hell? She threw it at them. It bounced off one of them and clanked to the floor. All it seemed to do was agitate them.

She wrapped her fingers around a thicker handle. A pair of pruning shears with eighteen inch blades. Fuck, yeah! The garage-things were almost on her. She jabbed the shears forward. One blade in the mouth. The other impaled the left eye, popping it. When the man fell to the floor, the shears impaled farther in. One down. She grabbed at another handle. This time, she got a spade shovel. Jude pulled it off its pegs and swung it at around. The blade hit one of the two remaining walkers in the side of the head with a satisfying thunk. He careened into his friend, sending them both into the wall. They recovered quickly, though, and closed in on her. She didn't have room to swing the shovel so she thrust the blade forward. It embedded into same garage-thing's chest. Jude backed up, the shovel handle slipping from her grip. He tripped over his dead friend, falling forward onto the blade. The tip of the handle skittered forward a few feet across the floor before it wedged itself into a wide crack. The blade plunged deeper into his chest—between his ribs, she guessed. He wasn't dead, but he had trapped himself.

The last garage-thing staggered around the other two. Apparently, they had better night vision to hunt her down—even with the cataracts. Office-thing started banging against the door again, startling her. Jude backed up away from the wall of tools, her heel bumping into something soft.

*Please, not another body.*

Bags of soil were stacked up in the corner. The animated corpse, his skin taut and ashen against his skull, swiped at her. She feinted left. Two steps later, her shoulder slammed into something large and unyielding. He was immediately on her. She didn't have a weapon, so she turned and straight-armed him in the chest. His fingers raked across her sleeves as he snapped his jaw at her—just like the others had.

*Why did they attack the living?*

She was trapped against what she had bumped into and the snapping garage-thing. He smelled dead, but smelled more of grass clippings, gasoline, and WD40. Ugh... gas again? Her elbows started to bend against his weight and pistoning legs. He lunged forward with snapping teeth. Jude whimpered, her strength failing way too quickly in this matter of life and death.

Jude bristled at the thought. What the fuck was wrong with her? Did she not have enough strength to fight for her own goddamn life? Had she survived her entire family just to be devoured in the maintenance garage of some cemetery she didn't even know the name of?

She looked at the silhouette of her attacker. His floating milky eyes cast off a faint luminance she hadn't noticed before. They looked lifeless, but had a strangely intense glowing focus. Like the eyes of a shark. 'Doll's eyes,' Quint had told Chief Brody of Amity Island. Mom had forbidden her from watching *Jaws*. She had said there had been too much nudity at the beginning of the film. Good thing she had friends with a DVD player.

Jude was the last Sawyer. No way she was going bite it in this garage. Instead of matching the garage-thing's wiry strength, she bent her elbows and side-stepped right. The corpse lunged forward to where she had been the moment before. Jude spun around the six-foot granite tombstone she had been pinned against, ending up on one side with the garage-thing on the other. It had a wide base, held upright by wood bracing on her side. That was why it hadn't toppled over when she ran into it.

She leaned into the front of the marker, her back and shoulders screaming in protest. She blocked out the pain, gritted her teeth, and pushed. The garage-thing reached around it and dug his fingers into her shoulders. She hissed in pain as he pulled her against the marker. She kept pushing. She thought she felt the stone move. She pushed and yelled at the top of her lungs. He pulled and growled at the top of what remained of his.

Like falling from the office steps, there was a split second of overbalanced equilibrium where Jude felt like she was floating. Then, just as quickly, the stone landed on the garage-thing and she slammed into the face of it. His fingers snagged into her clothing, but she was now safe above several hundred pounds of granite. His fingers suddenly fell away as the weight of the stone pressed into him.

Jude pushed herself off the stone. Her fingers felt the carvings on the face. She couldn't make any of it out in the darkness, but it was very ornate. She got to her feet and backed away from the stone and the still moaning garage-thing. It wasn't going to get up any time soon—hopefully, never. She stood there and waited for several seconds. Thankfully, there weren't any new moans coming from the darkness.

She felt around the other side of the work bench, finding a screwdriver—a flathead if her fingers were still able to discern such things—and a ballpeen hammer. Both should be just what she needed to get the battery out of the Bronco. She put them in her back pocket. Shuffling around the workbench so she didn't have to cross paths with any of the still-moving garage-things, Jude's left foot snagged the corner of something. She knelt down. It was a thick quilt. When she pulled at it, something plastic rolled off the other side, followed by several lighter pinging sounds.

In her head, she pictured an open prescription bottle with little white pills scattered across the floor. She imagined the three cemetery groundskeepers holing up in this garage after the power went out for good. She saw them make a suicide pact and downing a bunch of pills together—maybe chasing the pills with swigs from a warm bottle of Corona before they drifted off to their deaths. It was a sad notion, but endearing in a way. Three co-workers and, more likely, friends making the decision to face death together.

Of course, they hadn't thought through the fact they would be facing un-death together, too. Jude wondered if they would have succumbed to death so willingly if they knew they would end up shambling about in a concrete block tomb built to support their livelihoods. She shuddered to think about spending the afterlife trapped in a corpse's shell—let alone a dark tomb.

The rest of the left side of the garage was empty except for a large dark blob resembling a golf cart. Once, she got closer, she was able to kick the small knobby tires and rub her hand on the vinyl cushions of the driver's seat. The three maintenance workers must have used it to get around the grounds. While she would have enjoyed using the cart to get back to the Bronco and Lincoln, she was already armed with the tools she needed to get the town car running again.

Jude eased herself around the counters and benches and headed to the door. Moans still filled the space. She had only killed one of the three maintenance workers. Maybe, she was getting soft in her old age. The thing under the granite would never be able to escape from under it. The other one—the one with a shovel wedged between his ribs—was another matter. If he were to back up, the tip of the shovel would pull itself from the crack in the floor and all bets would be off. She pulled the hammer from her back pocket, hefted it, and approached him from behind. She had to put her free hand out in front of her, but worried her fingers would get bitten off as the sound of his growls grew louder. As soon as her fingertips felt the cold flesh of his back, she swung the hammer several inches above it. The sound of the thick wet thunk made her stomach queasy, but she swung the hammer several more times until the maintenance worker fell over and clanged against several other gardening tools hanging from the wall.

"Damn," she said with labored breathing.

She retreated to the door and unlocked it. Swinging it open, she was completely blinded by the glare of painful sunlight. She covered her eyes with the elbow of her free hand. The office-thing growled and rushed in.

"Shit!" Jude had completely forgotten about her. Jude slid left and blindly swung the hammer through the air at a slicing downward angle, pivoting her entire aching body into it. The hammer missed the office-thing entirely. Before Jude overbalanced completely, she rushed into the whiteness and slammed the door behind her. Let the office-thing and the pinned maintenance-thing spend their after-deaths in each other's company, protected from the elements. Jude would never know it, but when the door was opened, a slice of sunlight had exposed the name carved on the toppled tombstone—Sawyer.

Once her eyes adjusted to the outside world and she caught her breath, Jude started the walk back toward the vehicles. Jude got as far as the sidewalk joining the office and the garage before she stopped. She felt every muscle—not in a good way. She glanced back at the garage, its pristine white-painted concrete rectangle an inviting bunker.

"Goddamn it."

She sighed and walked back to the side entrance. The door wasn't locked, but she wasn't going to reach in to correct that oversight. No way.

Instead, she pulled out the screwdriver and gripped it like she was going to chip ice with it. After some thought, she started scrawling on the door. The paint came away easily enough, allowing for deep grooves for the sides of each letter. Once done, she stood back to check her handiwork. She mouthed the words a few times, using different inflections with each iteration. She shrugged to herself and nodded, thinking the message was serviceable.

She turned for the second and last time, her brain allowing her to walk away with the firm belief she had done all she could to warn the living future. As she walked off between the headstones across the green grass, Jude didn't realize she had left something of herself behind inside the garage. The message she had left on the door would serve as both a ward and a declaration long after the paint weathered and dulled. She had carved those letters with determination and intent, their grooves deep.

The message read,

Death Inside
Stay Out
And Alive

## 67
## *Negative Posts*
+4 Days – 7:29am EST

She returned to the scene of the vehicular suicides. They were just as she had left them, the hoods still raised. The gardener-thing was still crumpled up on the ground. He had been handsome in life, his broad shoulders and muscular features probably giving him many advantages Jude couldn't have even conceived of. It was a strange thought she shook away.

"I ain't going to last long this way." The huge tactical Rambo knife she thought she had lost was sitting right there on the radiator. She picked it up and chastised herself silently for her forgetfulness and recklessness. Her ongoing survival would be fleeting if she kept doing shit like that. The knife went back into its sheath and was secured. It occurred to her she had been on the verge of using it for swapping the batteries just when the gardener-thing had shown up. She shrugged into the backpack, not wanting to forget anything else today.

Another obvious thought popped into her head. She rushed to the driver's side door of the Bronco and pulled it open. The bench seat was clear of debris and supplies. Her old backpack—with her brother's Beretta and ammo—wasn't there. She checked the entire interior. It was clear of any debris.

Why hadn't she remembered it before now? Had Mr. Ritchie discarded it? Did he leave it somewhere—maybe where his children were? Had Mr. Ritchie stolen the Bronco from the person who had stolen it from her?

"Damn."

She had been so focused on exacting her revenge on Mr. Ritchie she had completely forgotten about her gun and gear. Why couldn't she see the big picture? Why did she get such tunnel vision, sometimes?

She took her new-found screwdriver and hammer back to the front of the Bronco. Even with her growing self-loathing, Jude ignored it enough to tap the terminals from multiple sides with the hammer. The corrosion from the battery acid flaked off in a grimy powder. Switching to the screwdriver, she scraped away the rest. It was the moment of truth. Jude wedged the screwdriver under the positive terminal and wriggled it up until it popped off. Success! She did the same with the negative terminal, although with a bit more trouble. Double success!

She almost ran over to the Lincoln, enjoying her moment of triumph. She quickly repeated the process and popped the terminals of the battery's posts, the Town Car in much better condition. She pulled out the battery and set it on the grass. She trotted back to the Bronco and lugged the heavier battery between the vehicles. She made sure the positive and negative posts were facing the right direction before sliding it into place. Except... the battery didn't fit. The tray for the Town Car was too small for the Bronco's battery. The bigger battery sat at an awkward angle, several inches above where the hood would need to latch into place.

"Are you fucking shitting me?" Jude yelled. They were both Ford vehicles. Swapping the batteries had been a good idea. Why couldn't things work out for her one time... just one fucking time? She pulled out the hammer and bashed it against the battery. Plastic flew in all directions as she shattered the housing around the posts. The negative post even bent with an errant blow.

Once she started panting and her shoulder screamed in sore protest, Jude threw the hammer on top of the engine and stepped away. Catching her breath took a few minutes. Rolling her shoulders hoping to work the soreness out of the muscles proved much more elusive. She had wasted energy and resources because of her overwhelming and blinding frustration. There were probably a dozen cars within walking distance with batteries she could have scavenged. Destroying the Bronco's battery was proof she needed to rein in her anger and start using the brain God had given her. Even if her gray matter was defective most of the time.

What really slid Jude's brain into gear was the pops of small weapons fire from somewhere beyond the deep line of trees serving as a border around the cemetery. She didn't remember what was out there. It could be an industrial area or a suburban sprawl. Or, maybe it was a retail area like the ones she had passed along the highway. There was really only one way to find out, wasn't there?

## 68
## *Family Matters*
+4 Days – 7:53am EST

The trees opened up quickly, relenting to a four-lane street. Across the asphalt were restaurants surrounded on three sides by blacktopped parking lots. Jude stood behind the last of the trees, still under cover. Her sightline limited her to the view of the backside of a Chinese food restaurant connected to two other shops. A pistol shot popped from beyond it. Taking a chance, Jude looked both ways before crossing the street and made her way to the rear corner of the restaurant. There were a couple cars in the parking lot—See? Cars!—looking a bit worse for wear. A Toyota Tercel looked like it had already been ransacked, its doors wide open. The other car, a Mercury Bobcat station wagon, sat on four slashed tires. Its windshield was shattered and its antenna was snapped off.

Another pop.

Jude crept up to the front corner of the restaurant. The empty parking lot opened up on the east side of the building. She looked back to the west—back across the road and to the safety of the trees and cemetery.

"I should just turn back."

No. Another road was before her. Literally. All of the restaurants had been built on the triangle created between the four-lane street and a service road—except a Denny's—while a Shell gas station, a Motel 6, a Men's Wearhouse, and a Starbucks occupied the plaza storefronts on the far side. The highway she had raced along just yesterday was to her north.

Another pop, louder this time.

At the far corner of the plaza were two people. One of them, a lanky teenage boy, was standing on top of one of the Starbucks patio tables firing at some unseen target with a handgun. Sitting at the same table was a just-as-young girl, looking up at the lone gunman with something akin to admiration. Or, maybe, infatuation. The girl smiled at him, whether he was squeezing the trigger or swinging the pistol around as he talked to her. For a while, they chatted without shooting anything.

Thank God.

There was no cover between her and them for her to make a safe approach. These two may be living people, but she sure wasn't going to get shot for the simple want of someone to talk to. Eventually, the boy hopped down from the table and quickly wrapped his arms around the girl to pull her close and give her a long kiss. Her knees caved just a little before she slapped him in the chest. They both giggled and headed inside the Starbucks.

As soon as they were out of sight, Jude sprinted across the road and through the parking lot. She flattened herself against one of the display windows with male mannequins wearing their trendy suits and sweaters. As she caught her breath again, the headless display models—for some reason—freaked her out more than facing the undead. She moved along the window until she could peek into the Starbucks. The door was propped open and she could hear them talking.

"Can't believe all these dead heads," the young man said, his arms tattooed and his face pierced.

"At least your shooting is getting better, Lenny," the girl replied with a laugh. "You really sucked when you started."

"Shut up," Lenny said in mock exasperation.

"Make me," she dared him.

"You don't want me to make you, April."

"Don't I?"

Lenny raced over to April and wrapped her up in his arms again. She squealed with delight as he picked her up and swung her around. He stepped into a wood chair, making it skid a few feet across the floor. They laughed as he dropped her to her feet in favor of catching his balance. Young people in love. Sigh. Young, dumb, and full of—

"Do you think our parents are in heaven?" April asked.

Lenny's smile flattened as he nodded. "I know they are. They were good folk. It wasn't their fault what happened. They couldn't have seen what was going on."

"You promise?" April looked like she was going to break down into tears any moment, but held her head up.

"You know I do." They hugged each other, April resting her head on his chest. She knotted her fingers into the back of his shirt, reluctant to let go.

If Jude was planning to make a move, now would be the time. She wanted to be around people again... but, she didn't want to be the one who had to put them down if the shit hit the fan. She was already beginning to lose count of the people—living and dead—she had killed over the past few days. Maybe it would be better to stay out here on her own? Stay away from other people who may start to rely on her to keep them alive? She didn't want to have to shoot either of these kids if the time—

Jude walked quickly and quietly through the door without thinking. "You really need to keep the door closed. The dead heads can be clever, sometimes."

While she spoke as softly as possible, Lenny whirled around with the .38 coming up. Jude side-stepped. She grabbed the top of the pistol with her right hand and jabbed his forearm with the stiff fingers of her left—just like Matty had taught her.

"Oww!" Lenny let go of the gun altogether. Jude easily pulled it away and spun it around in her grip. The business end was somewhat pointed at the two love-struck teenagers. Lenny swept his sore wrist back, keeping April blocked behind him.

Jude lowered the gun to the floor. "You doing okay? Would you like some company?" Lenny stared at her, April peeking out from under his arm. When they didn't speak, Jude grabbed the barrel of the .38 with her left hand and offered it back to Lenny grip first. "I just didn't want you to shoot me. Here."

Lenny tentatively took back his gun and put it in the front of his waistband. April stepped out from behind him. He took a look at Jude, noticing the blood splatter on her shirt and face. "How many dead heads you bang out?"

"Today?" Jude asked innocently.

"Oh, shit! You a gangsta?" Lenny exclaimed.

Jude laughed. A gangsta? That was the furthest thing from her mind. But, she had to say… her body count was piling up. In spite of the death behind her, she couldn't help but laugh until tears streamed down her face. Lenny and April's smiles turned into out-and-out grins as her mirth became contagious.

"Yeah," Jude finally said between somewhat nervous chuckles, "I'm livin' a thug's life."

"Right on." Lenny wrapped his arm around April's tiny waist and nodded. "You're alright with us."

Jude looked at their grins, so filled with hope and positivity—and love for each other—that her heart warmed up in her chest. Maybe, while she looked after them, protected them, and fostered their survival skills, they could teach her the meaning of what a family could be.

Maybe.

* * * *

Check out how Jude, Lenny and April meet up with John and the other survivors in the second book of the series.
***DAY ZERO: GAUNT MAN***

## *Coming in 2019*

Sgt. John Walken and what remains of his team
will return to continue their mission in the upcoming

### *DAY ZERO: BAD COMPANY*

## *Other Books by Charles Ingersoll*

### DAY ZERO

My name is Sgt. John Walken, Marine Corps Sniper.

I lost people in the sands of the Middle East. I lost my career there because of injuries. Now, I have been medically discharged, disgraced and forced back Stateside. I would have wandered aimlessly along the roads of America if I hadn't been picked up by a trucker who happened to bleed red, white and blue, too.

We soon found ourselves trapped on a barricaded island community after a strange and bloodied young girl wandered into the town square and attacked the residents. From there, things quickly went from bad to worst. I realized I was the only one with enough training to protect the island and its residents from the sudden hordes of invading reanimated human dead from the mainland, aggressive human threats, and unexplained deaths within the community.

The people of Rainier Island put their trust in me to keep them safe. I hope their faith in me doesn't get them killed... like it did for everyone else in my life.

## DAY ZERO: GAUNT MAN

My name is Sgt. John Walken.

The ghosts of those I failed to protect haunt me. The Gaunt Man, a new and persistent hallucination, claws at the cracks of my sanity. I must keep ahead of all of these phantoms. I need to get home, even if it means facing a road full of rotting walkers.

People on the road have chosen to follow me. Can they count on me for their survival or will the knights of a strange new kingdom tear us apart?

Will they be lost to me or will I be lost to them? Or will I simply descend into madness and be left as just another of the undead.

## DAY ZERO: CREEDMOOR

My name is John Walken.

I was a Marine Corps sniper once. Now it's a bit harder to know what I am. A series of shadowy events beyond my control have left me as something less than human... or, maybe, something more.

Roanoke & Raleigh spent considerable resources to hunt us down. Holding my people hostage, injecting another with an exploding capsule in her neck, and teaming me up with a woman I had thought long dead, the Man in the Black Suit secured my cooperation for one more mission.

Can we work together to exfiltrate a human target from one of dozens of buildings across hundreds of acres of the Creedmoor Psychiatric Institution—a crumbling mental hospital complex? Can I get the Man in the Black Suit's prize back before I lose all the people I care for? Or will I lose everything I hold dear in the process... including myself?

## REANIMATED WRITERS ANTHOLOGY: UNDEAD WORLDS

21 Authors.
21 Undead worlds.
1 Great Book.
Do you dare?

Read the short story, *In the Beginning, God*, where **Day Zero** all began.

All titles available in paperback and in most places where you enjoy downloading eBooks!

# DAY ZERO: FAMILY MATTERS

## *About the Author*

The love of zombies was in my blood immediately after watching George Romero's *Night of the Living Dead* at a far too young and inappropriate age. That feeling never faded, festering for forty years before the fever finally broke and beckoned me to write my own "Great American Zombie Novel". One story became a second. Two stories became an ongoing series.

I love comic cons, cosplay, movies and television, guns, the Marvel Cinematic Universe, and the supernatural. I currently reside in what the South Carolina locals call the Upstate with the two real loves of my life, my very own real-life Jude (Judy) and a certain fur baby canine named Holly—both straight off the pages of Day Zero universe.

A special *thank you* to my partner in crime, and to everyone who chooses to support my work to ensure my zombie universe doesn't die a horrible death.

## *Learn more and be social*

To find more information about Charles Ingersoll and the ***Day Zero*** zombie survivor apocalypse book series, please follow on:

Facebook @ https://www.facebook.com/dayzerozombies/

Twitter @ https://twitter.com/dayzerozombies/

Instagram @ https://www.instagram.com/dayzerozombies/

Website: http://www.dayzerozombies.com

bit.ly/dayzerozombies